"I'm here, Annabelle. It's all right."

Quinton touched her tattoo again, then soothed her with soft whispers.

She slowly opened her eyes and looked up at him, and he heard her thoughts as if she'd spoken them aloud.

She wanted him. A man who could kill coolly without blinking an eye, without an ounce of remorse, but a man who'd saved her life more than once now.

A man who made her feel more alive, more aroused, than she'd ever thought possible.

A threat to her—yes.

Would she have him?

She had to.

Quinton's gaze locked onto hers, his hunger evident in the deep blackness of his eyes. Sensations rippled through her in erotic waves.

"You're shivering," he mumbled in a fierce tone.

"Because I want you."

His jaw tightened. "You're in shock. Let's dry you off and put you to bed. I'm not a good guy. But I'm trying to do the right thing here."

She licked her lips, desperate, her body crying out for him. "Why in the hell would you start doing the right thing now?"

*Please turn this page
for praise for Rita Herron...*

Praise for Rita Herron and her previous book in this series, *Insatiable Desire*

"Experienced romance suspense author Herron...kicks off her new series with a bang."

—*Publishers Weekly*

"Rita Herron never fails to deliver a compelling story with memorable characters...Every scene is filled with emotion."

—SingleTitles.com

"Deep, dark, and tragic, *Insatiable Desire* will pull you in from the first page...Out of all the demon romances I've read recently, *Insatiable Desire* is the most plausible and most enjoyable...Herron writes a spooky and formidable romance—few do it better. I recommend reading it—and I'll definitely pick up future works from this gifted author."

—NightsAndWeekends.com

"Herron is a good writer who pulled me right in. I had to keep reading."

—JandysBooks.com

Also by Rita Herron

Insatiable Desire

Rita Herron

DARK HUNGER

FOREVER

NEW YORK   BOSTON

This book is a work of fiction. Names, characters, places, and incidents are the product of the author's imagination or are used fictitiously. Any resemblance to actual events, locales, or persons, living or dead, is coincidental.

Book design by Stratford, a TexTech business
Cover design by Diane Luger
Cover illustration by Franco Accornero
Typography by Ron Zinn

Forever
Hachette Book Group
237 Park Avenue
New York, NY 10017
Visit our Web site at www.HachetteBookGroup.com.

Forever is an imprint of Grand Central Publishing. The Forever name and logo is a trademark of Hachette Book Group, Inc.

Printed in the United States of America

First Printing: August 2009

10 9 8 7 6 5 4 3 2 1

To DragonCon fans for welcoming a new series!
Hope you like book two in The Demonborn!

Acknowledgments

Thanks once again to my wonderful editor, Michele Bidelspach, for her great insight and for making this book stronger; to the art department at Grand Central Publishing for a fabulous cover; to my critique partners Stephanie Bond and Jennifer St. Giles for all their support and input; to my sister for her never-ending faith and encouragement; to my husband, who loves me even when I scare him with my thoughts; and to Raven Hart for the vultures!

Chapter One

Quinton Valtrez was a killer.

A loner. A man without a conscience. A man who roamed the world as a ghostly gun for hire.

He needed no one. Wanted no one to need him.

But it was All Hallows' Eve, and dammit, he was going to get laid.

Still, the Glock inside his jacket rubbed against his chest, taunting him with the fact that he could never relax. That evil never died.

That it was his mission to stop it at all costs. Even if he didn't survive.

And All Hallows' Eve was the time when the veil between the world and the underworld was thinnest, when the spirit world could mingle with the humans and the ghosts of the dead came to life.

A buxom redhead in a pussycat costume smiled at him across the crowded Savannah street, and he put thoughts of the evildoers on hold as she glided toward him.

Even assassins deserved the night off.

"Hey, sexy," she purred. "Where's your costume?"

He cut her a sideways smile, letting his gaze dip to her

ample cleavage. "I am in costume. I'm going as a nice guy."

She threw her head back and laughed. "Want to head over to the party boat?"

"Sure." Despite the lust burning through his body, his heightened senses kicked in as he followed her through the dark, ghostlike alleys along River Street toward the lit-up ship.

The odors of refuse from the late-night partygoers—stale beer, cigarette smoke, and cheap perfume—permeated the air, along with the pungent aromas of fried fish, shrimp, and oysters floating from the pubs.

Suddenly the hairs on the back of his neck rose, and he paused and scanned the crowd, searching for the source of his unease. Kids, teenagers, and adults swarmed the streets in costumes portraying both colorful cartoon characters and the dark and macabre—everything from witches, zombies, pirates, werecreatures, birds of prey, and goblins to demons.

Twinkling orange lights, jack-o'-lanterns carved with scary faces, skeletons, ghosts, spiderwebs, and cardboard tombstones decorated the storefronts, while the sounds of spooky music, ghostly clanging, hooting owls, and moaning zombies added to the atmosphere.

Calling upon his chi, he focused on thumbing through the thoughts of various bystanders, searching for the evil one among them.

It was as natural as breathing, using his gift. He'd honed it when he'd lived with the monks. They'd taught him to access his inner being, drawing on nature and spirituality to strengthen his power. He'd expanded that power to a sharp tool in the military, searching and destroying the enemy on clandestine operations no one would ever admit existed.

His heart picked up its pace in recognition; he could feel the enemy, sense his presence. But an otherworldly sensation inundated the darkness of the enemy's soul.

Was this the demon the monks had warned him about?

Narrowing his eyes, he zeroed in on a stooped old man in a ratty green corduroy coat, his wire-rimmed glasses held together with duct tape. A terrible screeching sound suddenly reverberated from the dark skies.

He glanced up, sweat beading his brow as he spotted a vulture soaring above—not a new-world vulture but an old-world one, black with strong feet and a craving for carrion. And like the raven, this creature's bloodlust was for not only animal flesh but human meat as well.

Just like his own bloodlust.

A feeling of impending doom engulfed him as he connected with the vulture. The black bird was hovering above, ready to swoop down and gather the dead meat of an animal in its sharp talons and bury its bald head inside the carcass and feast on the remains.

Part vulture—part raven? Where had this creature come from?

He glanced through the crowd again, noticing a strange acidic odor emanating from the old homeless man in the green coat. Quinton pressed a finger to his temple, his head throbbing as he struggled to tap into the man's thoughts. His frail body trembled in the stiff wind, his mind a blank slate as if it had been wiped clean, all thoughts erased.

The old man's skin held a dull gray-black pallor, as if he'd already met death; his eyes were glassy and vacant, dazed, a shell of a human.

The redhead tugged at his elbow. "Aren't you coming, sugar?"

But a different woman's scent assaulted him. Delicious. Sultry. Enticing. "Go ahead, honey. I'll catch up," he murmured.

She raked her sharp nails down his arm. "All right, but don't make me wait long. I promise I'll destroy that nice-guy image of yours."

He chuckled. As if he'd ever had one.

She pranced toward the ship, and the enticing scent of the other woman quickly obliterated the redhead's cheap, flowery perfume.

Then his gaze fell upon the source.

Shiny, straight long blonde hair cascaded over slender shoulders. Intrigued, he forced his mind to drown out the sounds of the night. The party whistles and noisemakers prepared to ring in the celebration of the supernatural with witchcraft, séances, and pagan rituals that transcended time and worlds.

His body tingled with arousal, the fierce need he had to hunt stirring primal instincts he couldn't extinguish. He could almost smell the scent of her sex.

As if she sensed him watching her, she slowly turned, her gaze shifting through the crowd toward him.

His stomach clenched as their gazes locked. Shit.

It was *her*. CNN reporter Annabelle Armstrong. He'd watched her newsclips on TV, her do-gooder pieces on the homeless, her stories behind the stories.

A sliver of moonlight played across her face, her hair shimmering beneath the spilled light. He couldn't tear himself away. Her big blue eyes were hypnotic. Her pale creamy skin, exotic. And her rosy lips made him ache for a sinful taste.

A taste he could never have.

Because she was a damn reporter. A beautiful one, but falcons were beautiful, too. Still, they were birds of prey.

A bead of sweat slid down his neck. Had she discovered who he was?

Had she come to Savannah to expose him?

Annabelle Armstrong's gaze locked with Quinton Valtrez's. Damn. She'd come here to find him but hadn't expected to see him tonight. Not in the midst of a party in town.

And she certainly hadn't expected his penetrating gaze to rattle her. Or make her tingle with desire.

"Annabelle, are you listening?" Roland, her boss from CNN, barked over the phone. "Do you think you can get this story?"

"Yes," she said into her cell phone. "If Valtrez is this Ghost assassin working for some secret government unit, I'll find out."

She sucked in a sharp breath, well aware that the man hadn't moved since he'd spotted her. That his cold eyes and tightly set mouth screamed of danger. That every bone in her body warned her to run.

To forget this story—or she might end up dead.

"Annabelle?" her boss shouted.

"Yes, Roland, I'll do whatever I have to do to find out the truth."

She snapped the phone shut, smoothed down her skirt, and desperately struggled for a playful, flirty smile.

Quinton Valtrez was devastatingly and darkly handsome. Bigger than she'd imagined. His features were chiseled in stone, and his five o'clock shadow painted his bronzed stoic jaw with a hint of menace.

Her body tingled. Still, he was just a man.

And she was damn well tired of being at the bottom of the food chain at the station. Of being assigned human-interest pieces instead of the big stories.

She'd do whatever was necessary to get the scoop this time.

Even if it meant cozying up to a killer.

Suddenly a loud explosion rent the air, and the outer deck of the party ship exploded. Annabelle stumbled, the earth trembling below her feet as flames shot into the air. Wood and fiberglass shattered and spewed across the sidewalk as bodies collapsed into the burning rubble.

Quinton threw himself over Annabelle Armstrong, his heart hammering. What in the hell was happening? Were they under a terrorist attack?

And why in the hell had he tried to save her?

Pure instinct, he thought quickly.

A bloody arm landed beside them, its charred fingers reaching toward him as if begging for help.

Then a vulture swooped down and snapped up the arm, crunching it between its jagged teeth. A sinister look lit the bird's beady eyes, and in that split second, Quinton could have sworn the vulture smiled.

The rumble of the blazing fire continued as heat pelted him, and Annabelle's soft body trembled beneath his.

In the midst of the chaos and acrid odors of charred

flesh and burning wood, the horrific scent of evil splintered the air.

He had to do something.

He lifted his head slightly. "Are you okay?" he growled.

She moved slightly as if to push him off. "Yes, I think so."

Forcing himself onto his hands and knees, he stood, studying her. "Are you sure?"

"Yes," she said, her voice strained as she looked around at the mad chaos and dead bodies floating in the river.

Panicked screams jerked him into action. He dashed toward the burning ship, leaving Annabelle alone.

He needed to sniff out this killer. As he ran, he sent a text to his contact at Homeland Security to alert them of the attack.

The Death Angel flapped his black wings and bowed his bald head to Zion, paying umbrage to the new leader of the underworld. His belly was swollen from his recent meal, yet he still craved more tasty carrion.

The human bones and meat were especially delicious. The vulture-raven hybrid that was his demonic form for eternity had at first been punishment at its worst, but over the past century, he had embraced the predator's needs and urges, and now savored the agility of the bird's keen eyesight, flight patterns, and sharp talons.

Demons, shape-shifters, werecreatures, vampires, fallen angels, and other soldiers of Satan gathered in the underground cave of black rock lit by fiery torches.

Zion entered, his black cape billowing around his

demonic form, his orange eyes lighting up the darkness. The mortals would run in terror if they saw him now, complete with sharp fangs like claws, the devil's horns, flaming red scales, and cloven feet.

"The death toll?" Zion asked.

"In the hundreds."

Striking on All Hallows' Eve, the night of the dead, had been genius. All the Death Angel had to do was slide past the Twilight Guards, those with powers who guarded the portal between the mortals and demons, then he'd crossed into the mortals' world. Thousands of other demons had unleashed themselves tonight, their screeches unrecognizable to the humans but calling out to the others to announce their presence. The pagan holiday had also afforded him the opportunity to possess a human's body and walk among the masses unnoticed—the one he had chosen would serve him well.

And now that same one lay in a sleep-induced state awaiting his return. The bastard had been an easy mark, had been too weak to fight, his soul already black.

The Death Angel's power allowed him to crawl into the feeble minds of the weak on earth, put their minds to sleep, then bend them to his will. One touch and they became marionettes dancing on his string.

"I commend you." Zion's fiery breath rippled out in pleasure. "When I said spread evil and create chaos, you embraced the challenge."

The Death Angel flapped his wings with pride.

"And my sons?" Zion asked.

"The Seer found one of the twins, Quinton. He lives in the place they call Savannah, Georgia. This attack should capture the demonborn's attention."

Zion's red eyes flared, shooting sparks of crisp yellow flames across the black rock in jagged lightning-bolt-like lines. "Quinton should be easy. He has succumbed to his destiny already by choosing to be a killer."

The Death Angel refrained from comment. That was true, although technically the Dark Lord targeted only sinners.

But the fact that Quinton had no regrets, felt no remorse over his kills, worked in their favor and would ultimately be his downfall.

Unfortunately, the Dark Lord's cause also kept the balance of good and evil alive within him.

That balance had to be destroyed.

The Dark Lord had a weakness for that reporter. They could use her to trap him.

She would also bring attention to the Death Angel's victories with the mortals, keep a tally of the dead and create pain and misery with her stories.

He'd use her until she became dispensable, then he'd dispose of her. He might even be able to twist Quinton to the point that he killed the woman.

That would definitely earn Quinton his place in the kingdom of evil.

Chapter Two

A shudder of horror rippled through Annabelle as another vulture shattered the human bone and ripped off the flesh with its knifelike teeth, blood dripping. Where had all the vultures come from? There were dozens, swarming like gnats around the bodies.

Only vultures usually ate dead animals. She'd never heard of them feasting on humans.

And there were so many dead now...

Had anyone on the boat survived?

Tears blurred her vision, the images of flying body parts and terrified, dying innocents flashing before her.

Heat from the explosion seared her skin, lighting the heavens in a mountainous blaze of red, orange, and yellow. Smoke swirled and blanketed the sidewalk, clogging her throat and eyes. Sirens soon wailed and screeched toward the scene.

"Help me!" someone cried.

"Where's my little girl?"

"I can't move!"

The terrified screams and panicked shouts forced her back to the present.

She was alive, and people needed help. She had to do something...

A little girl lay crying beneath the bench near her, and she knelt and examined her for injuries. "Are you all right?" Annabelle asked.

"I lost my mommy," the child cried out.

"Come here, sweetheart. I'll help you find her." Annabelle held out her arms, and the trembling little girl climbed into them.

A man pushed past her, frantic and hobbling on a shattered leg, and hysterical teenagers raced by, too. Then she spotted a brown-haired woman staggering and searching the masses. "My baby...Jodie..."

The child in Annabelle's arms waved her arms. "Mommy!"

Clutching the little girl to her, Annabelle ran toward the woman just as she spotted them and stumbled forward.

"Oh, my baby, my baby," the woman cried. Mother and daughter sobbed, clinging to each other as they reunited. Annabelle smiled, grateful they were okay, then skimmed the lawn for others who needed help.

An elderly woman with gray hair dropped to her hands and knees, then pulled a man's head into her lap. "Herbert's not breathing," she yelled. "Somebody, please help us!"

Suddenly rescue workers and police stormed through, and Annabelle waved a paramedic over to the couple.

The next few hours she vacillated between being a reporter and snapping photos of the scene and helping the injured or lost. She'd seen footage of the war zones in the Middle East and photos of bombings and mass casualties.

But Savannah wasn't a war zone—the injured and dead here weren't armed soldiers prepared for attack.

Civilians had ventured out for a fun night with their

families, to celebrate the holiday with garish spooky costumes and gather candy, in total trust.

Her heart clenching, she snapped a photo of the river, which normally radiated beauty and peace but now looked like a scene from a horror movie, red with blood and death. Next to the body of a woman bobbed a rag doll, tattered and covered in grime, lost to its owner, probably a child who'd loved it as a friend.

A middle-aged man sat hunched and crying over his unconscious wife while the medics worked on her. Others searched frantically for their loved ones in the chaotic mess, women clutching children to their chests as police began to question the crowd for clues as to what had happened.

Charred and mangled limbs and bodies lay scattered in the murky grayness. Flames still ate at the boat as more emergency and police vehicles rushed onto the scene. Rescue workers and medical personnel transported bodies of the dead and the maimed while onlookers watched in stunned shock.

She had to focus. She'd come here tonight for a story, albeit Quinton Valtrez's, but now she had a different one to cover.

Yet as she approached the boat, she spotted Quinton on board. He paused next to a man who was trapped beneath a burning beam. She raised her camera to take a photo and snapped it quickly.

Quinton tried to lift the beam, but it must have been too heavy and didn't budge. Then he backed away, glanced around him as if searching for help or to see if anyone was watching. Slowly he fisted his hands and stared at the beam with his piercing eyes. His complexion seemed to take on a darker hue; his eyes turned glassy against the dark, then glittered with a strange silver glow.

She gasped at the transformation—he didn't look quite human at that moment, more like an animal about to attack.

She raised her camera and snapped another photo just as he flicked one hand up and, without touching the beam, sent it flying off the screaming man.

Annabelle blinked in shock, uncertain if what she'd seen was real.

It was almost as if he'd moved the heavy beam with his mind. But that was impossible.

Wasn't it?

Quinton helped the old man off to the side, glancing around to make certain no one had seen what he'd done. Dammit, he tried never to use his powers in public, but this was an emergency, and the man would have died in seconds had he not released him.

"Thank you," the man said with a cough as Quinton handed him over to a medic.

He nodded, then raced through the fire at superhuman speed, stopping to help more injured escape the burning rubble and carrying strangers to safety.

His senses remained alert, searching. He wanted to find the bomber. To know the source and reason behind this attack.

He placed his hand on the stiff body of a man but felt no evil vibrating from the man's soul, only the sickening sense of despair the man had felt just before he'd drawn his last breath.

A medic raced up, two firemen on his tail, dragging hoses to extinguish the flames.

"Move the bodies over there!" a suited man who looked like a cop shouted to him and a few other men who'd jumped in to help.

"I'm a doctor," a white-haired man said as he ran up. "Let's start a triage area so we can prioritize the victims according to their injuries."

Another team of medics appeared, along with nurses and more medical staff and began to organize the recovery efforts. Policemen flooded the area, attempting to establish order in the chaos and prevent any further injuries.

Quinton moved silently, like the Ghost he'd become, helping with the madness while still trying to sniff out the culprit.

In a pile of rubble, he spotted fragments of what appeared to be the bomb, then examined them, his temper flaring as he noticed a tiny piece of green corduroy fabric clinging to one of the small wires.

Though the remains of the body nearby looked less than human, he recognized the earlier distinct odor of the man amid the charred scent of his flesh.

He had been right about the homeless man being evil.

But what had caused him to turn into a suicide bomber?

His body humming with fury, he called over an officer, introduced himself, then pointed out the evidence so they could send it to forensics. While the officer grabbed a CSI, Quinton unpocketed his cell phone and disappeared into the darkness. With his near photographic memory, he recognized the type of bomb parts used. He knew where they'd come from.

In the periphery of his vision, he caught sight of Annabelle Armstrong helping an elderly lady to a gurney and turned away, finding safety within the sprawling branches of a live oak dripping in spidery Spanish moss.

Then he punched in the number for his handler and explained what had happened.

"I want to know where he is," Quinton said. "The bastard who sold these bomb parts is responsible for all these deaths. And he's going down when I find him."

EERIE, TENNESSEE

Vincent Valtrez clenched his jaw at the sight of the vulture perched on the edge of the windowsill. The bird of prey dipped its bald head and began to clean its feathers, licking pieces of carrion from its black wings. Then it lifted its beak and pierced Valtrez with its insidious eyes as if gloating over a victory.

Legend had it that a vulture's appearance meant death.

He cursed as a sharp wind rattled the panes and made the tree branches scrape the glass. The arrival of All Hallows' Eve had definitely brought in evil with a bang.

Vincent closed his eyes to the horror of the news footage scrolling across the TV screen. Clarissa had warned him earlier that something horrible was about to happen.

She had been right.

And in Savannah, Georgia, the town where he'd just learned one of his brothers lived. Quinton. Another Dark Lord.

Coincidence or not?

He didn't think so.

God, he hadn't even known he had brothers until recently. Until his dead mother had told him.

According to his information, Quinton worked for Homeland Security.

But he also belonged to a secret unit, one that the government would deny any knowledge of.

Quinton was a cold-blooded assassin. A Ghost who killed for hire. He'd been a trained sniper in the military. And he had continued carrying out vigilante killings ever since.

Quinton probably had no idea he even existed.

He had to set up a meeting. But he'd have to be careful.

His gaze veered to the seemingly endless footage of the dead. A ghostly gray mingled with the smoky haze, a gray he now recognized from his wife Clarissa's insight as spirits, Soul Collectors, who'd descended upon the refuse of bodies to offer immortality to the lost souls who lingered in shock over their sudden demise.

Was Zion responsible? Was his father rejoicing in the mass destruction and the number of soldiers he'd gained from the weak who traded their souls and joined him?

Clarissa moved up behind him and slid her arms around his waist. She fed his soul with her goodness, kept his dark side at bay with her tender loving.

Kept him satisfied in bed as he'd never expected.

For he craved sex constantly. And she never failed him. He would never grow tired of having his hands on her breasts, her flesh against his, her heat milking his cock.

"There are demons everywhere," she said in a low voice. "They slipped through the portal last night. I heard the cries of the lost souls as they struggled over immortality."

He nodded, fear making him edgy. Painful emotions that he still had trouble dealing with bombarded him.

Feelings he hadn't wanted any more than he'd wanted to fall in love with Clarissa. But he had, dammit.

Each night the black holes clawed at him. He heard the whisper of evil in the death-scented air, the footsteps of the demons clamoring to steal innocents, the screams of those who tried to escape but failed. The joyous cries of others as they broke through the gate barring their entrance to the mortal world to wreak destruction.

"I'm going to contact Quinton." He leaned forward with a sigh. "If he had something to do with those deaths..."

She stroked the tension from his shoulders. "Don't jump to conclusions, Vincent. Hear him out. Another demon might be responsible."

He nodded. "True. All the more reason he needs to know about our parents."

And their destiny.

But if Quinton had lost himself to the dark side as their father had, blood wouldn't matter.

Vincent would have to destroy him.

Chapter Three

Sweat trickled down Quinton's back as he aimed the M24 sniper rifle at his target, but he ignored the moisture as well as the insects buzzing around his mud-covered face.

Years of honing his concentration paid off on a mission like this. Nothing could distract him from the kill. And he was primed and ready to take this man's life.

The target was Carim Vigontol, an American-born terrorist who had single-handedly supplied massive amounts of weapons to terrorist cells that were responsible for the deaths of hundreds of innocent men, women, and children.

According to the latest intel in a phone call from his handler, Vigontol had provided the material for the Savannah bombings.

Quinton stared at the son of a bitch with hatred.

Dammit. *He* was partly responsible. If he hadn't let Annabelle Armstrong distract him, he might have stopped the old man and saved lives.

The images of the maimed and charred bodies congregated in his head, gnawing at his control and the rage eating his soul. The women and children shouldn't have been murdered.

And now, in the aftermath of their deaths, Vigontol was relaxing on a sunny, powdery beach feeding his slovenly, sick urges with expensive caviar, tequila, and women.

It was Vigontol's turn to feel pain. To taste the bullet as it sliced through his temple and exploded in his brain.

Quinton had stalked his movements the past year, detailing his habits, his likes and dislikes, his schedule. He even knew what time of day the man took a crap. Vigontol liked rough sex with young girls. Drugs. And flowers, for God's sake.

A sarcastic laugh caught in Quinton's parched throat. His target didn't mind killing people, but he tended his roses as if they were his babies.

His downfall—he thought he was safe.

A slow smile slid onto Quinton's face, and he gripped the M24 with ice-cold fingers itching to pull the trigger.

Then the woman appeared. Through the sliding glass doors, the whore slithered into the living room, her double-D breasts spilling over scraps of red lace, the thigh-high stockings covering her legs inching up toward a crotch shaved clean. He'd seen her before. Beautiful. Alluring. A woman who'd feed a man's every twisted fetish.

She knew what Vigontol was and gave herself to him anyway. And she'd helped him smuggle the fucking guns into the States.

Making her a child killer, too.

Still, his body hardened as the man tore the lace bra from her breasts, then used a pocketknife to shred the stockings from her legs. With a slap of his hairy hand, he shoved her to her knees. Though Quinton couldn't hear the target's command, he knew what the man had told her to do.

And she complied. She jerked his pants down and freed the man's stubby dick, then her tongue flicked out and trailed across its engorged head.

Quinton's own cock twitched in his pants. Raw animal sex was something he understood.

He especially liked to watch.

Yet he didn't let it distract him from tuning in to the sounds around him in case of a surprise attack. Security guards were, after all, everywhere. And armed heavily.

The whore sucked and licked, squeezing her hand around Vigontol's balls and teasing as she drew his cock deeper into her mouth.

Finally she pumped him until Vigontol began to come, then she cradled his dick and let him spray her face with his sticky white juices. Smiling, she lapped him up, cleaning him from head to base.

Finished, Vigontol pushed her aside, yanked up his pants, and poured himself a Bloody Mary.

Quinton braced himself, knowing the time had come. The man might have chosen to hide out in the Keys, but Quinton had easily found him. It was, after all, what he'd been trained to do since he was a child.

Track and kill.

Vigontol moved from the inside of the cabana to the brick patio where he stood, drink in hand. He clipped a bloodred rose from one of his prized bushes and sniffed it as he walked toward the hammock. Clear blue water lapped slowly against the shore, the waning sun streaking the majestic gardens with orange and purple rays, the air stirring with the scent of lush green life.

A beautiful day to die.

Then Vigontol's gaze shifted around the compound as

if he sensed Quinton was in hiding, waiting to strike. His beady eyes paused on the very spot where Quinton had staked his sniper gear.

Quinton's extrasensory perception kicked in, bombarding him with sensations. The scent of the man's fear swirled around him, vile and acrid in the heat. The sound of his target's blood racing through his veins pounded in Quinton's ears. The whisper of reality that Vigontol knew that he was about to taste death tickled Quinton's conscience.

But training kept him schooled and emotionless. The evil inside Vigontol had met its match in Quinton's cold-hearted, black side.

His hands were rock steady, his breathing low and steady as he inserted his earplugs. He had one shot before the man's security came running.

He had to get it right.

All thoughts fled except for the kill as Quinton aimed the M24 and fired. The Bloody Mary fell to the patio, the glass shattering. Brain matter and blood splattered across the white brick as his target's body spasmed and jerked, then slumped to the ground and went still.

Methodically, Quinton reached for the grenades to thwart the security as Vigontol's hired guns shouted and scurried about in shocked panic.

Vigontol's black cat darted onto the patio just before he tossed the first explosive. Mentally, Quinton connected with the animal, telepathed the feline a silent message to run into the sea of palms beyond. The cat perked up its ears, arched its back and hissed, then lurched away through the gardens to safety.

Quinton tossed one, then another grenade into the

compound, brick and mortar and bodies exploding and shooting toward the heavens in a fiery blaze. Red rose petals fluttered through the air and rained down around Vigontol's body like blood drops from the sky.

The thrill of the kill sluiced through Quinton as he loaded his weapon system, then turned and jogged toward the chopper he had waiting.

His job was done. All he needed now was to pound out his tension into the body of a willing woman.

Annabelle Armstrong's face materialized, taunting him. He'd wanted to fuck her senseless for months.

But having her was not an option.

A frisson of unease traipsed up his spine. Keeping his identity secret was imperative.

If she tried to expose him, he wouldn't fuck her. He'd have to kill her.

Where was Quinton Valtrez?

Annabelle rubbed the back of her neck, massaging the tension knotting her shoulders as she walked through the now desolate Savannah streets toward the B and B where she'd rented a room. Even twenty-four hours later, the acrid smell of smoke, charred grass, booze, shock, and fear permeated the streets, the lack of crowds a definite sign that tourists and locals alike were terrified of another strike. Only a few curious and brave souls ventured out, some morbid seekers snapping photos of the area roped off as the crime scene.

The cleanup crew still hadn't had time to remove all the debris; the shattered pumpkins, pieces of Halloween decorations, tattered paper ghosts and strands of spiderwebs, and bloody plastic and cardboard tombstones looked even more garish in the aftermath of the violence.

She'd looked for Quinton today as she'd scouted the town, conducting interviews and meeting with the police. She'd even driven out to his cabin, but he was no place to be found.

She wanted him to explain how he'd moved that beam without touching it. Wanted to know more about the killer who'd rushed around saving lives.

She hunched her shoulders beneath her coat as the fall wind rustled the bare trees and tangled her hair around her face. The gnarled branches of the ancient live oaks cast snakelike shadows across the sidewalk with their sweeping webs of stringy brown moss.

Weary, Annabelle hurried into the bed-and-breakfast, then pulled out the files she'd gathered so far on the Valtrez men.

She scrolled through the notes she'd taken a few weeks ago when she'd done a follow-up story on the serial killer in Eerie, Tennessee, then clicked on her recorder.

"Deputy Bluster of Eerie, Tennessee, confirmed that the serial killer used women's fears to track and capture them. People in town also hinted that something supernatural was going on in Eerie. Many recounted spooky legends of monsters who live in the place they call the Black Forest. According to locals, Special Agent Vincent Valtrez grew up in the area, and was the only person to ever go inside the forest and survive."

She paused and took a deep breath, then continued.

"Agent Valtrez was also the FBI agent who tracked down the killer. A local medium named Clarissa King helped solve the case through communication with the dead victims. But Vincent and Clarissa refused to talk to me or be interviewed.

"On my way out of town, I stopped near the edge of the Black Forest and met an old man who rented out cabins on the mountain. He claimed that demons and monsters lived in the Black Forest, and that the only way Vincent survived was because he was part demon himself. The man even claimed that Vincent came from a family spawned by the devil.

"That he had the power to make things explode with his hands."

She shook her head, disbelieving that myths and legends still thrived in the Tennessee hills, that people ran scared of them.

Then again, she was a reporter, and yet she'd wondered if she'd really seen Quinton move that beam with his mind.

She clicked on the mike again. "My interest was piqued, so I did further research and discovered that Vincent has a brother in the military. This led me to my current project, Quinton Valtrez."

She clicked off the mike and stared at the photos of three different terrorists Quinton had supposedly eliminated.

Back to the mike. "Getting information on Quinton has been nearly impossible, but I finally found a soldier who talked. He admitted that Quinton was a trained sniper.

"He also stated that he thought Quinton possessed some kind of mind power that went beyond explanation.

"I am currently investigating this matter and must find details to prove it."

She clicked off the mike and massaged her temple.

Was the old man in Eerie right? Were Vincent and Quinton demons?

She stood and stretched with a groan. She was a by-the-book kind of girl, saw the world in black and white. Did she really believe demons existed?

No, of course not.

She glanced at the clock. It was only midnight. Maybe she'd drive out to Quinton's cabin again. He had to come home sometime.

And if he wasn't home, she'd sneak into his house and find some information for her story.

Dr. Jerome Gryphon combed the rows of beds in the hospital ward, checking on the subjects, who mumbled incoherently and begged him for help.

Their ramblings relayed a hodgepodge of broken memories and traumatic events from times past.

Most had already lost their minds to the cruelties of the aging process, just as their feeble bones and weak limbs had robbed them of agility and speed.

Perfect targets for a predator.

And the perfect fodder for his experiments.

"Please, help me," the old man cried.

"I will," he said gently.

He touched the old man's forehead, his wrinkled skin like sandpaper, and thought of his own father so long ago, of the way his rangy body and mind had disintegrated over time until there had been nothing left but knotted bones and the empty shell of a half human.

Bitterness left an acid taste in his mouth. Memories of being dragged from one ratty cardboard box to another for shelter. Of digging for food from garbage cans, sleeping on the ground with his empty belly growling. His ears ringing with strangers' nasty taunts.

Those bitter memories had shaped him into the man he'd become.

A doctor who intended to do something about it. His research would aid many in the future.

"Just relax, my friend," he said quietly, soothing the man with his calm voice. "You will only feel a tiny pinprick of pain, then relief will come shortly."

Chapter Four

Finally, Quinton was going to get laid.

His body twitched with arousal as the voluptuous bleached blonde slid her clothes to the floor, then sank onto the chair in front of him and spread her legs. He'd arrived back in Savannah in the early morning hours, rented a cheap hotel room—he never brought women to his house—showered, and called Fancy.

Her friend was on her way.

She licked lips painted a bold shimmering red, a reminder of the red roses and blood dotting the target's white brick, and he moaned, his body coiled with heat.

"I'm here to please," she said in a seductive voice.

Her tits bounced as she gyrated around him, dancing so he could watch her sultry moves, and she shook her ass in front of his face until he could barely keep his hands glued to the damn chair.

Then she strutted in front of him, teasing him as she brushed her breasts across his face. Her dark nipples puckered and begged for his mouth, and he drew one in and bit the tip, then suckled her until his cock throbbed inside his jeans.

The door swung open. "Hey, let's get this party started." Her friend strutted in, throwing off clothes as she sashayed toward him, her straight brown hair spilling over her pale back.

Fancy stroked her pink clit, parting her legs so he could see her fingers moving over her heat. His tongue thrust out, hungering for a taste.

But she shook her head, denying him as she would over and over again. Until he ordered her to do as he said.

Her friend moved behind her and began to knead Fancy's breasts, the two of them dancing together like lovers as they titillated each other with fingers and tongues.

He wanted part of the action. To taste and be tasted by them.

But they forced him to wait while they pleasured each other and then wiped their cum on his lips. He groaned, his control slipping as his orgasm teetered near the surface.

"Now," he finally ordered, his patience snapping as dark thoughts churned in his brain. Thoughts of punishing them.

Thoughts he had to extinguish to thwart the animal inside him from being unleashed on innocent humans.

"You are horny, aren't you, you bad boy?" Fancy teased.

He groaned and Fancy laughed like a vixen, then fell to her knees and sucked his cock into her mouth. He closed his eyes and imagined Annabelle Armstrong going down on him, her tongue on his hot skin.

Fancy's friend straddled him, rubbing her clit on his face. Fancy deep-throated him at the same time, and his fantasies of Annabelle sent him over the edge. With a guttural groan he came, his body shuddering as she pulled away and let him spray her breasts.

Relief poured through him, his mind a sieve of evil thoughts. Excitement came from pain. Death triggered pleasure beyond relief.

The past few months, a voice had intruded in his head. An evil voice that called his name as if searching for him, as if it had splintered the earth to rise from the grave.

The monks had warned him when he was a child that one day demons would find him, that they'd try to trap him.

That was the reason they'd sent him to that training camp.

The reason he'd been isolated. Taught to rely on his chi, to hone his skills, to recognize the evil.

And to kill. He enjoyed the kill, maybe too much.

The memory of the vultures the night of the Savannah bombing flashed into his head. More death was on its way. A new dark force walked the earth, one more terrifying and deadly than any he'd encountered to date.

One that wasn't human.

"You're done." He pushed the women off him, stood and yanked on his jeans, then tossed cash onto the table and stormed into the chilly night.

Cramming his hands into the pockets of his jeans, he climbed in his Land Rover and drove toward Tybee Island, the one place where he found peace and quiet.

And a reprieve from the evil.

Yet as he crossed the bridge to the island, fear crawled along his spine. He checked the perimeter of the secluded house, the dark stretches of beach beyond, closed his eyes and inhaled the wind and marsh.

Danger lurked nearby. So close.
Had the demons found him?

Annabelle paused to look around, her nerves on edge as she used her hairpin to break into his house. She was surprised at his lack of security. It was almost as if he thought he had nothing to hide.

The door squeaked open and she inched inside, tiptoeing as she waved her flashlight around the room. Simple basic furniture, all black and chrome—cold, just like the man.

A black lacquered desk occupied the corner, but there was no TV or sound system, only built-in shelves against the wall housing books. The den opened to a small kitchen and a bedroom sat to the left, but it was empty except for a mattress on the floor. His place seemed minimalistic, as if he didn't want any comforts.

She didn't know what she was looking for, exactly, but she'd hoped maybe he kept some kind of journal or file on his kills.

And what else? Perhaps evidence that he might be a demon or have supernatural power?

She still couldn't believe it. Although she could have sworn he'd moved that beam...

She zeroed in on his computer, sat down at the desk and flipped it on, rifling through the contents of the top drawer. A stack of mail drew her eye, and she glanced through it. Typical bills. Curious, she opened the latest bank statement, expecting to find a huge advance for services rendered. She found a few thousand dollars, nothing suspicious.

She spent the next few minutes searching his computer

and desk, hunting for hidden files, a calendar, anything to point to his work. Zilch. Frustrated, she stood and went to the bookshelf, surprised to find books on spirituality mingled with others on martial arts and maps of various places all over the world. Then she noticed a leather-bound book wedged behind a work on meditation.

Her interest piqued, she pulled it out and frowned at the handwritten words.

Deadly Demons.

Her pulse clamored as she flipped through the book. Sketches of supernatural creatures, demons, monsters, and pagan gods filled the yellowed pages.

Perspiration dotted her forehead as she studied the drawing of the Death Angel, an ominous, sinister-looking black shadow that could appear as a vulture, a crow, or a raven.

Just like the vulture she'd seen last night after the explosion.

Another page detailed purgatory and the levels of hell. The punishments for evil that matched the sins, punishments that were horrific.

Then a drawing of the Soul Collectors. She frowned as she read the notations:

The Soul Collectors barter and buy souls off the street by offering immortality to those near death or recently deceased.

Some of the undead become vampires and zombies. Others shift into animal forms—werewolves, werecats, and other werecreatures.

On All Hallows' Eve, a portal is opened that allows demons and Soul Collectors to enter the Earth and ravage the innocents.

Anxiety knotted her insides as she flipped to a sketch of Pan, the god of fear, a hulking black shadow with orange eyes.

One touch and he knows your worst fear, then he uses it to kill you.

Her mind spun with questions. Why did Quinton have this book?

She flipped to another page and read about the Dark Lords, the spawn of Satan and an Angel of Light. Men who possessed superhuman powers.

Suddenly a noise startled her. The faint sound of wooden boards squeaking.

Damn. She quickly shut off the flashlight.

Quinton Valtrez had returned.

If he was a killer as she suspected, he wouldn't hesitate to put a bullet in her head. All he had to do was cart her body out to the ocean, and no one would ever know.

And if he was a demon or a Dark Lord?

Her heart tripped in panic.

No, she didn't believe in demons. Still, Quinton Valtrez was dangerous. She felt along the desk edge for a weapon and grabbed the letter opener as she eyed the sliding glass door. Clenching the letter opener in one hand and the book of demons in the other, she raced to escape.

But Quinton moved at lightning speed, jumped her from behind and slammed her against the wall, pinning her with his body. His knee jabbed into her lower back so painfully she gasped, and he karate-chopped her hand, making her release the letter opener. Pain shot through her wrist, and her legs buckled.

Then the cold barrel of a gun raked across her cheek.

Her heart hammered against her breastbone as she choked on a cry of pure terror. "Please...don't hurt me."

His hot breath bathed her neck as he tightened his grip. "What in the hell are you doing here?"

A sob escaped her. "I...wanted to talk to you."

"So you broke into my house and went through my things?"

"No..."

He wrenched her arm behind her back, twisting it so hard she whimpered and braced herself for the sound of bones shattering.

"Don't lie to me," he growled in a menacing tone. "Who are you, and what the fuck do you want with me?"

A tear slid down her cheek. "Please...you're hurting me..."

"If you don't tell me the truth, I'm going to do a lot worse."

She shuddered, growing nauseous from the pain. "All right, just let me go, and...and I'll explain."

He dragged her from the wall to the sofa and threw her down onto the edge. Her vision blurred as her head snapped back. Outside, the wind roared and the waves crashed against the shore; thunder clapped above. The sound of her own heartbeat drowned them all out, though, her mind scrambling for a feasible lie.

He flipped on the lamp, the dim light streaking the room in sharp yellow lines that slashed the walls, dust moats floating in the light.

With a grunt, he pressed the gun into her chest as he towered over her, a hulking shadow dressed in all black—black leather jacket, black T-shirt, black jeans—his black eyes making him look even more intimidating.

She rubbed at her arm, which throbbed from his punishing grip. What had she been thinking?

She was an amateur, had been a fool to break in.

But if she'd found something concrete, she would have had the story of her life. She'd finally win the respect she wanted and prove she could do hard-core stories.

"I'm waiting," he said in a lethal tone. "Who are you?"

"Annabelle Armstrong," she said.

His voice was just as husky and dark as the rest of him. She'd never seen a man with such raw intensity. His shaggy hair added to his renegade look, the raven locks shimmering in the light. His nose had been broken at least once, and a razorlike scar stretched from his ear down his neck into the top of his T-shirt.

God, he was sexy.

He closed in on her again, rammed his broad face in front of hers, eyes gleaming with coldness. "Go on. You've got five seconds before you become shark bait."

Her breath rushed out, but she met his steely gaze with as much courage as she could muster. "You know who I am, Quinton."

"An intruder, that's what I know."

"Then maybe you should call the police," she said in challenge. "Or are you afraid they'll find out who you are?"

"I'm not afraid of anything," he hissed.

She inhaled against the pain in her wrist and arm. If he was going to kill her, she wanted the truth first. "Why? Because you're a cold-blooded killer? Some kind of monster or demon?"

His gaze fell to the book she'd dropped in her haste to

escape, and his eyes turned that same strange glittering silver they had the night before.

"You believe in demons?" he asked with an ominous eyebrow raise.

"No, I deal in cold, hard facts, blacks and whites. Demons are mythical legends people made up to explain the unexplainable." Her voice cracked, but she forged on, determined not to let him intimidate her. "History and research have shown that people who might have once been deemed possessed or demonic were in reality suffering from a mental illness such as schizophrenia, or another disease, such as syphilis."

"Is that so?" He took a step toward her, his breath bathing her face as his gaze pinned her.

She slid back into the corner of the sofa and shivered. God help her.

He was going to kill her.

Quinton narrowed his eyes, trying to probe Annabelle Armstrong's mind to see how much she knew about him. In spite of her gutsy attitude, she was terrified of him. Thought he was a hard-edged killer. And maybe a demon.

But sexy...

That realization momentarily threw him off guard.

Made his cock twitch and his blood run hot.

Even in danger the night before, he remembered what it had felt like to have her sinful body beneath his.

But, hell, she'd broken into his damn house.

Where had she gotten her information?

She couldn't have found anything concrete here. He was a professional. He left no evidence, no paper trail, nothing that could link him to any of the terrorists or their deaths.

Except for that damn demon book...

Which had nothing to do with his job.

Just his personal life.

"You know, lady, if you really think I'm a killer or a monster, you must be pretty damn stupid to break into my house."

His fingers tightened around her wrist, and he clenched his jaw as she paled. He had to scare her off. "Either that or you have a death wish."

She winced but jutted up her chin, those cobalt-blue eyes boring into his. "No, I don't. But I want the truth. I know you're an assassin. I have photos of three of your kills." She hesitated. "So I don't understand why you ran around saving people last night."

He cursed. "You wanted me to stand by and let innocent people die?"

"No, of course not." She hesitated, confusion marring her face. "Just tell me one thing, Quinton. Do you ever regret what you do, that you kill for a living?"

How could he regret killing bad guys? But he didn't acknowledge her question, and he refused to admit to anything, no matter how much proof she thought she had.

"Photos can be misleading." He squeezed her wrist harder. He'd use his gift against her. Climb in her head and figure out how to keep her from exposing him.

Her memories became his—her mother had died recently. Her father had abandoned her. She was trying to make it in a man's dog-eat-dog world.

"You think you have something to prove," he said in

a gruff voice. "And you'd jeopardize your life to do it. That's not very smart, Annabelle."

She stiffened. "I just want the truth. I saw what you did last night," she said in a strained voice.

He narrowed his eyes. "What are you talking about?"

"You moved a beam off of that man without touching it," she whispered. "You did it with your mind."

He threw his head back and laughed sarcastically. "You must have hit your head. You were obviously seeing things."

Her mouth tightened. "I didn't hit my head."

Her gaze latched onto his, the sultry look in her eyes daring him to argue.

"Then you're delusional."

A crooked smile curved her mouth as her gaze swung sideways to note the demon book. "That's not what your book says. Which one are you? One of the demons? A Dark Lord or a Soul Collector?"

He smirked. "Like you said, they're childhood stories. Not real." He released her abruptly. "Get out," he snapped. "And stay out of my life or you'll be sorry."

She heaved a breath and strode toward the door, tugging her shoulder bag over her arm. It suddenly hit him that she probably had a recorder.

He caught her before she could leave, jerked the bag from her and rummaged through it.

Cold rage shot through him as his fingers slid around the small metal recorder. She flinched, trying to mask her fear as he ripped out the tape.

She glared at him, then snatched up her bag. "You're not going to scare me off, Quinton."

He gripped his hands into fists, the darkness inside

him tearing at his calm veneer, and he barely held himself in check.

Something in his eyes must have frightened her because she suddenly hurried toward the door.

Damn, the woman had brains and guts. But she was too close to the truth for comfort.

Instinct told him to kill her now, but rationale warned him to wait. He watched her as she sprinted down the drive and onto the road. She must have parked her car on another street, the reason he hadn't seen it when he'd arrived.

He rubbed his head, contemplating how she could have gotten her information. The only person who knew his identity was his handler. And he would *never* divulge the truth. He'd be a dead man if he did.

So who had sent her those photos and given her his name?

His training kicked in and he swept the cabin in search of a bug, then checked his phone as well. Thankfully the search turned up nothing, so he punched in his contact number, then left the coded message for his handler to call him back.

Had someone discovered he was the Ghost? If so, what had the person hoped to accomplish by telling Annabelle?

His home phone trilled, and he checked the caller ID box—a Tennessee number. And the name Valtrez.

What the hell?

He didn't have any family . . .

His heart racing, he snatched up the handset. "Yes?"

"Quinton Valtrez?" a deep voice asked.

"Yes, this is Quinton Valtrez. Who is this?"

"My name is Vincent," the deep voice said. "I'm your older brother."

Chapter Five

Quinton clenched his jaw. Was this some kind of joke? Or a trap?

"I don't have a brother," he ground out. "In fact, I don't have any family at all."

"That's not true." The man cleared his throat. "I know this comes as a shock, but I was a toddler when you were born, and our mother sent you away. I only recently found out about you myself."

Quinton didn't believe him. This had to be a setup. Maybe the man who'd sent the tip about him to Annabelle was behind this.

"I want to meet you, then I'll explain everything," Vincent said gruffly.

Quinton checked his watch. He'd already had one visitor too many in his place. "I'll come to you. Tell me where you are." And he'd be ready and armed, prepared this time.

"Eerie, Tennessee," Vincent said. "It's in the Smoky Mountains."

"I'll be there tomorrow." He jotted down the address, then hung up, his suspicions mounting. If he'd had a brother, the monks would have told him. But they'd sworn he had no family.

No, he was an island unto himself. And he didn't intend to let anyone invade his territory.

So who was this man? One of the demons the monks had warned him about?

He would find out. And if this man had fed Annabelle Armstrong information about him, or if he was a demon, Quinton would kill him.

His pulse pounding, he strode to his bedroom, retrieved a duffel bag from the closet, and tossed in some jeans and shirts. Then he stripped and showered, but he was too wired to sleep. He'd trained his body long ago to do without, and now the adrenaline racing through his veins from his encounter with Annabelle and that bizarre phone call kept the questions ticking in his head.

His cell phone rang again, and he checked the number—his handler, Keller.

"Valtrez, good work on number 343."

For security purposes, they always referred to the targets by number, not name.

"No problem."

"What's going on?" Keller asked.

Quinton explained about Annabelle's visit. "How the fuck did she find out who I am?"

"I don't know," Keller said, his voice edgy with concern.

"You haven't had any security breaches?" Quinton asked.

"Absolutely not. If I had, I would have alerted you."

"Maybe you should check your contacts," Quinton said. "Someone has leaked information to her, and I want his name."

"Right. I'm on it."

"I've got another problem, too. I received a strange call from a man who claimed to be my brother."

The roar of an engine, then a loud whirring sound cut into the background, and he realized Keller must be catching a chopper. Always on the go.

He started to ask where but bit back the question, knowing the answer would be cryptic. Information was dispensed on a need-to-know basis.

"This man called himself Vincent. It has to be a trap." Quinton scrubbed a hand over his face. "I'm going to Tennessee tomorrow to check him out."

"I'll see what I can find out about him, if it's a fake name or if Vincent Valtrez exists," Keller said. "Be careful."

"Don't worry," Quinton said, the ice back in his veins. "If it's a trap, he won't walk away alive."

When he met the man tomorrow, he'd probe his mind. Find out his real agenda. And if he posed a danger or a threat, he'd dispose of him just as he did his usual marks.

Then once again the Ghost would be safe. That is, unless Annabelle Armstrong decided to talk.

No . . . she wouldn't. He'd do whatever was necessary to keep her quiet.

Annabelle shivered as she drove to the bed-and-breakfast, an antebellum mansion that was supposedly haunted by the spirit of a war-torn lover.

According to the legend, the woman had stayed behind to wait on the man she loved, but he had betrayed her and never returned home. Guests often claimed they heard her sobs at night as she roamed restlessly through the attic, and some said on a foggy night you could see the silhouette of her face pressed against the attic's oval window.

Annabelle scoffed at the story. The woman should have known not to trust the man. Annabelle's own father had taught her that lesson well when he'd deserted her.

She gripped the steering wheel of her VW tighter. She'd been convinced that she could handle a confrontation with Quinton because he had saved her life.

Then he'd threatened to take it.

She'd never met anyone like him. Cold. A loner. A man with secrets.

A man who intrigued her because he both aroused her with his dark sensuality and terrified her with the fury simmering in his brooding, intense gaze.

She wanted to know more about him.

Damn her curious nature, her thirst to unveil the facts and find the story behind the story.

Because if Quinton had killed those suspected terrorists, he was an assassin. And if demons existed, if he was a demon...

God, she would be crazy to go up against him.

What was she thinking?

She parked in front of the B and B and climbed out, searching the shadows as she rushed up the oyster-shell walkway, then inside. The house was eerily quiet, the wooden steps creaking as she climbed to the second floor. The whisper of the wind echoing off the ocean whistled through the eaves of the empty hallway. A cold chill crawled along her nerve endings, the soft sound of someone crying floating to her from the attic.

The woman's ghost...

She'd never stayed in a haunted place, but the prospect had fascinated her when she'd first arrived. Now, the thought unnerved her.

Hand trembling, she jammed the key into the lock and opened the door. The second-floor rooms had been built in a square surrounding a garden area below, each with French doors and a wrought-iron patio overlooking the garden. A faint stream of moonlight streaked the room, the window sheers flapping from the heat vent below.

Her foot hit something, though, and she glanced down. A plain manila envelope lay on the braided rug in the entryway. Someone must have slipped it under her door while she was out.

Nerves gathered, catching in her throat as she picked the envelope up and flipped it over in search of a name or return address, but as she expected it was blank. Forcing air into her lungs, she flipped the clasp open, biting back a gasp at the sight of the photo.

A dead man, shot once in the temple, lay on a sea of white bricks with bloodred rose petals surrounding him, his house behind him in shambles and flames from an obvious explosion.

She recognized the man immediately—Carim Vigontol, a well-known suspected terrorist who had escaped the law on technicalities.

Now he was dead.

Was Quinton Valtrez responsible, or was her information incorrect?

A second photo was inside the envelope, and her heart hammered as she pulled it out. The scene in the picture wrenched her heart all over again—the bombing on Halloween.

Suddenly her phone vibrated at her belt, indicating she

had a message. She flipped it open, and her heart lurched as she read it:

Like the fireworks? Stay tuned. More on the way.

NOVEMBER 2, ALL SOULS' DAY

Quinton steered the Range Rover around the Tennessee mountain roads, his Glock weighing heavy against his chest where he'd stowed it inside his shoulder holster.

He had no idea what he was going to encounter, but he had to be ready for anything.

Gigantic trees and sharp ridges climbed and rolled, the bare branches swaying with the force of the fall wind, reminding him of the Tennessee mountains where the monks had told him he'd grown up. He'd heard tales of the Black Forest and the strange, inhuman creatures that lived within the dark woods, the serpents and screaming vines that ate humans, the place where no life existed, only shadows, darkness.

The stories of evil and sin thriving across the land, of the Twilight Guards, who guarded the realm between the mortal and demonic worlds, of the Soul Collectors, who preyed on the weak to steal their souls for Satan, the werecreatures and monsters who lived in the shadows, the Night Stalkers, who could shape-shift into demons or humans at will, the legends of the Sacred Places and the Wasteland for Lost Souls...

He had been terrified as a kid.

Because he'd seen into the monks' minds and known the stories were true.

With his gift, he didn't doubt there were others among him who possessed supernatural powers, both good and bad.

But he had learned to channel his fear of demons because they'd never shown themselves to him. Then he'd escaped the mountains and tales, only to come face-to-face with human monsters.

Those he could fight.

Yet the monks had predicted that the demons would come in time. That he must train and focus so he could fight his enemies.

Was this the time?

He maneuvered the narrow, winding road, the stiff peaks and ridges swallowing him in their folds as he neared the address Vincent had given him.

The log cabin sat at the top of the ridge, its back deck jutting over the cliff, offering a breathtaking but terrifying view of the miles of rugged terrain stretching below with its dangers and unforgiving rock.

He visually assessed the isolated area. If Vincent intended to kill him, he could easily dump his body into the forest and let the animals feed on his remains, and no one would be the wiser.

He patted the Glock inside his jacket, checked his backup pistol and the knife strapped to his ankle, then climbed out, adjusting his shades as his eyes were sometimes supersensitive to light, a product of being locked in the dark for long periods of time as a child.

He scanned the periphery of the log cabin, his senses kicking in. A vulture soared above as if waiting on death to strike.

The scent of the forest engulfed him, the trees, the

animals, the stench of blood and death. The sound of scampering squirrels foraging for food, the growl of a mountain lion in search of prey, the flap of a hawk's wings against the frigid air. A rattlesnake hissed in the distance, followed by the undeniable screech of one animal attacking another.

Memories of his days of isolation in the monastery and the mountains returned, along with his sniper training, and he steadied his breathing. Calm. Cool. Detached.

Trust no one. Suspect everyone.

The front door opened and he squared his shoulders, automatically moving one hand over the weapon inside his bomber jacket, bracing himself for attack.

The man who walked out was an inch taller than him, and Quinton was a big man. Vincent had black hair and eyes . . . eyes just like his own. Black. Cold. Emotionless.

Quinton forced a mental connection, but for a moment, his telepathy hit a brick wall. Then he saw darkness and pain. A soul struggling with inner demons just as he did himself. And an endless, bottomless pit beckoning him to plunge into its abyss.

Was this man a demon?

Then a woman appeared by the man's side. Small, with long, curly russet-colored hair and a heart-shaped face. An expression akin to surprise flitted in her eyes, and then she smiled.

He mentally sifted through her thoughts, read relief that he had come. A deep love for the dark man by her side.

Then a sudden screech of lost souls screaming in her head.

He swallowed, adopting his expressionless mask although his pulse clamored at the horrific cries.

We shouldn't have died.

A monster killed us.

There's another demon in our midst.

Her gaze met his, the same pain and suffering reflected in her eyes. Finally the voices fell silent as if she'd shushed them in her head.

He studied her intently. She must be a medium.

"Welcome to our home, Quinton." She nudged the man beside her, who was staring at Quinton, sizing him up. "Vincent, aren't you going to invite your brother inside? It's cold out, and he's come a long way."

Vincent strode toward Quinton, his movements as precise and controlled as Quinton's. In spite of his skepticism and distrust, Quinton's heart thundered in his chest.

His physical resemblance to this man was uncanny.

"Vincent Valtrez," the man said as he extended his hand. "This is my wife, Clarissa. Come inside now. We have to talk."

His voice was more a command than an invitation, and Quinton hesitated before he shook his hand. But the gesture opened a doorway into the man's mind, and Quinton bit back a smile.

Vincent was just as distrustful of him as he was of the man.

Then, in a flash of darkness, he heard a war raging in the man's head. Vincent thinking about making things explode with his hands. Killing animals.

Grief as he'd watched his mother die. Then Vincent as a boy driving a stake into a man's heart.

No, not a man, a black shapeless beast.

One that was back now to spread his evil.

Drip. Drip. Drip.

Dr. Sam Wynn smiled as he watched the blood drain from the corpse. So much blood. Steel pans were filled with the thick rich substance, the smell vile and coppery.

Adrenaline churned through his bloodstream. The autopsy was a fascinating process. First the Y incision to open the body cavity. Then the saws and scalpels.

Next the process of removing the organs. One by one. Weighing them. Holding them in his hands.

He smiled as he contemplated watching the fluids *gush* and stream from the lifeless body. He could feel the warm liquids *seep* through his fingertips as he dug inside the internal cavities. Could hear the bones shattering as he sawed his way through cartilage and tissue.

Ah, those lovely bones...

Brittle, filled with marrow, with the blood of a life that no longer existed.

Science was his calling. Slicing bodies to study the cause of death, his playing field.

Now he had so many decimated bodies to study. The ones from the mass bombing intrigued him. Flesh had literally been ripped from bones, muscle and tissue exposed. An arm here, a leg there, a headless body.

Like a puzzle, he'd spread the pieces out, labeled each one, run tests, and pieced them together to make the bodies whole again. Although for some it was too late to be put back together. The poor bastards.

But he would do what he could for them. Attach a name to them so families could be notified.

He pulled on his protective goggles, then narrowed his eyes as he spotted the jagged teeth marks etched into the woman's femur. Like needle marks in a junkie's arm, but these were jagged in places, more brutal.

The markings of a bird's talons.

He grabbed his camera and snapped a photo. He had to add this bone to his collection.

After all, no one would ever miss it.

Chapter Six

Quinton entered the log cabin, wary, alert for a trap.

On the surface, the small cabin looked homey, with soft leather couches, braided rugs, a wedding photo on a pine sofa table, a crocheted afghan in blue and red, and a fire roaring in the stone fireplace. A shepherd mix stood up and growled then moved to Clarissa's side as if to protect her.

Before Clarissa or Vincent could quiet the dog, Quinton squatted down and held out his hand, soothing the animal's fears with a silent command.

Clarissa's eyes widened as if impressed, but Vincent simply studied him with narrowed eyes. Quinton tried to tap into Vincent's mind again, but suddenly a wall slid up, shutting him out.

"His name is Wulf," Clarissa said. "Let me take your coat."

She reached for his jacket, and Vincent strode to the bar in the corner and poured two drinks. Scotch, an expensive brand that Quinton often purchased himself.

He accepted the highball glass, their gazes locking.

"You're going to need that," Vincent said.

"What I need is answers," Quinton said. "And the truth about who you are and what I'm doing here."

Vincent gestured toward the sofa but Quinton shook his head. He moved to the fireplace and claimed the wing chair facing the door and window, his training kicking in. He never placed his back to the door, never in the line of attack.

"You were in the military," Vincent said. "And now you work with Homeland Security."

Quinton gave a clipped nod, then took a small sip of the scotch and let it slide down his throat, warming him as he assessed Vincent. "And you?"

"FBI." Vincent produced his identification, then handed him a folder.

Vincent said nothing else, simply waited while Quinton examined the file. Detailed notes and photos of past cases Vincent had worked on for the government filled the folder. His heart hammered at the most recent story—the serial killer who'd stalked and killed several women in Eerie.

Annabelle Armstrong had done a story on the case, although she hadn't mentioned anyone by the name of Vincent Valtrez.

He glanced up at Vincent. The files looked legit and would be easy to check. "I heard about that serial killer case," he said, "but a deputy named Bluster solved it. Your name wasn't mentioned."

"I don't like the press."

Quinton chewed the inside of his cheek. "So you work for the FBI," Quinton said. "That's how you found me." Meaning his cover was definitely blown, and the Ghost unit might have to be disbanded for safety's sake. He wasn't their only agent.

Vincent nodded. "Trust me, your cover is safe. I didn't call you about that."

"Then what?"

"Like I said, we're brothers."

Quinton forced his voice to be calm. "What makes you think that?"

Vincent's gaze remained steady. "My...our mother told me."

Quinton drained the scotch, set the glass on the table with a thud, and stood. "Now I know you're lying. My mother is dead."

"I know," Vincent said in a low voice. "But Clarissa is a medium, and she spoke with her from the grave."

Quinton hesitated, then pivoted to study Clarissa. So he had read her mind correctly—there had been lost spirits crying out in her head.

Could she have communicated with his mother? And if so, was this man telling the truth—did he have a brother he'd never known about?

Annabelle's hands shook as she entered the police station. She had to report the text message. Although she wished the messenger had given her more information to go on.

She'd tried to send a reply, but it bounced back. Apparently no address from the sender could be located.

A twenty-something blonde receptionist smiled at her as she stepped up to her desk. "How can I help you?"

"I need to speak to a detective."

"Just a sec."

She punched an intercom button, relayed the request, and five minutes later, a husky man in a baggy suit and flashy tie appeared through a steel door. He was scowling, his balding head shiny beneath the fluorescent lights.

"Detective Crawley, ma'am." His head bobbed slightly. "You asked to speak to a detective?"

"Yes," she said, then introduced herself. "I'm Annabelle Armstrong, CNN News."

His bushy eyebrows rose. "Oh, yeah, I recognize you from TV. You come for a story about the bombing?"

"Actually, I was here on vacation and happened to be on River Street at the time of the explosion." She gestured toward the back. "Can we talk?"

He shifted awkwardly, then led her through the door to a small interrogation room with a metal table and chairs. "Coffee?"

She nodded. "Thanks."

He poured them each a cup, then straddled the chair across from her. "We already had a press conference, and I covered everything we have so far."

She placed a photo of Quinton on the table. "Do you recognize this man?"

Detective Crawley nodded. "Yeah, Quinton Valtrez. He works for Homeland Security. He found bomb parts in the explosion and pointed them out to our CSI."

So he was working with the police. Interesting.

She laid the photo of Vigontol on the desk next. "How about this man? Do you know who he is?"

He narrowed his eyes at the dead man's picture. "No. Should I?"

"He was a suspected terrorist."

"You think he had something to do with the bombing?"

"I'm not certain, but it's possible."

"You know where he is?"

She produced the second photo, the one of Vigontol lying in a pool of blood. "Dead. As of last night."

His gaze lifted slowly to hers. "You know who killed him?"

"Again, I can't say until I have proof."

He grunted. "Well, if he was responsible for all those people's deaths, then I say he got what he deserved."

So he believed in meting out justice like Quinton. Annabelle clenched her teeth. "There's something else." She removed her PDA. "I received a disturbing text message that you should see."

He unfolded reading glasses from his pocket, put them on, then read the small screen with a frown. "Who sent it?"

"I don't know," Annabelle said with a hint of frustration in her voice. "That's why I'm here. We need to try and trace it."

He pulled at his chin. "Don't you think it's probably just a prank?"

She rolled her shoulders. "That's possible. But what if it's not?"

"Why send it to you?"

"Because I'm a reporter," she said, "and he's seeking attention. He wants his five minutes of fame."

He frowned. "It doesn't say when or where the next one will strike, does it?"

"No, but we should see if we can trace the message."

He made a grunting sound. "I guess you're right. Although I just got word that Dr. Wynn, a forensic specialist the Feds brought in from DC, ID'd the man they thought was the suicide bomber as Warren Ames. Some locals who survived witnessed an old man in a green corduroy jacket set it off. Seems he was homeless, had been sleeping in the graveyards. Says here he lost an arm during his stint in the service and suffered from post-traumatic stress syndrome. Police are trying to locate his family members or friends for questioning." He heaved a breath as if the explanation exhausted him. "So it doesn't sound like a terrorist cell."

She shivered. "Why would a homeless man kill himself and others?"

He gave her an impatient look. "He was probably mentally ill or had a substance abuse problem."

"But how would he get the parts or have the knowledge to build a bomb?"

Crawley consulted the fax on his desk. "He was a veteran. Probably learned how to make a bomb in the military. And if not, anyone can read about it on the danged Internet these days."

Annabelle pursed her lips, thinking. "If he's homeless, he wouldn't have access to the Internet."

He made another sound in his throat. "Right. And he's dead, so he couldn't have sent you a text."

Annabelle frowned. "But someone else could have put him up to it. And they might be planning another attack." She gestured to the phone, determined that he listen. "Do you want more deaths on your conscience?"

He sighed, then reluctantly picked up the phone. But another thought struck her. If Quinton worked for the government taking out terrorists, maybe he already had information about the bomber.

The man scared her, but she'd find him and make him talk to her. More lives might be lost if she didn't.

Quinton didn't need Vincent, didn't want anyone needing him. He liked his life just fine.

No ties.

No one to answer to or worry about being used as a means to get to him.

No one to distract him as Annabelle had that night in Savannah.

"This is bullshit," Quinton said. "How do I know this isn't a trap?"

"You don't," Vincent said in a deadly calm voice. "Just as I'm not sure I can trust you. For all I know, you may already have given in to your dark side."

Quinton tensed. Vincent knew that he struggled with the darkness? Was he a mind reader as well?

"Please, listen to him," Clarissa said softly. "Your mother wanted Vincent to find you. You need each other to fight the evil threatening the world."

Vincent refilled Quinton's glass as well as his own, then turned, his penetrating gaze boring into Quinton's. "Our father was a spawn of Satan, our mother an Angel of Light, of goodness." Vincent unrolled his right palm to reveal a scar, the imprint of an angel's wings. Then Clarissa removed an amulet from around her neck—an angel's wings with a bloodstone set in the heart of the angel.

"This amulet belonged to our mother," Vincent said. "I took it after her death. She told me that she also left one with you when she gave you away."

Quinton's head churned. He did have one—it was pewter with a clear quartz stone.

"The amulet is for protection," Vincent said. "My bloodstone stands for courage. Your stone stands for the mind, clairvoyance, because you have that gift."

So he had done his homework.

"The amulet proves that we're tied together and symbolizes the fact that we have Mother's blood as well as our father's." Vincent unbuttoned his shirt and angled himself to reveal the back of his right shoulder. "Just as this serpent birthmark means we're brothers, that we're demonborn."

The symbol of the serpent eating its tail . . . The monks claimed the birthmark represented the universe and how it destroyed and re-created itself in the cycle of life and death.

Vincent sighed. "Of course, we'll want to test your blood to verify that we're actually related."

Quinton nodded. "And if I don't agree?"

"You will," Vincent said.

Clarissa smiled gently. "You have to know the truth about your past to understand your destiny."

Quinton's patience snapped like a thin rubber band. "Just cut the cryptic shit and get on with it. You said our father was evil. What do you mean by that?"

"He was brutal, abusive, and cruel. He took his temper out on me and turned on Mother toward the end," Vincent said sharply. "When I was ten, he tortured her and burned her at the stake, because he allowed his dark side to possess him completely."

"His dark side?" A side Quinton knew well, one the monks had referred to and warned him about.

Vincent cleared his throat. "Yes, he was a Dark Lord." He paused and sipped his scotch. "Just as you and I are."

Quinton remained stone still, refusing to react.

"But Father allowed his evil side to triumph over good." Vincent blew out a breath. "It's a constant battle for me, as I assume it is for you."

Quinton's jaw clenched. He didn't want to admit

anything to this man. Had kept his secrets too long. "I don't know what you mean."

"Of course you do," Vincent said, a hint of a sinister smile gracing his lips. "You're a sniper. You kill for a living because you have a hunger for blood; you crave the kill."

Suspicions reared their head. "Did you tell CNN reporter Annabelle Armstrong about me?"

Vincent frowned. "Hell, no. I refused her request for an interview. Why do you ask?"

"Because she came to Savannah and said an anonymous source fed her intel about what I do."

Vincent cursed. "And she wants to expose you?"

He gave a clipped nod.

"Our secret can't be made public, Quinton. Imagine the panic that would occur if we announced that dangerous demons are entering the mortal realm."

He was right. Complete terror would prevail.

"Our father has risen in power now," Vincent continued. "Those killings started when it was announced that Zion was being named the new leader of the underworld. The upheaval and destruction will continue until we stop him."

Chapter Seven

"Our father is the leader of the underworld?" Quinton asked.

"Yes. And one of his worshippers is responsible for the deaths in Savannah." Vincent spread the photos of the Savannah ship bombing in front of Quinton. "See that gray cast, the shadows?"

Quinton nodded. He'd noticed it the night of the bombing. "I assume it's some sort of an illusion from the smoke."

Vincent shook his head. "Those are spirits, the Soul Collectors, who converged to steal souls while the dead were still in shock over their demise."

"Come with me, Quinton," Clarissa said. "There's something you need to see. Then you might believe that Vincent is telling the truth."

Quinton probed her thoughts and read sincerity, not subterfuge. So he followed her and Vincent up the stairs to a small attic with sloped ceilings. For a brief second, his claustrophobia resurfaced, the memories of being locked in the closetlike rooms at the monastery, the nightmares of his imprisonment underground when he'd been beaten savagely—the heat, the stench, the rats and bugs nibbling at him . . .

Clarissa closed the curtains, bathing the room in darkness, then knelt and lit a circle of candles on the hardwood floor. The scents of lavender, rosemary, vanilla, and other spices filled the air as the candles fluttered to life.

He scrutinized her as she closed her eyes and chanted,

To the present
From the past
Bring this spirit
To speak at last.

Suddenly cool air swirled around him, adding the aroma of otherworldly creatures to the mix. The curtains fluttered, and a shimmering mass of golden sparkles lit the darkness, first floating randomly, then gelling into the silhouette of a woman. A warm glow replaced the chill, and a peacefulness settled over the room.

"It's our mother, the Angel of Light," Vincent said quietly.

He stared at the shimmering creature in shock. She was beautiful. Long golden hair flowed around her white-gold silhouette, her face almost translucent, soft, lovely.

"Quinton, I'm glad Vincent found you. Your brother brought you here because it's time you all know about one another." She turned to Vincent. "Where's Dante?"

"Who is Dante?" Quinton asked.

The Angel hesitated. "Your twin. You were separated to keep you safer."

"I have people looking for him now," Vincent said.

Anger mounted inside Quinton, born from years of bitterness toward her for abandoning him. "Don't you think it's a little late to act like you care about me now?"

"I don't blame you for being angry," the Angel said. "But I gave you up to protect you, son. To keep you safe from your father and the demons. Each of you has powers. Vincent has the power in his hands to make things explode. You, Quinton, are telepathic. And you can make things move with your mind."

Quinton tensed.

"You have goodness in you, Quinton, as Vincent does, but you fight that inner evil every day. It's going to grow more difficult to resist now that your father, Zion, is in control, because he will play upon your weaknesses." She paused. "He's issued orders that the three of you must be turned and brought to him. And he'll do anything to win you over. There's a demon after you now. The Death Angel—you may have seen him in his demonic form. The Death Angel appears as a vulture or a raven."

Quinton fisted his hands, his heart hammering in his chest. Fuck. He'd seen the vulture at the bombing in Savannah, then others had swarmed. And he'd spotted another one above Vincent's house. "Let's say for a minute that I do believe you. What then? Do I go around and kill vultures?"

"No. The Death Angel has the power to possess the body of a human. Find him in that form, and you can kill him more easily. You must use your power to destroy him."

The Death Angel watched the Valtrez brothers through the window as they met for the first time.

The devastation and death he'd already wrought made him lift his head in regal glory. So many bodies to devour, so much blood and maimed flesh.

So delicious.

He licked his feathers, cleaning blood and juices from the strands, already anticipating his next feast.

The men could not stop him. Death was inevitable.

Unless they caught him in human form...

But he was too cunning and fast. Could shift into and out of demonic form in the bat of an eye.

A tasty morsel of flesh rolled down his throat, and he savored its succulent flavor, wishing he could taste the decaying flesh of Zion's sons.

He might one day.

If he couldn't turn them, then he would take their lives.

The Seer had prophesied that if the Angel's plans failed, Quinton would join with the woman, and she would strengthen his noble side.

He would stop the Dark Lord before that happened. And he'd use the woman to lure Quinton into his hungry hands.

Annabelle sighed into the phone. The detective had finally connected her with another agent from Homeland Security. "So you weren't able to trace where the message originated from?"

Agent Keller cleared his throat. "No, ma'am. It could have come from a throwaway phone or the sender has a scrambling device, but we tracked it back to the server and found nothing." He paused. "You know this could be a prank."

"But what if it's not?" Annabelle said in frustration. "I'm a reporter. Maybe that's why he sent me the message. He wants me to publicize the fact that he's not finished, that this is a terrorist attack."

The agent cleared his throat. "I can put a tracking device on your phone in case you receive another message."

"What good will that do if he's using a throwaway phone or a scrambling device?"

"None," the agent conceded. "But if you receive another message, especially any specific information, you will pass it on?"

"Of course," Annabelle said. "I want the story, Agent Keller, but I certainly don't want a repeat of the Savannah scene. I was there and witnessed the horror."

"I understand. And I will be in touch with my sources to see if any talk of a new terrorist cell has cropped up."

He started to hang up, but she stopped him with her next question. "What can you tell me about Quinton Valtrez? Does he work for Homeland Security?"

A tense second of silence stretched between them. "I'm assuming you know that he does or you wouldn't be asking."

"Yes, but in what capacity does he work for you?"

Another pause. "He's an investigator, one of our best."

"Then you'll inform him of my call?"

"Yes."

"What about his unit, the Ghost team?"

"I have no idea what you're talking about, Miss Armstrong."

Annabelle's fingers tightened around the handset. No guts, no glory. "They're a secret group of assassins who work for the government, aren't they?"

"I don't know where you got that information, but your source is incorrect. The government certainly has no such unit."

"If they did, they wouldn't acknowledge it, would they?" Annabelle pressed.

"If they did," he said in a lethally calm voice, "trying to dig into it would be very dangerous."

Annabelle seethed with anger.

"Now please let me know if you receive another text, especially if you discover information on when and where another attack might occur." Without waiting for a response, he hung up.

Annabelle sighed. She hoped the bomber did contact her again. If another bomb was due to go off, she wanted to help stop it.

Detective Crawley returned and she thanked him, then hurried to her car. As she settled inside, she phoned Quinton Valtrez's number. She let it ring and ring, but he didn't answer.

Of course, Agent Keller was probably calling him now, warning him about her inquiry. She'd track him down; she still needed answers to many questions.

But first she'd drop by the local homeless shelter, see if anyone there had known Warren Ames and what would drive him to kill himself and hundreds of others.

Storm clouds darkened the sky, casting shadows along the winding mountain road as Quinton drove back to Savannah. He'd stopped by BloodCore and given a blood sample to find out if he actually was biologically related to Vincent Valtrez.

Would his demon blood show up in the tests?

His phone rang and he noticed it was Annabelle Armstrong, so he let it go to voice mail. She was a problem that he hadn't figured out what to do with yet.

Just as Vincent Valtrez was now. Dammit, he'd liked his life as it was. Ordered. Controlled.

Unencumbered by family.

He got his assignment, tracked the target, made the kill. No personal involvements. No one to answer to.

No one wanting him to work with them.

He worked solo.

He was the hunter.

Now, Vincent wanted him to believe that someone was hunting *him*. Not just someone, but a demon. That he had to connect with family he'd never known and fight his father, the leader of the underworld.

His phone trilled again, and he checked the number. It was his handler this time so he connected. "Yeah, it's Valtrez."

"We've got problems. I just got off the phone with that nosy reporter Annabelle Armstrong."

"Hell, what did she want?"

"Two things," Keller said. "Information on you. She asked about the damn Ghosts, Quinton."

His fingers tightened around the steering wheel. Fuck. She had balls. "I told you she was a problem. What did you tell her?"

"Nothing."

"Good. She has no proof, or she wouldn't be asking you."

"Yeah, but there's more. She received an anonymous text message saying that the Savannah bombing was only the beginning."

Quinton ground his teeth, his blood running cold. "Any specifics?"

"No. I tried to trace the message, but it was impossible."

"Where is she now?"

"Still in Savannah. She was at the local police station. The detective also told me she was asking questions about you. I covered your ass, but she's getting way too close."

"Don't worry. I'll take care of her." He didn't like it, but he'd have to. "What about Vincent Valtrez? What did you find out about him?"

"Everything I've been able to dig up says he's legitimate. His ties to the Feds run deep. And three months ago, he solved a serial killer case in Tennessee."

"I know." He tightened his hands around the steering wheel as his handler continued, relaying the story of how Vincent's parents supposedly abandoned him at age ten, that Vincent had accused his father of killing his mother in the Black Forest, but that her body had never been recovered.

Because Vincent had said his father, quite possibly *their* father, was a demon that had killed their mother. And he'd witnessed it.

"So what do you think?" Keller asked.

"I don't know," Quinton said. "I need more time to investigate."

"All right. Honestly, Quinton, with your cover in jeopardy because of that reporter, I can't give you any assignments right now. We can't risk exposing the team."

He clenched his jaw. He knew the rules. Had known the moment he'd signed on.

He hung up, heart pounding. By the time he reached Savannah, his muscles were in knots and his dark side had emerged with images of men and bloodbaths. He craved the taste of violence, of the kill. Of vengeance.

He had to find out if Annabelle was his enemy. Just how much she knew. Steeling himself for whatever he discovered, he swung by his cabin and picked up surveillance gear, then drove to the bed-and-breakfast where she was staying. A quick check and he discovered she wasn't inside.

Using skills he'd honed on the job to become invisible, he climbed up the railing outside her room and jimmied the French doors, then slipped into the room. He searched the drawers and her suitcase first but didn't find a weapon. Her computer and files were not in the room, so he assumed she'd taken them with her.

Methodically he installed hidden cameras in every room. Watching his targets afforded him the advantage. He learned their routine, their contacts, their plans, their weaknesses. Surveillance of Annabelle would be no different.

Footsteps sounded outside in the hallway, and he slipped quietly outside, down the rail, and through the garden and thick foliage surrounding the antebellum house. He'd go to his cabin now and watch her. He would track her every movement just as he did a target's.

And if he discovered she intended to expose him, he'd add her to his hit list.

Chapter Eight

Quinton breathed in the salty ocean air as he climbed from his SUV outside his cabin on Tybee Island and visually scanned the perimeter. Night shadows plagued the back, the palm trees swaying in the breeze, the ocean waves crashing against the shore in a thunderous roar.

Shoulders squared, he tuned in to his surroundings as he walked up the shell drive to the door, then he flipped on the light and entered.

A quick scan of the interior and he breathed a sigh of relief. Nothing seemed out of place. No intruder or demon waiting in the shadows to attack. No Annabelle Armstrong.

Although he had to deal with her now. Was someone really sending her messages regarding the bombing, a warning there would be more? Or was it a prank?

He went to his bedroom dresser and removed the wooden box. His hand shook slightly as he opened it, and he stared at the angel amulet.

Except for the stone, the amulet was identical to the one Vincent had shown him. The monks had explained its symbolic meaning, that the clear quartz represented soul realization, clairvoyance, wisdom, and continuity of consciousness. All related to his chi and the spiritual lessons he'd learned from them.

Breathing through clenched teeth, he picked it up in his hand and held it. Suddenly the amulet vibrated in his palm and the stone lit up, sending a swirl of intense clear light through the dimly lit room.

He slid the amulet around his neck and fastened it. It glowed and sparkled, warm against his neck, for another moment, then turned cool again, the glow slowly fading. It felt oddly right, as if it connected him to something he'd lost a long time ago.

Feeling more in balance, he immediately went to his surveillance camera to watch Annabelle.

She was seated at the oak desk in the corner of the room reviewing computer files, ones containing photos from her homeless exposé.

He frowned, wondering at the significance, then tried to tap into her thoughts. He rarely could do so at a distance, but sometimes if he concentrated hard enough, it worked.

This time he was unsuccessful. Then she clicked on a photo of a man named Warren Ames. He skimmed the information on the man, then noticed that he had been identified as the Savannah bomber.

So Ames was the homeless man he'd seen near the ship.

Then she clicked to a different file, and his picture appeared. Her face twisted as she studied the information scrolling on the screen. His background. His stint in the service.

Photos of his recent hits, three terrorists who had deserved to die.

Anger knotted his stomach, and he gritted his teeth. Who in the hell had sent her the information?

She clicked back to his photo and another one appeared beside it—Vincent's. Shit. She had done her homework.

Had connected him to this man when Quinton hadn't even known he existed. Was that the reason she'd gone to Eerie, to research him? To find out if the two men were connected?

Then she clicked on a site about supernatural phenomenon and began to research demons, starting with the nine circles of hell.

"Who are you, Quinton Valtrez?" Her expression softened as she lifted her hand and traced it over his face.

He froze, unnerved by her gesture.

Then she rose and walked to the bathroom and began to strip.

His gut tightened as she slowly unfastened each button of her silk blouse. He felt as if he was watching a slow striptease, only she had no idea she was performing.

She would be furious if she did.

But the dark side, the man with an unquenchable thirst for sex, couldn't drag his eyes away as she slid the silky fabric over her shoulders, revealing full, tantalizing breasts encased in thin wisps of black lace.

Good God, she was breathtaking.

Her skirt came next, the black fabric hitting the floor in a puddle. His gaze zeroed in on the strip of lace serving as panties, the sheer material revealing a crotch that made his mouth water.

He'd fantasized about her, but she was even more beautiful in the flesh. Her skin was exotically creamy-looking, her luscious breasts spilling over the bra, her stomach flat, her hips flaring into shapely thighs that could suck a man in by holding him between them. Although petite, she looked muscular, well-toned, and . . . sinful.

He wanted her so badly his cock pushed against the fly of his jeans.

Tilting her head sideways, her glossy hair cascaded around her bare shoulders as she unfastened the front clasp of her bra, allowing her breasts to spill free. His heart hammered, his sex twitching with arousal.

Pink-tipped globes swayed as she pushed her panties down her hips and kicked them off. Her hips flared, and he zeroed in on the tiny triangle of blonde curls between her legs. He wanted to touch her, sift through that silky softness.

Watching had always been his weakness. And he'd dreamed about seeing her naked for months. Having her beneath him, his cock pumping inside her until she cried his name and begged him not to stop.

He stood with a curse. Dammit, he was in trouble. Keller wanted him to get rid of her.

But he wanted to fuck her instead.

Annabelle undressed, her body coiled with tension, her emotions on a roller coaster. The last two days had been hell.

Her trip to the homeless shelter had proven fruitless. Then she'd combed the cemeteries asking the homeless people who slept there if they'd seen or talked to Warren Ames, but came up empty. If she could find his family, she'd do a human-interest piece.

Was the bombing an isolated event?

Could someone have put him up to the bombing? Drugged him into committing mass murder?

Had that text been a prank?

If it was real, when would the next bomber strike and where?

Needing to relieve her tension, she stepped into the

shower and let the warm water sluice over her. Unbidden images came to her of Quinton's dark, brooding face, his smoky eyes, his hands trailing over her, stroking her, massaging the ache from her shoulders, arousing her with his fingers and pressing his lips where he'd touched her.

She hadn't been with a man in ages, had closed herself off from relationships after her mother's death and her father's desertion. She couldn't contemplate the pain of another loss.

So why did she find Quinton so damn attractive?

His black eyes stole into her thoughts, and she pictured him crawling above her, kneeing her legs apart, settling himself between her thighs. Lowering his head to taste her mouth, then lower to her breasts, where he'd suck her until she bucked and begged him to fill her.

Then he'd free his hard length and thrust it inside her, stretching her until she thought she'd come apart.

Her hand moved, her fingers caressed, gentle featherlight strokes over her clit, then quickened, slid deeper, deeper, adding pressure as if they were his sex.

She sighed and moaned as titillating sensations rocked through her. Heaven help her. She couldn't get involved with Quinton.

He was a government assassin.

A man who might be a demon...

Still, she had to go to him. Find out what he knew. If he had an idea where the bomber might attack again.

Fuck.

Hunger shot through Quinton as he watched Annabelle caress her body.

It was the most erotic sight he'd ever seen.

He zeroed in on the small tattoo of a rose on her hip and wanted to touch it.

Kiss it. Ask her the significance of the tattoo...

Unable to stand the tension, he unzipped his jeans and freed his hard length, then wrapped his fingers around his rigid penis and stroked.

He imagined ramming it inside her, watching her body buck as he plunged to her core. She parted her legs wider, her body quivering as her orgasm rocked through her. His body jerked and spasmed, pure hot pleasure rippling through him as cum shot from his tip.

He envisioned the sticky fluid flowing down her legs, the milky white bathing her crotch and thighs, and he groaned her name, mindless with erotic sensations.

Shit. No other woman had ever stirred his hunger to such intensity or aroused emotions like this in his chest.

His phone jangled, and he cursed, quickly cleaned up then grabbed the handset and checked the number. His handler, Keller.

He connected the call, automatically assuming his professional persona. No emotions. Killer mode. "Yeah, Valtrez."

"We had a meeting."

A film of cold sweat broke out on his brow.

"It's time to get rid of the Armstrong woman. We can't allow her to expose the team. If she does, it will have to be disbanded."

Quinton ran a hand over the back of his neck.

"You'll take care of her?" Keller asked.

A bead of sweat trickled down Quinton's back. He was an eraser, a sniper. This was no different. Another assignment.

The darkness in him rose, hungry for blood, protective of his tribe of killers.

He'd sworn to take care of the team, the mission. He had no regret over the other hits. No remorse. And he'd never disobeyed a direct order.

But he glanced at the camera and saw Annabelle climbing from the shower, water droplets clinging to her skin, her face flushed from arousal, and he hesitated.

She wasn't a terrorist or a soldier. She was a civilian.

He closed his eyes, banishing the image. He never hesitated. Hesitating would get him killed.

If he didn't do this job, Keller would consider him disposable, would send someone after him. And after Annabelle.

Either way, her days were numbered.

He hissed in a sharp breath. "No problem. I'll call you when it's done."

He retrieved his weapon system from the closet, then unlocked the case and pulled out the M24.

CHARLESTON, SOUTH CAROLINA

Reverend Narius spread his hands, waving them in a wide arc as he addressed the crowd in Charleston, his diamond-and-onyx ring glittering beneath the lights. "Turn your life over to my command, and you will be reborn. Follow me now, and redemption is yours."

Women, men, and children alike bowed their heads and listened to his prayer, then stood and began filtering out of the Charleston chapel.

"Thank you for coming, Reverend." The white-haired

woman wiped at the tears in her eyes. "We heard you were in Savannah. God bless those people. Those bombings were just awful."

He clasped her hand between his, pasting on the appropriate compassionate smile. "Yes, a tragedy. Another reason for each of us to ask to be saved. One never knows when our earthly time is up and the Lord will call us home."

She shivered and he patted her gently. "You have been saved haven't you, Miss Erma?"

"Oh, yes, years ago."

Another elderly man approached, and he released Erma's hand, then extended it to the old man. "You're a godsend, Reverend," the old man said. "I once was tempted by evil, but I've resisted."

"In Matthew, even Satan tempted Jesus, but he overcame temptation through the word of God," Reverend Narius said smoothly. "So many are lost and need salvation. In fact, I'm on my way now to visit the homeless shelter nearby."

"You're a good man," a young woman with twin toddlers tugging at her legs said. "So kind of you to stop and see them."

He shrugged. "It's my mission to serve."

Gratitude and admiration flickered in her eyes, and his chest puffed up. He was the first to admit that he enjoyed the accolades. "I work for the Master," he said softly. "And I will be an obedient servant to the end."

But salvation came at a cost. And the ones who followed him had to earn their way. He smiled.

So easy to twist their minds and persuade them to follow.

Chapter Nine

Annabelle had to talk to Quinton. If he had any idea who was behind the bombing or threats and where they might attack next, something had to be done.

Of course, working with him would be akin to making a deal with the devil, but lives depended on their stopping another attack.

She flipped on the news while she pulled on a robe, wondering if another station had accessed information she didn't yet have.

"Reports that vultures attacked the bombing scene in Savannah are disturbing. Witnesses said they preyed on the humans as if they were animals.

"Folklore says the vultures are an omen of impending death. Oddly, reports are now flooding the lines from Charleston, South Carolina, saying there have been at least a hundred sightings of the predatory birds hovering above the town. Residents are wary, and veterinarians and environmentalists have been called in to address the problem. Some are worried that the vultures may be a mutant strain that preys on humans, or that they may carry diseases that could be passed to humans."

A shudder coursed through her as she remembered the

vultures greedily eating human flesh and cleaning the bones.

A tapping sounded at the French door, and she glanced up, expecting the wind to have rattled it, but a black vulture hovered on her patio, pounding the glass with its sharp, pointed beak.

Then a shrill screeching sound erupted from the bird, and she jumped backward, terrified it was going to break the glass and attack her.

Traffic crawled by as Quinton drove across the bridge and into Savannah toward the B and B and his target. The tourist crowd that had been bustling on Halloween now seemed minimal, although some curious souls had ventured out to see the ruins of the ship left after the bombing, and the homemade memorials people had made. Flowers, trinkets, teddy bears, toys, and other memorabilia decorated the area, reminders of the individuals who'd died such violent and needless deaths.

He turned on the radio news.

"People in Charleston, South Carolina, are reporting a disturbing number of vultures within the city limits as well as on the outskirts of town.

"Oddly, the vultures are described as having the bodies and heavy, sturdy feet of old-world vultures, not the more common turkey vultures prevalent in the U.S., which have chickenlike feet for running on the ground. Old-world vultures are normally found in Europe, Asia, and Africa.

"Also, in South Africa, hundreds of headless vultures have been found. Poachers have been killing the vultures, then removing their heads and putting them through a drying process to sell, because of beliefs that the vulture's

keen eyesight enables it to see into the future. Unscrupu-
lous dealers are selling the heads for up to $1,000. Due
to the fact that vultures are an endangered species, bans
have been placed on killing the animals."

Quinton's shoulders stiffened, and he flipped off the
radio as he parked down the street from the B and B in
an alley where he wouldn't be noticed. He had to focus.
Couldn't make any mistakes today. Couldn't get caught.
Had to be invisible.

Dry leaves crunched beneath his boots as he walked
to the inn. A damn vulture circled above, as if watching,
waiting for someone to die.

He moved stealthily into the gardens, through the rows
of topiaries and giant azaleas, scoped out an empty room
across from Annabelle's, then climbed the rail, jimmied
the door, and slipped inside.

He set up his M24 with its attachable telescopic sight
and aimed it at Annabelle's window. Through the lens, he
watched her. She was sitting at the desk in her robe, sipping coffee and tapping on her computer. He forced himself to tear his gaze from her body and zeroed in on the
screen.

She was researching vultures.

Determined to finish the job as quickly and painlessly
as possible, he aimed the weapon. He had a clear shot.
Could take her out quickly. She would never know what
hit her.

Then she clicked to a file of the bombing and more photos appeared. Pictures of the explosion, of people maimed
and dying. Women and children crying. The blazing fire
and smoke pouring from the ship.

Then another of him on the ship, reaching down to

help an injured woman off the burning deck. Dammit, he shouldn't have been photographed. Shouldn't have put himself in that position. But his humanity had surfaced, and he'd wanted to help that night.

He swallowed, slid his finger over the trigger. Felt the cool metal against the pad of his thumb. Could already smell the scent of death. Could hear the glass crashing and see Annabelle's body jerk with the impact. Blood spewing from her pale forehead.

His throat convulsed. The darkness ate at him, urging him to do it. He had to in order to protect the team. She was simply a casualty of the cause.

But he thought of her as Annabelle, not the target, and his hands began to shake. His palms grew sweaty. His vision blurred.

His breath came in pants, erratic. Lifting one hand, he wiped the sweat on his jeans and swallowed hard.

Shit. His control was slipping.

Anger churned through his blood. He *never* lost control. And certainly not over a woman.

He hated her for it.

He closed his eyes, mentally willing himself back in the game. She could destroy him and his team, endanger their lives and the lives of hundreds of others.

But images of her on the news haunted him. The way she'd helped the needy the night of the bombing.

Memories of her in the shower followed along with the sight of her shivering as she ran from his house to her car the night he'd met her.

Dammit, he was thinking too much. He relied on instinct while on the job; he demanded perfection.

But now he was rethinking his plan.

What if she had sent files on him to another source?

She had talked to the local police about him. If she went missing, would they come after him? Shit.

He'd have to figure out a way around it. The unit would be his alibi.

He curled his fingers around the handle, moving his trigger finger into position, and focused. Mentally channeling his energy into the zone, he looked through the viewfinder again and found his shot.

He lived for the kill. He liked the sound of the bullet zooming through the air. The startled look in the victim's eyes the moment they realized they'd been hit.

That death had come calling.

Good-bye, Annabelle. It's time to die.

Annabelle's cell phone jangled, and she hurried to retrieve it, hoping it might be a lead on the bombings, that the man who'd sent her the text message might be trying to make contact again.

But she checked the number and saw it was her boss. She bit her lip, debating over whether to answer, but knew he'd keep hounding her until she did.

Resigned, she punched the connect button. "Hello, Roland."

"Annabelle, why haven't you called me?"

She sucked in a sharp breath. "I've been busy," she said through gritted teeth. "In case you've forgotten, I'm in the middle of putting together a story about a bombing, interviewing witnesses and victims and their families." And she hadn't divulged the fact that the bomber had contacted *her*.

"So what is the story?" he asked. "Some homeless man set off the bomb in Savannah?"

"Apparently so," Annabelle said. "But I think there's more to the story, Roland. I just need more time."

"We have to report something, Annabelle."

"You have what I can verify so far. Warren Ames, a homeless man, was the suicide bomber in Savannah. He suffered from PTS. That's all you can print for now."

Roland's agitated breath reverberated over the line. "What are you holding back?"

She sighed. "You know I'm still digging. As soon as I know, you'll have my story. Until then, you're going to have to trust me."

"Then at least send me a human-interest piece or two to work with to distract the public."

"Fine. You'll have a couple of pieces tomorrow."

"What about Quinton Valtrez?"

She hesitated and went to stare out the window, her nerves on edge. "I'm still working on that story. He's not as cut-and-dried as I thought."

"You aren't going soft, are you?" Roland barked. "Because I can send someone else to get the story."

Her stomach tightened and resolve set in. "I'm not going soft. But this story is complicated, and I can't work with you breathing down my neck."

Irritated, she hung up and dropped her forehead against the cool windowpane, confused and nervous as hell.

Was she going soft? Starting to see Quinton as some kind of hero instead of a killer?

Quinton's fingers tightened around the gun, but his gaze caught Annabelle's as she angled her face and stared out the window. For a moment, he wondered if she could see him.

Her eyes were luminous, innocent, wary, probing. Her face delicate but determined. Her hair flowing as she raked a hand through the glossy long strands.

Then her thoughts came to him—she was thinking about the bombing, the vultures, the homeless man, wondering how the three were connected.

And she wanted to talk to him.

Because she thought the killer had contacted her. And she suspected there was more to this than a single suicide bomber, that another person might be behind it.

That there would be more victims.

Her thoughts came again, this time as if she'd spoken directly to him.

She wasn't going to rat him out. At least not yet. She wanted the whole picture.

How do you fit into the puzzle, Quinton Valtrez? Just who are you—a savior or a killer?

"Not a savior, sweetheart, that's for damn sure," he muttered.

Forcing himself to focus, he inhaled deep breaths then slid his finger away from the trigger.

Dammit, he couldn't kill her.

He was acting impetuously, on emotion, on fear that she'd expose him instead of thinking clearly. So had Keller.

Taking her out here would draw too much suspicion.

She wasn't a terrorist. She was a public figure. People knew who she was and where she was staying.

And what if the demon had contacted her? What if she proved to be a link to this bomber?

The smart thing to do would be to play along. Find out just what she knew. Who she might have already passed information to. Then he'd do whatever he had to do to convince her to keep quiet.

Hell, seducing her would be more effective than murder.

Smiling at that thought, he reached for his cell phone with steady fingers and punched in her number. She fidgeted but answered the phone.

"Annabelle Armstrong speaking."

"It's Quinton Valtrez."

She drew a sharp breath and tightened the belt of her robe as if she sensed she was being watched.

Now that he knew what lay beneath the robe, no matter what she wore he'd have a permanent picture of her naked in his mind. Lush and inviting . . .

She rushed to the window and moved the sheers aside, searching the gardens. "Yes?"

"We need to talk."

"I thought you didn't want to talk to me."

"I don't." He hesitated. "But since you're still here, I figure I have to."

She seemed to be searching the street for him. "How did you know where I was?"

"I have my sources." He grinned, enjoying the way his tone unnerved her. Damn, he was a bastard.

But if she exposed the unit, she jeopardized dozens of lives, including innocents the team protected.

"Come to my place," he suggested.

She shook her head, a frown marring her brow. "Too isolated."

"Then I'll come to your room."

She ran a hand through her hair. "No. Someplace neutral. How about Colonial Park Cemetery?"

An odd place to meet. "All right." He disconnected the call, then took his weapon system and went to his car to wait. He'd parked under a row of big oaks down the street a ways, but near enough to see her exit.

Moonlight streaked the asphalt, a vulture sweeping in front of her as Annabelle hurried outside. Was Quinton finally going to talk to her and tell her the truth?

Did he know more about the bombing than he'd told her? Could they possibly work together to identify the person or persons behind the bombing?

She scanned the street near her car, her nerves suddenly kicking in as she spotted a vulture perched on the roof.

Breathing in to calm herself, she hesitated several feet away and clicked the unlock button.

A second later, a loud roar rent the air, and her car exploded.

Annabelle screamed, the impact throwing her to the concrete. Her head hit the ground and she collapsed, metal and glass pelting her.

CHARLESTON, SOUTH CAROLINA

The cold wind shifted through B. J. Rutherford's paper-thin skin and gnawed at his bones, frail bones riddled with arthritis in a body that had seen nigh on eighty years. Hunching the weathered gray coat someone had donated to the shelter around his shoulders, he hobbled through the streets of Charleston, scrounging through garbage for a crust of bread to go with his booze. His knees ached and his back throbbed as he clutched the bottle of cheap wine and took a sip. The alcohol warmed his insides and soothed the ache in his joints.

But he had to make the bottle last. He'd begged for money for two days just to buy a gallon jug of Gallo, and he hated begging in the streets. Hated the way people looked at him with pity as if he wasn't worth spit. Just because he'd fallen on hard times a few years back.

Sorrow welled in his chest as the painful memories assaulted his feeble mind. When Haddie gave in to the cancer and left him ten years ago, he'd wanted to join her in the grave.

But God had punished him for doing bad things when he was younger by leaving him alone and making him suffer. Yes, he'd been a sinner. Had lusted for young girls. Even cheated on Haddie. But he'd tried to atone for those sins in his old age.

Reverend Narius had helped him. Had offered him redemption and he'd taken it.

Ominous gray clouds floated across the moon, robbing any light, and the stench of garbage and urine filled his nose as he neared the shelter. Oddly, the smells welcomed him as if he was home. He stumbled to the grassy area behind the shelter and dug a spot to bury his bottle.

One day soon B.J. would join Haddie in death. Then he'd feel no more pain, and he'd never be cold again.

A man with eyebrows so thick and black they looked like bird feathers stood in the shadows of the entryway, wearing a long black duster. His eyes were close together, narrowed and beady in his oddly shaped face, the top of his head bald with a long black ponytail trailing down his back.

B.J. frowned. Who was this guy? He didn't look homeless, not with that gold watch on his arm.

"What do you want, mister?"

The man smiled, revealing a row of jagged teeth, then pressed a feathered hand to B.J.'s temple. B.J. tried to jerk back, but sharp talons sank into his skull and unbearable pain splintered through his head. Shaking with the force of it, he sank to the ground and screamed in terror.

"Please, I'll do whatever you want. Just stop the pain."

The shadow laughed in answer.

Laughter bubbled from the Death Angel's throat and echoed around him as he literally fried the man's mind, stealing his thoughts and his dreams, turning his brain into a blank slate to accept the commands that he would issue.

With a sweep of his wings, he sailed outside into the dark evening, leaving the old man to rest until his body woke from the trauma. Then the man would do as he commanded because Satan owned him.

More deaths for the Angel tonight. More lost souls for the Soul Collectors to offer Zion.

More bodies to be cleaned of flesh.

He soared upward and perched on a phone line, then licked his talons, his hunger mounting as his eyes zeroed in on the Charleston market.

Tomorrow night, another big one. Midnight.

It was many hours away. But he could wait.

The feast would be worth it.

Chapter Ten

Quinton's heart pounded as he jumped from his Land Rover and ran toward Annabelle. The few people on the street screamed and raced away in panic as smoke and the scent of burning metal and rubber clogged the air.

Through the chaos, the roar of a siren, and his own curses, the screech of vultures reverberated in his ears, a horrific noise like mocking laughter.

Annabelle lay facedown on the sidewalk, blood trickling from her head, her body limp. He quickly placed two fingers to her neck to check for a pulse but felt nothing.

Fear shot through him.

Dammit, was she dead or alive? And who had done this?

Did this bombing have to do with the demons who'd invaded the earth on All Hallows' Eve? Were they after him or Annabelle?

And if they were after her, why?

Unless somehow they'd tapped into his head and realized he'd connected to her.

Shit. His heart practically stopped. Was that possible?

If he could read minds, maybe the demons could, too...

He leaned over and listened, waiting, praying for a breath.

But she wasn't breathing.

Hell, he should let her die. Her death would solve his problems with the Ghost unit.

But sweat beaded on his skin. Her tempting mouth made him physically ache. The innocent stubbornness in her face roused protective instincts that he had never known he possessed. And memories of her naked body sparked a pure primal thirst that couldn't be quenched if she died.

He tilted her head back, checked her air passage, and began CPR. The moment his mouth closed over hers and he gave her a breath, a bolt of warmth spread through him, another foreign feeling he didn't recognize or want.

Yet the heat spurned him on, and he pressed his hands to her chest and pumped rhythmically.

"Come on, Annabelle," he muttered. "You're too tough to die."

Around him, chaos descended. Sirens roared. The fire blazed. Some people fled while others raced to watch the horror. A camera flashed, catching him in the light, and he cursed at it, wanting to throw the onlooker against the concrete wall. But he had to hear Annabelle breathe first.

Finally the blessed sound came. The moment where her throat convulsed. Her chest heaved. She fought to return to life. For the first time in his life, instead of his blood churning from the kill, it raced from the exhilaration of saving a life.

A totally foreign feeling.

She choked and coughed, then her eyes fluttered open, and he heaved a sigh of relief. But the scene around him suddenly burst into life.

"What happened?" Annabelle asked, blinking as if to focus, her face wan and pale.

"Your car exploded."

Oblivious to anything but listening to the sound of her voice and the rasp of her breathing, he barely realized the firefighters careening onto the scene to extinguish the car fire, that the paramedics and police had arrived.

An officer appeared with Detective Crawley behind him. "Valtrez?" Detective Crawley said in surprise. "What happened here?"

He stood and stepped aside with the detective as the medic team rushed up and began to examine Annabelle.

A little old woman fanned smoke from her face. "Detective, this man saved the woman's life. He's a hero."

Quinton threw up a hand to ward off any more accolades. If she knew he'd been sent to kill Annabelle, the police would be handcuffing him right now.

"Someone obviously bombed Miss Armstrong's car," he said to the detective. "She'd called me and asked me to meet her so I was here."

"Is she all right?"

"She's alive, but she'll probably have a hell of a headache."

"Did you see anyone near her car before or after the explosion?"

Just a vulture, but he couldn't very well share his suspicions. "Afraid not."

The big man glanced back at Annabelle. "Looks like someone didn't want her asking questions. Maybe that text she received was real after all."

Quinton nodded. "Obviously someone wants her attention." Unless this bomb was one the Ghost team had planted?

With the recent violence in town, an explosion would provide the perfect smoke screen.

But he'd been so focused on watching Annabelle and lost in his own thoughts, he hadn't thought to check her car.

A major mistake.

One he couldn't repeat, or both of them would end up dead.

Annabelle opened and closed her eyes, battling the resounding throbbing in her head and ringing in her ears. She was so disoriented. Dizzy. Terrified.

What had happened?

She'd left the room to meet Quinton. Then suddenly bright lights and noise. Fire. Shattering glass. Metal pelting her.

And she'd hit the ground.

Then darkness.

Quinton's words finally registered. Someone had planted a bomb in her car . . .

She blinked against the smoky haze around her. Heard someone say he was a paramedic. That the police were there.

"Possible head trauma," one of the medics shouted.

"Mild lacerations. Start an IV drip!"

A sharp jab as a needle pricked her arm. The IV. Fluids dripped and burned as they flowed into her veins. A stinging pain in her head and arm followed. Her chest felt heavy. Her limbs numb.

The past few minutes flashed back. She had seen the bright light, beckoning, calling her name. Promising peace. Her mother's face floating in the light, her eyes glowing with unshed tears. "Go back, darlin'... It's not your time."

Her father... She searched for his face but didn't see him. Did that mean he was alive?

She'd had to come back and find him. But a sudden rampage of darkness had swallowed her, and another voice had called to her. A sinister but enticing voice that had offered her immortality in exchange for her soul.

The black monsterlike image had terrified her, and she'd run back toward the light.

Then a masculine voice had penetrated her mind. A voice that sounded gruff. Worried.

Then she'd felt soft lips on hers. A breath inside her chest.

And the will to survive had become stronger than anything she'd ever experienced in her life.

She'd fought her way through the tunnel of darkness and climbed from the depths.

Quinton had saved her life again. Where was he now?

"Quinton?" she whispered.

A female voice spoke instead. "Ma'am, we're going to transport you to the hospital. You probably have a concussion, but you're going to be all right."

She coughed, her throat raw. "Where's the man who saved me?"

"The police are questioning him now."

She nodded feebly.

Had Quinton seen the person who'd tried to kill her?

Quinton let his hands dangle by his sides, adopting a calm, detached expression as Detective Crawley called for a crime scene unit and ordered another officer to rope off the area to keep the spectators away.

He followed Detective Crawley to the ambulance.

"How is she?" Detective Crawley asked the medic.

A twenty-something blond man stepped to the doorway of the ambulance. Quinton looked past him and saw Annabelle on the stretcher, with an IV attached.

"She should be all right," the medic said. "She sustained some lacerations, and she probably has a concussion, but she's conscious. The doctors will run tests when we get her to the hospital."

"Can I talk to her for a minute?" Detective Crawley asked.

The medic nodded, then the detective climbed up into the ambulance. "Miss Armstrong?"

Annabelle moaned but mumbled, "Yes."

"Ma'am, did you see anyone by your car who looked suspicious?"

Quinton held a steady breathing pattern, wondering if she'd reveal what she knew about him. She could have him arrested now and get her story.

"No," she whispered.

Crawley cleared his throat. "Any more odd text messages?"

Her strained cough resounded through the ambulance interior. "No."

"How about enemies? Someone you pissed off from another story."

She hesitated for a brief second. "Not that I know of."

He grunted. "If you think of anything, let me know." He glanced at Quinton. "And don't leave town without letting me know."

Quinton nodded curtly. He waited to follow the ambulance to the hospital, dialing Keller as he went.

Keller answered on the third ring. "Is it done?"

"Dammit, Keller, did you send someone else to kill Annabelle?"

A tense pause. "We thought you might be too involved."

"Well, I'm not. But she's a public figure. We can't kill her. That would only bring attention from the cops."

"But what if she exposes us?"

"Trust me. I'll find another way to keep her quiet."

He let the implication stand and Keller laughed. "You cocky bastard, you. Good luck. And if it doesn't work..."

"It will," he said quietly. "She wants me."

And he wanted her.

But she'd almost died tonight right in front of him. And that had scared the hell out of him.

The next few hours in the ER passed in a hazy blur for Annabelle. The doctors examined and treated the small cuts and abrasions on her hands, arms, and knees, then she was wheeled to another area for X-rays and a CAT scan.

Thankfully, all the tests came back clean, although her head throbbed relentlessly. The doctor insisted she stay overnight for observation.

Finally, they allowed her some painkillers, and she closed her eyes and dozed but jerked awake a few minutes later with the image of her car bursting into flames haunting her. If she'd gotten inside it a minute earlier, she would be in a million pieces, splattered all over the sidewalk like the glass and metal from her car.

The detective had asked if she had any enemies...

She definitely did. Quinton. He was a hit man. He'd called her and asked her to meet him. Had he set that bomb?

No. He'd saved her.

She glanced around the room then and saw him sitting in the corner in the dark, his long legs stretched out in front of him, his gaze pinning her to the bed. He looked angry as hell.

"What's wrong?" she asked.

"You nearly got blown up, and you're asking me what's wrong?"

She tried to sit up, then winced. "I figured you wanted me dead."

His frown deepened, and she saw the truth in his eyes. "Oh, my God. You did. You tried to kill me, didn't you?"

His lips thinned, but he glanced away. "I didn't plant that bomb or set off that explosive."

She twisted the sheets between her fingers, reading between the lines. Finally she summoned the courage to ask. "Is there a hit out on me?"

His gaze swung back to hers, steady, detached, unemotional. "I called it off," he said simply.

Shock rolled through her. "Then you *were* sent to kill me?"

He stared at her but didn't respond, and a shudder coursed through her, leaving her feeling naked and vulnerable.

"Why didn't you finish the job?" she finally asked.

"I don't know. The monks' teachings." He stood and walked toward her, their gazes locking, heat rippling between them. He almost reached out to touch her but pulled back. "I have a code. I kill bad guys." He shrugged.

"You're nosy and a pain in the ass, but you don't fit into that category."

She'd studied serial killers, had read the profiles. They had troubled pasts, had been abused, suffered from medical or psychiatric disorders that drove them to violence.

She wanted to learn more about him, and his past. How he could be so cold one minute and tender the next?

Her phone buzzed from her purse on the side table, and she scrambled to reach it. Quinton handed it to her, a frown on his face.

Then she flipped it open and read the message:

Midnight tomorrow. A different city.
More to die.

Quinton jammed his hands into his pockets. He'd thought he'd made peace with the monks' teachings and with his path in life.

But Annabelle's questions bothered him.

"Oh, my God," she whispered. "He's going to strike again."

He grabbed the phone from her and his blood turned to ice as he read the message.

Then suddenly a premonition swept over him, and the room faded as he envisioned the future event.

Another bomb. Dozens of people running and screaming. Another old man lying dead, one who held the same odor as the homeless man in Savannah. He struggled to make out details of the scene—where was it?

Suddenly the vision ended as abruptly as it had come upon him.

He jerked his gaze to Annabelle's. "Do you have any idea who sent this?"

She shook her head, then swung her legs to the side of the bed as if she was going to get up. "No, but I received one after the first bombing. The message said there would be more."

He cursed and paced to the window, then stared out at the night sky. A bloodred moon hung heavy, the inky darkness endless.

"Did the message say anything else?" he asked.

"No. I took it to Detective Crawley, and an agent named Keller from Homeland Security tried to locate the sender, but it appeared to be a throwaway phone and he couldn't trace it."

The same thing Keller had told him.

She touched his arm, turning him to face her. "Quinton, do you know where the bomber might strike next?"

He struggled to think, to pinpoint something from his premonition that might help, but came up empty. Then the answer hit him. "Charleston."

"Why do you think that?"

"The vultures," he said in a dark tone. "They're swarming the town." He pulled away from her and headed to the door. "I have to go there. Figure out where he'll attack next."

"I'm going with you." Annabelle reached for her clothes in the bag on the side table, but he shook his head.

"No, you have a concussion. You need to rest."

"I'm not staying here," she said emphatically. "Whoever is behind this is sending me messages. I have to follow up. It's my story."

She threw off the hospital gown, mindless that she

was wearing only her underwear, and began to dress. He swallowed at the sight of her voluptuous body, fisting his hands by his sides to keep from going to her.

"You'd risk your fucking life for a story?"

"I want to stop this guy," Annabelle said. "And I'm good at what I do, Quinton. I can help." She buttoned her blouse, then her skirt. "Now, either take me with you or I'll go alone."

Chapter Eleven

Quinton wanted to argue. To tie her down and force her to stay here, where she was safe.

Being with him would put her in more danger. If Vincent was right and he was like his father, his demonic side might try to take over one day. It had in the past, and his dark hungers ate at him.

At least that darkness had tried to control him for years. But he'd called upon his nochd and the monks' teachings.

And now being around her was doing something bizarre to him.

He just needed to screw her and get her out of his system. Then he could focus.

But he didn't have time for that either. Not if this bomber was going to strike again.

And in less than twenty-four hours.

"All right. But you won't print anything about my work for the unit."

She hedged, a war raging in her eyes. "Let's stop this killer, and you'll be the hero of my story."

He barked a laugh. A demonborn hero—yeah, right.

But he didn't have time to worry about what she'd report.

The clock was ticking. They had to figure out where this next strike would take place.

She winced slightly as they took the elevator and then battled the wind as they walked to his car. But she didn't complain as she settled inside. He drove to his place first and threw together a bag, went to the B and B where she retrieved her things, and then hit the road toward Charleston.

On the way, he called Detective Crawley to inform him of his plans, then his contacts at Homeland Security to tell them about the message Annabelle had received.

"We'll get on it," Chief Tarrington said. "I'll try to pinpoint possible locations where the bomber might attack."

"Anything on the terrorist-cell side?" Quinton asked.

"Nothing so far. But all our operatives are working with the CIA and FBI trying to locate the source. Meanwhile, meet with the locals and let them know you're on the job."

"Copy that." Quinton hung up, worry gnawing at him. So far, they'd found no connection to a terrorist group. And they might not.

Not if they were dealing with a demon.

Annabelle sighed and rested her head back against the seat. The bruise on her forehead made the thirst for revenge tap at the brink of his control.

He imagined finding the man responsible for putting Annabelle in the hospital and for cruelly taking so many lives. He'd tie him down and beat him until blood poured from his nose and mouth. Then he'd torture him as he himself had been tortured before. He'd strip him naked, make him lie in his blood, make him taste it, make him beg to be released.

The corner of his mouth tilted upward. He could hear the man's screams and curses, the screech of his voice begging for mercy. A mercy that wouldn't come, not at Quinton's hands.

Nightmares haunted Annabelle. Her car exploding. A faceless madman chasing her.

A man clothed in black about to kill her. A demon... Quinton.

No, she didn't believe in demons...

She struggled through the bleak memories to a time when she was safe, when nothing could harm her and her future was anything she wanted it to be.

She was five years old, sitting by a blazing fire, happily playing with the new train set Santa had brought her, the twinkling white Christmas lights dancing along the caboose. Her father rose from his chair, then knelt on the floor beside her and grinned. "That train will take you any place you want to go, Annabelle. All you have to do is dream."

Her mother, who'd been relaxing in the big overstuffed chair sipping tea, joined them. "Where do you want to go, sweetie?"

"All over the world." She'd jumped up and grabbed the camera her parents had given her and snapped a picture of them. "And I want you to go with me."

Her father had clasped her mother's hand and kissed it. "We'll always be a family," her mother said.

"Sandwich!" Annabelle said with a laugh. It was her favorite game. She squeezed between her parents while they hugged, pretending they were two slices of bread and she was the bologna, and they all laughed.

She jerked awake, a well of sadness engulfing her as reality crashed back. It wasn't real. Her parents were gone. She'd been dreaming.

Then she inhaled a masculine scent, the raw primal one that had been driving her crazy the last few days, and she glanced at Quinton.

God, the man was mysterious. Still, he intrigued her and stirred wicked fantasies in her mind.

At the same time, he terrified her.

His steely gaze met hers, and she swiped at the tears, embarrassed at her display of emotion.

"Nightmares?" he asked.

She nodded. "I was thinking about my father."

"Where is he?" Quinton asked.

"I don't know." Annabelle sighed. "My mother died about six months ago. The night of the funeral, he disappeared. I haven't heard from him since."

"He hasn't contacted you at all?"

She twisted her hands in her lap. "No."

Quinton lapsed into a sullen silence as she turned to look out the window.

"What about your family?" she asked.

He gave her a sharp look. "I don't have family."

"What about your brother, Vincent?"

A muscle ticked in his jaw. "Get some rest, Annabelle. We'll be in Charleston soon, and it's going to be a long day."

She twisted her hands together, disturbed at the way he'd cut her off. Quinton was one person she couldn't trust.

So why did she feel drawn to him?

It didn't matter. She had to guard her emotions and

protect herself against him. His avoidance told her more than he realized. And she would find the story behind him before this was over.

But he was right. Her head was throbbing and when they got to Charleston, they had work to do. It was already early morning.

Midnight was only hours away. They had to stop this bomber before more lives were lost.

Quinton momentarily tapped into Annabelle's thoughts. She didn't trust him. And she'd vowed to guard herself against him.

Smart thinking. She *shouldn't* trust him.

But she wanted him, found him desirable.

Hmm... interesting. He could use that attraction to his advantage.

Wind whipped the trees into a frenzy, scattering dead leaves across the grass and sidewalk in a flurry of red, orange, yellow, and brown as they neared Charleston.

He swiped a hand over his neck, then turned to study her. Her blonde hair lay in waves against the seat, her bruises more pronounced in the early morning sunlight. Everything about her was light to his darkness, her blonde hair to his black, her ivory skin to his bronzed.

Her soul to his lack of one.

For once in his life, he wanted to soothe someone's pain, not inflict it.

He had to stop this bomber today. The sooner they discovered who'd orchestrated the attacks, the sooner he'd be free from Annabelle's spell.

Because he would never be free from the darkness that ate at his soul.

And when he killed again, he didn't want her around to interfere, or to endanger her because of it.

Or to make him question his actions.

He pulled into a hotel on the northern side, went inside and reserved adjoining rooms, and quickly installed cameras in the room where Annabelle would stay so he could watch her every move.

He didn't trust that she wouldn't pass on her story or suspicions. Besides, he needed to see if anyone approached or tried to attack her.

When he returned to the car, he nudged her awake. "I got us a room. Let's go inside, rest a bit, and clean up before we talk to the police."

She nodded sleepily, her mouth pinching as she climbed out. But again, she didn't complain. She tried to grab her suitcase, but he yanked it from her and carried their bags inside. As soon as she crawled into the bed, Quinton called his chief to let him know he was in town.

"I'll meet you at the local police station," Chief Tarrington said. "Then we'll try to narrow down target areas."

Quinton agreed then hung up. He only hoped they found the location in time.

Although Annabelle could have slept for days, the short nap and shower revived her. She and Quinton grabbed coffee and doughnuts on the way to the police station, where a burly bald man named Detective Barbaris met them.

An FBI agent named McLaughlin joined the team in the conference room, along with a man whom Quinton introduced as Chief Tarrington, his boss from HS.

"What do we have to go on?" Detective Barbaris asked.

Quinton spoke up. "Miss Armstrong received a text warning of an impending attack tonight at midnight."

The detective frowned. "And you know this is for real?"

Quinton exchanged a look with Annabelle, then nodded.

"Why do you think it will occur here?" Detective Barbaris asked.

"It's really a hunch," Quinton said, earning him an odd look from the chief, "The vultures gathered in Savannah before the attack. We have to follow every possible lead and take precautions. You don't want a repeat of Savannah, do you?" Quinton's steely voice drove home the point. "To be accused of negligence or the press to reveal that you were warned but did nothing?"

The detective shifted and rubbed at the top of his shiny head. "Of course not."

"Let's take a look at a map of the city," the chief said.

The detective nodded, then rolled down a wall map that they all began to scrutinize.

"Charleston is one of the most historic cities in the States," Barbaris said. "Although it's a fairly small city, a walking one, the Battery could be a target. There's also over a hundred restaurants, carriage tours, the shopping district, Market Hall, the churches, the famous houses..."

Frustration lined Barbaris's face. "Without knowing where this person is going to attack, it's like looking for a needle in a haystack."

"Since the bomber chose the waterfront area in Savannah, perhaps that's where he'll attack here," Agent McLaughlin suggested.

"It's possible," the chief said. "But maybe too predictable."

"Any special activities planned tonight in the town?" Quinton asked. "A parade? Political function? Celebration?"

"It is Saturday night," Detective Barbaris said. "The downtown will be alive with activity. That is, if those damn vultures don't scare people away."

Annabelle booted up her computer and googled a list of the city's events.

"Maybe you should consider shutting down the town," one of the local officers suggested.

"We can't ask business owners to do that," Detective Barbaris said. "We're talking about their livelihood."

"Paralyzing the town, its businesses, and creating fear and panic are other forms of terrorist attack—more subtle, but something the perpetrator may be aiming for," Annabelle pointed out.

"I'll call neighboring counties for backup," Detective Barbaris said. "Have local and plainclothes officers stationed all over the city. Maybe someone will see something suspicious."

"Let's look at major events again," Quinton said. "Something that would draw hundreds of people together at once."

Detective Barbaris snapped his fingers. "Two things I can think of. That preacher, Reverend Narius, is in town. He'll be at the First Baptist Church tonight. I'll put men there."

"And there's a football game at the Citadel," Annabelle added.

Quinton glanced at her with a nod. "The stadium could be a viable target. It definitely has to be covered."

"I'll get some agents to search the stadium," Chief Tarrington said. "And extra security will be posted tonight."

Barbaris scraped his hand over his jaw. "This is a nightmare."

"That's what we're trying to prevent," Quinton said.

Annabelle cleared her throat. "There's also a concert at the North Charleston Coliseum tonight. The venue is sold out. Thousands of teenagers and young adults will be flooding it to party."

"Let's get to it," Quinton ordered. "Midnight is only a few hours away."

Quinton cornered Annabelle while Barbaris debriefed the local officers and coordinated with other precincts for extra security.

"Thanks for the help in there," Quinton said.

"You really think we can stop this attack?" Annabelle asked.

Quinton clenched his jaw at the daunting task. It was difficult to safeguard and predict a crime like this, especially when they hadn't ID'd the unsub yet, but if a demon was involved . . . "We'll do our best."

Then his mother's words echoed in his head: *The Death Angel has the power to possess the body of a human. Find him in that form, and you can kill him more easily. You must use your power to destroy him.*

But what if he shape-shifted into another form? And if he was a vulture—hell, there were vultures everywhere.

"I keep thinking about that homeless man, that he was suffering from post-traumatic stress syndrome," Annabelle said. "I'm wondering if whoever is behind this convinced him to do the bombing. Maybe he paid him. Or what if the man was mentally ill and was convinced he was going into battle?"

Quinton considered her theory. "I agree that there is a mastermind, and that it's possible our perpetrator brainwashed the homeless man."

Annabelle rolled her shoulders. "Maybe he's going to find someone else like Ames to use. Another homeless man?"

"Or one suffering from PTS." He snapped his fingers. "I'll check military records, contact the VA hospital and see if I can get a list."

"And I'll check out the homeless shelters in the area," Annabelle said. "See if the social workers know of anyone preying on them. I've heard of cases where people fear the homeless and attack them."

Protective instincts kicked in as Quinton glanced at her. The bruise on her cheek looked stark against her pale skin, and she had dark smudges beneath her eyes. She needed rest, to be in bed recovering from the explosion, not out chasing leads.

But she was strong and gutsy, here working alongside him, trying to find this killer.

Admiration tightened his chest, and he reached up and stroked her arm. "Are you sure you're up to it? We have officers and agents working on the investigation."

"No, I want to do this," she said. "I have to. We can't let this guy win."

"We won't," he said. "But we go together."

No way he'd allow Annabelle to go up against a possible demon on her own.

You have powers, the Angel of Light had said.

But would his powers be strong enough to fight this evil?

⌒

Disturbed by the overwhelming scent of evil in the air, Father Robard called a meeting of the monks. They gathered in the monastery churchyard, the news of the recent unleashing of demons on the world weighing heavily on all their minds.

His fellow monks strolled in, wearing their doboks, culottes, or earth and wind garbs, depending on their level of training.

He greeted them accordingly. "Duno (brother), Duna (sister)," he murmured. "Ra-duno," denoting an older monk or big brother. His comrades were referred to as Fe duno or Fe duna.

Yet, Father Robard was the oldest and most revered.

After the Angel had brought the Valtrez boys to him, had told him of the prophecy of the Dark Lords and the danger to them, they had separated them for their own safety.

He had personally watched over Quinton and guided him to be a great fighter. Had shown him how to use the power of body and mind for survival and to prepare for the demon rising. Had taught him to survive off the land, to respect and love nature, to use herbal plants for healing and food, and also to mix the herbs with wine for potions.

"The demons have gotten past the Twilight Guards," he said as the monks bowed to listen.

Concern rippled through the group.

He cleared his throat. "We have trained the demonborn Valtrez to use nature's nochd—life energy—to call upon all the elements: light and darkness, fire, water, air, and earth.

"He has been trained to sense the energy of all living things by opening his mind and channeling nature to make himself stronger. But we must pray, for his soul is torn in two from the bad blood in his veins."

He paused and the monks nodded solemnly, obedience being key to their inner balance.

"He must use that energy as a weapon."

"Is he prepared?" Duno Florence asked.

"I believe so. He was put through a series of grueling physical tests to prepare his mind for the journey early on. And when he left here, he received more rigorous training.

"Now let us pray and meditate in silence for the remainder of the day. We must channel our faith into him. He will need it."

He held up his hands in a wide arc, his robe billowing around him as he silenced any more doubts, and led them in prayer using the ancient language.

It was important that the Dark Lord survive and defeat the demon after him. If he failed, they would all be in danger.

Chapter Twelve

An odd look twisted Quinton's face as they approached the Safe Haven homeless shelter. If the situation weren't so dire, Annabelle would have laughed at the irony of a hired gun visiting the needy.

The shelter was in an older cement building attached to one of the local churches, with one central room for meals and sharing, and two rooms in the back for overnight stays. A social worker ran the shelter, utilizing volunteers from the community and local churches for donations and assistance.

The lunch line was already forming as they arrived, and Annabelle spoke to several of the men and women as she approached, shaking their hands and offering a kind word.

Quinton remained silent behind her, looking uncomfortable, his mouth set in a grim line.

"Hi, I'm Emily Nelson," a vibrant young blonde said as she approached them. "I'm the social worker on staff."

"Quinton Valtrez, Homeland Security," Quinton said.

Annabelle extended her hand. "And I'm Annabelle Armstrong, CNN. Can we talk?" Annabelle asked.

"Sure. Step into my office." Emily gestured to a tiny room that looked as if it had once been a closet.

Quinton gestured that he'd wait outside. She nodded, watching him move through the crowd as if he was searching for the bomber. His look bordered on belligerence and made Annabelle wonder at his thoughts, wonder what it was like to suspect everyone you met. Had his entire life been built on violence and distrust?

"What can I do for you?" Emily asked.

Annabelle explained about witnessing the Savannah bombing, and the young woman's eyes grew sad. "That was horrible."

"Yes, and we have reason to suspect that an attack is planned for Charleston tonight."

"Oh, my goodness," Emily murmured. "Do you know where?"

"We're working with locals and the FBI to pinpoint a possible target."

"I don't understand how I can help," Emily said with a frown.

Annabelle had to guard her words. "The Savannah bomber was identified as a former war veteran who suffered from post-traumatic stress syndrome. He was also homeless."

Emily's blue eyes widened. "What are you implying? That someone here may be a bomber?"

"No, not exactly," Annabelle hedged. "Actually, I think that someone else was behind the first attack, and somehow they drugged, hypnotized, or brainwashed Mr. Ames into setting off that bomb."

"You mean someone is preying on the homeless?"

"Yes." Annabelle licked her dry lips. "Have you seen anything suspicious?"

She shook her head.

"Do you know of anyone here suffering from PTS?"

"Not right offhand," Emily said. "Of course, there are a couple of mentally impaired men and a junkie or two who stop by for meals."

"What about any other visitors?" Annabelle asked. "Maybe someone who looked like they didn't belong?"

"That's hard to say," Emily said. "We're not judgmental here. We get folks from all walks of life, from all socio-economic levels, with a variety of problems. We don't turn anyone away."

"Of course not."

Emily's eyebrows pinched together as she thought. "The only other visitor we're had lately was that televangelist Reverend Narius. He came by and offered to pray with individuals." She paused. "He said he was in town and is speaking at the First Baptist Church tonight."

Annabelle considered him for a moment. Some preachers had been known to brainwash their followers. And in some ways the reverend fit the profile of a serial killer. She'd researched him a few months back for a story. According to her sources, he'd been raised in a strict religious family and was a religious zealot. In fact, he might have a God complex. He liked public attention and had spoken in Savannah after the bombing, offering prayer sessions at local churches.

Serial killers often entrenched themselves in a crime scene or stayed to watch. And what better cover than to offer solace to the victims' grieving family members afterward? Reverend Narius also made visiting the homeless part of his mission. He planned to travel worldwide to wipe out sinners.

A bead of perspiration chilled her neck. No, he'd done

too much good in the world, saved lives and donated to charities. She couldn't possibly look at him as a suspect.

Quinton ignored the rancid odors of unbathed skin, sweat, and urine as he combed through the shelter, listening to conversations and probing people's minds. Some talked about the food, the weather, and the deaths the last few days, while others seemed lost in their own world of turmoil.

Jagged moments of their past lives, their jobs and broken families, the craving of booze or pills, splintered their tumultuous thoughts. He dug deeper, searching for someone who might be planning suicide, but the only thoughts of death he picked up were those of some of the elderly, who seemed to be looking forward to reuniting with lost loved ones.

Remembering the sickly pallor and sightless white eyes of the Savannah bomber, he studied each individual for signs of possession. Two or three people struck him as virtually brain dead, but he lingered beside them and realized they were simply too drugged and disease-ridden to think clearly.

Annabelle finally said her good-byes and approached him. "Did you learn anything?" he asked as they headed to the car.

"Just that Reverend Narius stopped by and offered private prayer sessions."

"So he could have hypnotized or drugged one of them when they were alone, and no one would have suspected a thing?"

Annabelle nodded grimly. "What about you?" Annabelle asked. "Did you learn anything?"

"No. I didn't sense that the killer was here either."

"Is that part of your supernatural power, too? You sense things?"

"So you believe I have supernatural powers?"

"I don't know," Annabelle said. "I've never believed before. But...I saw you move that beam." She narrowed her eyes. "What else can you do?"

A smile curved his mouth. "Sometimes I can read minds."

Her mouth gaped open. "You read minds?"

His smile widened, teasing her as they got in the car. "Yes."

She settled in her seat, fidgeting uncomfortably. "Have you been reading my mind?"

He twisted a strand of her hair between his fingers. "You want me, but you don't trust me. And you're afraid of what I am."

"That's not mind reading," she said. "Naturally I'd be wary of you. You're an assassin, and what else...I don't know yet."

He chuckled. "I'm not going to hurt you, Annabelle."

You will if I let you get too close.

"You're right," he said, reminding himself that he had no place in his life for a relationship. Not with his job.

And not with a demon attack.

As if she realized he had indeed read her thoughts, she shifted to look out the window, shutting down in front of him.

He didn't blame her. He wouldn't want someone in his head any more than he wanted anyone in his heart.

They drove in silence to the veterans hospital on Bee Street, parked and went inside. The place resurrected memories of Quinton's own hospital stay after injuries he'd sustained in the military. The smell of pain and suffering, the sound of silent cries and horrors filled his head as they made their way to the administrator's office.

A woman in her forties with copper-colored hair greeted them, and Quinton identified himself and explained the reason for their visit.

"We need you to look at your list of outpatients, consult with therapists, and see if you can pinpoint a name for us."

"Let me get this straight," Ms. Duffy said. "You believe someone is preying on a man with PTS or a homeless person, somehow convincing them to commit murder?"

"It's a theory," Quinton said. "And we don't have much time. We expect the bomber to strike again tonight at midnight."

"But you're talking about violating these veterans' privacy. And the numbers alone are impossible."

Quinton ground his heel into the thick carpet in frustration. "I understand that. But at least speak to your team of therapists. See if a name jumps out as someone suspicious. Someone who already is exhibiting signs of violence or who is suicidal."

She sighed and tapped her pen on the cluttered desk. "I'll see what I can do."

"Has Reverend Narius visited the hospital?" Annabelle asked.

The woman pursed her mouth. "Yes, as a matter of fact he did. He held chapel early this morning."

"Did he counsel anyone privately?" Quinton asked.

She shook her head. "Not that I'm aware of. But you can't possibly think the good reverend would hurt one of the veterans? He's trying to save their souls."

Quinton frowned. Was he? Or was he a demon in disguise, using religion as a way to weave his way into their psyches and steal their souls instead?

Annabelle considered another theory. "Ms. Duffy, do you have any doctors or psychiatrists conducting research here with the patients?"

"What type of research?" she asked.

"I'm not sure. Maybe someone researching Alzheimer's or memory problems. Or perhaps a doctor who uses hypnosis in his therapy? Or someone studying mind control?"

Ms. Duffy closed her eyes, pressed two fingers to her temple as if to massage an ache away, then opened her eyes and frowned. "I'm not going to impugn any of the doctors or therapists who work here for some ridiculous speculation on your part." She stood abruptly. "Now, if you come up with something concrete to show me or a warrant, please come back."

"We're just trying to stop another attack," Quinton said.

She fidgeted with the ruffle at the neck of her blouse. "I understand and I really want to help you. But again, I have protocol to follow."

Annabelle sighed and pushed her business card into the woman's hand. "We understand. But if you come up with a name or see or hear anything suspicious, please call."

"Confer with your staff and see what they tell you," Quinton said. "We're not the bad guys here, Ms. Duffy. We're trying to save lives. I think you'd want that, too."

"I do want that," she said sharply. "Or I wouldn't be working here."

Annabelle thanked her, and Quinton followed her through the corridors to the outside.

"Well, that got us nowhere," Quinton muttered with a curse.

"Maybe, maybe not," Annabelle said. "We planted the seed of doubt. She'll start thinking. And she may come up with something for us."

"I just hope it's in time," Quinton said as he glanced at his watch.

Fear crawled up Annabelle's spine.

Only a few hours until midnight. And they had no idea where the bomber would strike, or who the one pulling the strings would use for the attack.

The next few hours Quinton and Annabelle combed the streets, the market area, the Battery, visited the main hospital, and talked to locals in the cemeteries and parks. Quinton used his power to listen to people's thoughts, searching for signs they might be dealing with a demon.

He also checked in regularly with the local police and the Homeland Security agent, but the day was wearing on and they still had nothing.

As they parked at the Citadel stadium and walked up to the entrance, Quinton touched a railing, hoping for a premonition. Concentrating, he closed his eyes and allowed his senses to take control. Vultures soared overhead, the sound of their hungry cries shrill in the midst of the crowds gathering to tailgate for the game.

But he was only one man. And the noise of the crowd, the excitement, the anxiety of the undercover police and agents, all created a mass of emotions, blocking out details.

"Are you okay?" Annabelle touched his arm gently.

He nodded then looked at her and saw the same frustration mirrored in her eyes.

They were no closer to finding a viable suspect.

And he couldn't share his fear that the perpetrator might not be an average Joe this time but a demon.

"Detective Barbaris was right," Annabelle said, rubbing at her sore rib. "We're looking for a needle in a haystack."

"We're doing everything we can," Quinton said. Although he wondered if that was true. He was still behaving like an agent, a military spy.

If a demon was behind these attacks, Homeland Security, the local police, and logic alone might not be able to solve the crime.

He needed help from someone who understood demons and the demonic world.

Vincent and his wife, Clarissa.

No. He still didn't know if he could trust Vincent. For all he knew, he might be orchestrating this as a trap for him.

But the monks? The ones who'd warned him about demons from the beginning.

Maybe they would have answers.

He would contact Father Robard, the one who'd encouraged him to document the demons in the *Deadly Demons* book. He could tell him if Vincent was really his brother. If he could be trusted.

Or if Vincent was a demon himself.

Trust no one. Everyone is the enemy.

He couldn't forget that rule of combat.

But contacting Father Robard meant traveling back

into his past. To a dark, lonely place he thought he'd left behind.

The military had trained him to compartmentalize. To endure torture, punishment, deprivation, and repress emotions in order to do his job.

Even when the darkness pulled at him, he'd learned to channel it into destroying the enemy. The ones preying on innocents.

Killing them triggered no remorse. No guilt. No regret.

And kept the balance within him. The monks had taught him the importance of that balance.

Maybe they would be able to help now as well.

Maybe they'd be able to tell him how to recognize the demon, and how to destroy him when he did.

He stepped aside and searched through his address book, then punched in Father Robard's number. When he answered, the man's familiar voice brought a sense of comfort. The monks had been the only family he'd ever known.

"Quinton. It's been a long time. I've been waiting on your call."

A vulture soared above the stadium, making Quinton tense. "I need to ask you something important. Who brought me to you?"

"Your mother," Father Robard said quietly. "It was a sad day for her and she was most troubled by her decision, but she had to give you up to protect you."

"Was I alone?"

Another pause. "No, you had a twin. Your mother warned us of the dangers and we separated you early on."

"What dangers?"

"You don't remember my teachings?" Father Robard asked. "My warnings about the demons that would one day come for you?"

How could he forget? "Yes, I do remember. And recently a man named Vincent contacted me. He claimed he was my brother."

"Yes, Vincent is the oldest of the Dark Lords, the one who knew your father and just how evil he was."

"So it's true that he's my brother?"

"Yes. What else did he tell you?"

Quinton relayed the story Vincent had shared about his mother's death. "Is it true?"

"Yes. And since your father took over the underworld, we've felt the rumblings below, have been praying non-stop for the innocents, and for you and your brothers."

"Then I can trust this man Vincent?"

"Trust? I'm not certain. As far as we know, he hasn't succumbed to his dark side. He even defeated the god of fear a few months ago, which was a good sign. The medium he married feeds his goodness. Zion was not pleased. He has sent a demon to win you."

"The Death Angel?"

"Yes. Be careful. Stay strong, my son. And use your power to stop him."

Laughter bubbled from the Death Angel's demonic chest.

Torturing the Dark Lord was pure pleasure.

He raised his bald head and screeched to the vultures nearby, calling them to antagonize Quinton and the reporter.

The Dark Lord was struggling over whether or not to accept his destiny. He'd listened to those damn monks.

Fools. They might be God's soldiers, but they would lose.

Zion was too strong.

And the Dark Lord was starting to care for the woman. He would use that against him.

Quinton had promised to protect her. Would he join Zion's side if it meant sparing her life?

Soon they'd put him to the test.

And Zion would win.

Chapter Thirteen

"Have you found anything?" Quinton asked Detective Barbaris.

The cop shook his head, his expression worried. "Security is all over the city. We had bomb dogs search the entire Citadel stadium. Your chief and one of our officers are stationed in the security office now watching the feed."

Quinton nodded. The fans were pouring toward the stadium, excited and oblivious of the fact that their game might draw a crazed killer.

But calling off the game would give the bomber too much power. And what if they were wrong? What if there was no attack?

They had no concrete lead on a terrorist cell or a location for an attack.

"Let's review the security tapes," Quinton said.

Annabelle followed him, and for the next two hours they studied the cameras.

"I feel helpless," Annabelle said quietly.

He squeezed her arm. "We've done everything we know to do. Security is all over the place." But the threat of one lone bomber slipping through undetected was very real.

Annabelle sighed and rubbed her forehead. "He may be at the coliseum or even at the church where Reverend Narius is."

"True," Quinton said. "Unless Narius is part of this."

Annabelle's cell phone jangled, and she quickly answered it. "Yes, Annabelle Armstrong." A pause. "All right, Ms. Duffy, we'll check out those two names."

"What?" he asked as she disconnected the call.

"Ms. Duffy said she spoke with two of her therapists and gave me the names of a couple of patients they were concerned about."

"Really?" Quinton said. "What about her strict rules and patient confidentiality?"

Annabelle frowned. "If anyone asks, we didn't get this information from her."

"What about these men made the therapists think they might be suspect?"

"The first one, Tobias Longfellow, has been suicidal for weeks. And the second, B. J. Rutherford, is bipolar. When he's in his manic state, he leaves home and lives on the streets."

Quinton nodded and took her arm. "Let's check them out. Maybe we've finally got a lead."

Annabelle's heart raced as they drove toward the Isle of Palms where Tobias Longfellow resided. Finally, they might have a clue.

Grandiose two- and three-story mansions lined the coast, and Tobias's house was an impressive beachfront antebellum with wraparound porches on three levels.

Three rings of the doorbell, and a woman wearing a maid's uniform answered.

Quinton flashed his ID and Annabelle introduced herself. "We're looking for Tobias Longfellow."

"I'm sorry, but he's not here."

"Where is he?" Quinton asked.

"His brother came this afternoon and drove him to his place. Mr. Longfellow has been depressed lately, so Mr. George thought it would do him good to stay with him for a while and help with his business."

"Can you call and verify that he's there?" Quinton asked.

The woman frowned. "Why would I do that?"

"We just want to make sure he's safe," Annabelle said.

Her hands fluttered to the collar of her uniform. "Is there some reason he wouldn't be?"

"Just check," Quinton said in a commanding voice.

She looked irritated and worried but hurried to get the house phone, and dialed the number. "Yes, Mr. George, I'm calling to check on Mr. Longfellow. How is he?"

Relief softened the lines on the woman's face as they conversed. Tobias was obviously safe—not the man they were looking for.

The housekeeper disconnected the call and gave them a smug smile. "Mr. Longfellow is doing fine."

"Thank you." Annabelle took Quinton's arm and pulled him down the steps toward the car.

"Where to next?" Quinton asked as he started the engine.

She gave him the address of an apartment building on the outskirts of Charleston, and he raced toward the address. A few minutes later, she spotted the run-down building and sighed.

She checked her watch as they parked. Eleven p.m. Only one hour until midnight.

Both feeling the time crunch, they jumped from the car and hurried to the apartment door, but the interior was dark, and no one answered their knock.

Quinton used his credit card to break into the apartment. Annabelle frowned but stood in the entryway as he combed through the small, dark rooms. Weathered ancient furniture, the stench of stale beer, an empty fridge. He checked the desk for notes that might offer some information on the man but found nothing except a newspaper.

Then he glanced at the open page—a feature on the band Death's Door that was performing at the coliseum. B. J. had drawn a big red circle in marker around the name of the group. Death's Door apparently rapped about devil worship.

"That's it." He turned to Annabelle and waved the paper. "The coliseum in north Charleston—that's the target."

Annabelle's pulse pounded as they drove toward the coliseum. Quinton phoned Agent McLaughlin and told him that he suspected the concert was the target, and to secure a photo of B. J. Rutherford and pass it to all the security guards and police.

Traffic crawled by, clogging the road to north Charleston.

Quinton honked his horn and maneuvered around cars, sometimes taking the shoulder in his haste. Midnight was less than half an hour away when they arrived. Fans had filled the coliseum, a mixture of teenagers and young people with no idea that they might die tonight. Dozens of vultures had gathered atop the building, with more soaring above as if in anticipation.

The parking lot was packed, and people were jammed inside as rock music blasted the coliseum. Quinton ran the car up on a curb near the closest entrance.

A nasty black vulture dove toward the windshield of his car, its wingspan casting an ominous shadow across the glass, then pecked viciously at it.

Normally Quinton connected with animals. He felt a connection now, except this connection wasn't friendly. The vulture had only fierce hunger for carrion on its mind, and it craved human flesh.

Quinton's. Annabelle's.

It was almost as if the bird knew him. As if he'd come for some kind of sinister revenge.

"You're not going to win," Quinton growled.

But as he climbed out, the vulture swooped down in attack. Soon another bird joined in, and he shouted at Annabelle to stay in the car. Two more appeared, diving toward the glass and pecking it viciously.

He focused his eyes, and his mind, on the creatures and suddenly sent them bouncing backward off the glass. Annabelle gasped in shock but jumped out, burying her head in the crook of Quinton's arm to shield herself from others who attacked as they raced toward the building.

He met a security guard, identified himself, and asked to be patched into the head security station. A team had arrived with dogs and began to comb the stadium. Meanwhile, he continually searched for someone suspicious. For the smell of death he'd noted in Savannah. For a person with suicide on his mind.

For B. J. Rutherford.

But there was too much noise and too many people, the stands pulsing with the heavy-metal beat.

He glanced at his watch. Almost midnight.

They hurried into the security office on the main level, and he introduced himself to two officers who were watching the feed from numerous sets of cameras situated on the various levels of the coliseum. Thousands of people overflowed the stands, singing and dancing in their seats.

"You haven't noticed anything suspicious?" Quinton asked, his nerves on edge.

"Are you kidding? Have you seen the way half these kids are dressed?"

One camera panned the stage—the members of Death's Door wore black T-shirts with "Purgatory" in red letters on the front, letters that appeared to be dripping blood. Many of the fans were dressed similarly, and sported the goth look with their chalky faces, black lipstick, and garish makeup.

McLaughlin ran in with an army photo of B.J. on his PDA and showed it to the guards. "If you spot this man, let me know."

Quinton scowled. What if they'd been wrong? What if the suicide bomber wasn't B.J.? What if this time the demon had chosen a teenager? If the Death Angel could bend a person's mind to his will, a young, impressionable kid would be the perfect subject.

And if these kids were into devil worship as the rock band professed, their souls were already half lost.

"Hey, wait a minute," one of the guards said. "I see an old man up on the third floor. He's pushing a cleaning cart, but it looks like he might have something beneath his jacket."

"Get him and start evacuating!" Quinton ordered.

He pushed Annabelle toward the exit to safety, then jogged toward the stairs. He had to find this guy and stop him.

But suddenly an explosion sounded, the building shook, and pieces of concrete began to crumble.

The vulture hovered above the North Charleston Coliseum, watching as hundreds of mortals raced from the stadium, a host of teenage humans and college students.

A wicked sense of delight had bolstered him when he'd heard the name of the group.

So fitting tonight, when death would greet them into its welcoming, endless darkness.

More delicious bloody bones to clean, and all from young, youthful bodies. So many more souls to join Satan—Zion's kingdom would grow exponentially.

The reason he'd chosen this venue for his mark.

He screeched his call, alerting his fellow vultures to join him for the party so they could fill their bellies with the human remains.

The sight of the dozens and dozens of vultures soaring above the North Charleston Coliseum roused Quinton's dark side, yet at the same time, knowing they had come to bury their ugly bald heads inside human carcasses made his skin crawl.

He understood the predator's natural instinct to hunt. Related to the bird's senses tuning in to the smell of blood and decomposing flesh. His own mouth watered for the taste of death.

And now justice.

Dammit, they'd been so close to catching this guy. Maybe stopping him.

Dilapidated sections of the building lay in concrete and stone rubble, the scent of smoke and burned bodies nearly suffocating as he moved through the mess to assist in the rescue. Paramedics rushed onto the scene to carry victims to safety and to ambulances. Police, security, and FBI agents swarmed the coliseum, as well as crime scene units who began to comb the massive area, trying to piece together exactly what had happened and identify the bomber as well as the victims.

He made it outside and helped a young woman to an ambulance, then Detective Barbaris approached, rubbing soot from his forehead. The Homeland Security agent joined them. "Did anyone see the bomber?" Quinton asked.

"We're still questioning witnesses," Barbaris said. "But half of them are so in shock they don't know what the hell happened."

"It's a cluster fuck," the other agent muttered.

Quinton noticed Annabelle working her way through the crowd, stopping to interview various witnesses and offer sympathy and help where needed. She was amazing. Obviously upset over the senseless deaths but strong and willing to help those in need. Her stories weren't written simply for purposes of sensationalism—she really wanted to do what was right.

"Make sure CSI collects all the security tapes,"

Quinton said. "I want to view them myself." And verify if B. J. Rutherford was their man.

Detective Barbaris pulled his hand down his chin. "They may be damaged from the explosion."

"Get them anyway," Quinton said. "Some of our techs may be able to restore the images."

"I'm on it." Detective Barbaris clapped his thigh with his hand. "What about you guys? Any idea what's going on here? You think these perps got together and planned this?"

"We're looking at an online support group for veterans," Quinton said. Although he refrained from adding that he believed a demon was responsible. Instead, he let the other agent handle the question, and he headed into the crowd, forced himself to focus, to zero in on the people's thoughts.

Pain, shock, anger, and fear dominated their minds. And the overpowering scent of death permeated the air.

He spotted the black vulture perched on the sign in front of the coliseum, its beady eyes boring into his. The Death Angel was taunting him, a sign that Vincent had been right. That demons roamed the earth now, trying to destroy it with evil. A gray mist shrouded the area, telling him that Soul Collectors had also swooped in to steal souls from those who died.

Quinton glared at the bird of prey, his demonic side emerging. Then the vulture squawked and flew away from his attack, screeching again as if mocking him.

He cursed.

The Death Angel thought he'd won. Maybe he had tonight.

But he'd met his match.

Soon Quinton would destroy him. Then he'd laugh at the vultures as they fled in terror.

The vulture buried its head inside the decomposing body, savoring each tasty morsel of bloody carrion as if it were his last meal.

Although he could always find food later.

Because death couldn't be stopped.

And there were dozens of bodies tonight, enough to feed him and all his friends.

Delicious death. A constant part of the natural order of life. So why did people fight it as if they could actually defeat the inevitable?

And why had the foolish reporter gone toward the light in Savannah when immortality waited in the darkness?

Frustration made him flap his wings wildly and screech his fury. Why had Quinton Valtrez saved her? Was the Dark Lord turning...good?

They had to force him one step closer to his destiny as a Dark Lord, force him to join the underworld and scrap the rules of humanity.

Evil had no rules.

It played to win and it would.

Eventually Valtrez would realize it and cross over. If not, he'd take him against his will.

After all, he was Death. And no one could stop him.

Chapter Fourteen

A feeling of déjà vu along with memories of the Savannah bombing struck Annabelle. Although the coliseum was large enough that the damage seemed to be contained to the upper area, people raced from the building in a steady rush of panic. She searched for Quinton but didn't see him.

Knowing she had to help, she rushed over to assist two young girls who were frozen in fear, hunched over and trembling against a large chunk of concrete.

As they stumbled outside, she noted moments of heroics as a young man or woman stopped to help another, as teens carried the injured to safety. A young woman knelt and ripped off the tail of her shirt to bind the wound of a stranger.

But the vultures soared above, dipping and attacking the dead.

One of the policemen glared at her as if she were a vulture herself, and she glared back. She realized some people viewed reporters as leeches, but she wasn't callous or unsympathetic.

Still, she would ferret out the truth about this bomber anyway she had to. People deserved to know the truth.

Two teenagers huddled together beneath a blanket,

their surface injuries already attended to. She stopped to tell them she was sorry.

"Did you see anyone suspicious?" she asked.

The young girl buried her head in her boyfriend's shoulder. "No, we just came to the concert." Her cell phone buzzed and panicked eyes shot up. "Oh, God, that's my mom. She's probably freaking out."

Annabelle patted her gently on the shoulder. "Answer it and assure her you're all right."

She moved on to another group of teens gathered in a circle, waiting on their parents to arrive. "Did anyone see anything suspicious tonight?"

"The guy behind me was snorting coke," one girl said.

"And a guy had a big backpack," another boy said.

The redhead with tattoos beside him rolled her eyes. "He had a twelve-pack in that backpack, not a bomb."

"Miss, miss!" a woman dressed in a cleaning lady's uniform waved at her, and Annabelle veered toward her.

"Are you all right, ma'am?" Annabelle asked.

"Yes, yes, but I saw a man pushing a cleaning cart. He wasn't from our company." She gestured toward the logo embroidered on her uniform. "His clothes smelled like sweat. And he looked glassy-eyed."

"Can you describe him? Did he say anything?"

"He had gray hair, wore work boots, and he favored his right leg." She rubbed at her arm, now bandaged and in a sling. "But he didn't say anything. Just pushed that cart along slowly. Then suddenly I heard a noise and the bomb exploded."

Sounded like the man security had zeroed in on earlier. B.J. Too bad they hadn't reached him in time.

Annabelle squeezed her shoulder, then took her contact information and glanced up, searching for Quinton.

She finally spotted him, ran to him, and relayed what the woman had told her.

Quinton nodded. "CSI is supposed to bring us the tapes to verify his ID."

The next two hours passed in a blur. Finally they left the site for the rescue workers and CSI to process while they went to the police station. The crime scene unit had gathered pieces of what they suspected were the bomb and the clothing from the man who'd set it off. His body had been transported to the medical examiner's office. Dr. Sam Wynn, the ME who'd worked on the Savannah case, had been called in to do the autopsy and help identify other victims.

"B. J. Rutherford is the man we believe to have been the bomber," Quinton said. "The director of the veterans hospital told us he was bipolar."

Detective Barbaris nodded. "I'll tell Dr. Wynn to obtain the man's medical records for comparison. That will speed up the ID." He fidgeted, his gaze raking over Annabelle. "You think these are connected through that online group?"

"Maybe. The Savannah bomber was a homeless man who suffered from post-traumatic stress syndrome," Annabelle said. "B. J. Rutherford also suffered from PTS and when in his manic state, lived on the streets. I think someone is taking advantage of these men's mental problems and using them to commit the crimes. Whoever did it found the men through that chat group."

He rubbed his chin. "Interesting theory."

He excused himself to contact Dr. Wynn, and Annabelle turned to see Quinton glaring at her.

"What's your problem?" she asked.

"Just how far would you go to get your story?"

Anger slashed through her, and she jammed her face close to his.

"How dare you suggest I'd do something immoral when you have no morals yourself."

Quinton silently cursed himself. Why in the hell had he said that?

Because he hadn't liked the way the detective looked at her.

"I do have morals," he said in her ear. "I choose who I kill. I also want to fuck you," he murmured, "and so does every man who sees you, so you should watch whom you're being nice to."

"Being nice is my nature." Annabelle's eyes blazed. "And we were simply discussing the investigation."

He moved closer to her as if staking out his territory, and Annabelle's eyes flickered with unease. But Detective Barbaris loped back into the room, cutting their conversation short.

"Come this way." He led them to another room with a monitor for viewing. Special Agent McLaughlin had just arrived.

"What have you found out about the bomb materials?" Quinton asked.

"Our EDU-BDC unit has collected small fragments of the explosives at the crime scene, and forensics is conducting tests now," McLaughlin said. "We're comparing them with the bomb in Savannah to see if they were created by

the same source and where the materials might have originated from, if they were homemade or if we're dealing
with a terrorist cell." McLaughlin paused and set up the
tapes. "We're also cross-checking for matches across the
States."

Quinton folded his arms. "You have any leads?"

Agent McLaughlin sighed. "I'm afraid not. We've
alerted security at airports, federal buildings, and other
possible targets designated in studies by Homeland Security." He dropped down in a chair. "Unfortunately, since
these two attacks occurred only days apart, we may be
looking at another one soon."

He was right.

McLaughlin scrolled through several sets of tapes from
various areas of the coliseum first, showing feed of hundreds of teenagers and college students entering the stadium, along with vendors, security, and cleanup crews.

"Here's our person of interest." McLaughlin pointed
out a gray-haired gentleman dressed as a janitor. Quinton frowned and leaned closer, noting the deathly pallor
of the man, the glassy-eyed look, the way his movements
were robotic.

"Yes, that's B. J. Rutherford," Quinton said. "But I
couldn't reach him in time."

McLaughlin fast-forwarded through several more sections of tape, then focused on the immediate area where
the bomb had exploded. A vulture hovered above, others
circling and preparing to feed.

Detective Barbaris returned, rubbing his eyes. None of
them had slept, and he looked bleary-eyed and exhausted.
"Ms. Duffy is faxing over B. J. Rutherford's medical
reports so we can verify the ID. She said his therapist

had referred him to Dr. Gryphon, a specialist working on research regarding dementia, Alzheimer's, and PTS. She didn't think they'd met yet."

Annabelle and Quinton exchanged looks.

"Maybe we should talk to Dr. Gryphon," Annabelle said. "He might be able to offer insight into how someone could brainwash two former soldiers into strapping on bombs and walking into a public place and setting them off."

Quinton knotted his hands. They had been brainwashed. Been subjected to mind control. He knew the techniques, and given the men's already troubled mental states, it probably hadn't been that difficult. A combination of drugs and hypnosis?

A doctor certainly would have the knowledge to do it.

And so would a demon who possessed the ability to bend a person's mind at will.

The weight of the night settled over the car like a thick, hot blanket. Annabelle lapsed into silence again as they drove into the heart of Charleston and back to the hotel.

News of the explosion had obviously spread, and human nature and self-preservation had kicked in. The residents huddled in fear within their homes, their private sanctuaries where they were safe.

She had always thought in blacks and whites. She'd gone to Savannah to expose Quinton because what he was doing was wrong. Yet now she was relying on his help.

"I feel sorry for B. J. Rutherford," Annabelle said.

Quinton grunted. "Even though he killed tonight?"

She sighed. "I think he was a victim himself."

Dawn was cracking the sky, but Annabelle located the

number for Dr. Gryphon and phoned him anyway. His voice mail picked up, and she left a message saying it was urgent that she speak with him.

When she hung up, she shivered, wondering if she'd ever feel safe again. So much pain and sadness.

And anger, too. She hated feeling out of control. Knowing another attack might occur and that this killer was using her in a game of cat and mouse to draw attention to himself.

It was ironic that she had teamed up with Quinton, an assassin, in order to stop this bomber. Quinton, a man with supernatural powers.

Although the idea of supernatural powers didn't fit into her orderly world, she couldn't deny it. She'd witnessed their use twice herself now.

Did Quinton have other powers he hadn't revealed? More dangerous ones?

Her gaze met his, and the smoldering intensity in his eyes sent a shocking thrill through her. His words at the precinct, that he wanted to fuck her, reverberated in her head, eliciting hot sensations in her belly.

How could she be so attracted to such a dangerous man? To a man who killed for a living and had no remorse for his actions?

Yet he was strong and protective and he was fighting to save innocents.

How could she not be attracted to him?

Exhaustion and adrenaline warred with each other as they parked and went inside the hotel. They were both tired, the lingering scent of sweat and smoke cloying, so she climbed into the shower.

Yet as she brushed the soap over her naked body, she

closed her eyes and imagined Quinton's fingers touching her instead.

Quinton showered quickly, then, unable to help himself, tuned in to the camera in Annabelle's room, desperate to make sure she was safe.

And hungry to see her, touch her, be inside her, reminding them they were both alive.

More vultures soared outside in the sky like dark-winged inhuman demons. They were everywhere, perched on lampposts, building tops, gathering above the cemeteries as if they'd risen from the graves to stalk the residents, waiting silently, intensely, their keen eyesight alert for an innocent to walk outside so they could attack.

"The demons feed on humans," the monks had told Quinton. "They will try to rule the world one day, and you must be ready to fight them."

Quinton couldn't shake the feeling that the demons had arrived, like devious terrorists hiding among the innocents, adopting various insidious shapes and forms that he might not recognize. That no one was safe now. Especially Annabelle.

That he might become one of them.

His hand rose to the angel amulet lying against his bare chest. The heavy weight served as a reminder of his conversation with Vincent and their mother's spirit.

That good blood ran through his veins as well as demonic blood.

He'd felt only the sting of bad blood before, the darkness, the obsessive need to kill, to taste blood, to destroy and rid the world of vile creatures. To feed his lust and constant craving for sex with any willing woman.

He felt the darkness mounting, engulfing him like a black cloud that sucked the light from his soul as he hungered for vengeance for the dead innocents.

And another fierce need—a need for Annabelle.

In light of the death they'd seen tonight, the urge to protect her battled with other primal urges. The urge to sate himself with her sweet, luscious body.

Just like the vile predatory creatures hovering above the town, his thirst for flesh stirred, exciting him.

Was she thinking about him, fantasizing about his fingers touching her as she bathed?

He itched to put his fingers on her skin, too. To feel the turgid peaks of her nipples against the pads of his thumbs. To suckle her like a baby and slide his fingers into her warm wet flesh. To have her quiver beneath him and cry out his name in the heat of passion.

To make him forget that he was part demon. That the Death Angel was stalking him, and that in order to fight him, he might have to let his dark side win.

Then Annabelle stepped from the shower and his mouth went dry, thoughts of the Death Angel taking a momentary backseat as desire spiraled through him. The past hours had been a harrowing, nerve-racking ride as they'd rushed to try to stop this killer.

The tension in his tightly wound body needed a release. He wanted that release to be inside Annabelle.

Dammit, he sensed she wanted it, too.

So what was stopping them?

Chapter Fifteen

Annabelle stepped from the shower and dried off, then slid into a cool satin gown and robe before she dried her hair. Her body ached and she felt fatigued, but she doubted she could fall asleep.

The images of the victims were still too fresh in her mind.

And so were Quinton's words. *I want to fuck you.*

He hadn't said *make love.*

No, he'd been crude and raw and...so damn sexy that she didn't care right now if he loved her. She wanted to feel alive. To be caressed and stroked, and to erase the terror-filled screams in her head with mindless pleasure.

She opened the bathroom door and stepped into the bedroom, her heart fluttering as the door adjoining Quinton's room opened. He stood in the archway, a picture of angry, steely male strength, his broad shoulders squared as if braced for battle.

His hair was damp from his shower, brushing his neck, and her gaze zeroed in on an amulet around his neck, the stone glowing a bright amber against his bronzed chest. Her breath caught at the feral look in his eyes.

With a growl low in his throat, he walked toward her.

When he stood only an inch away, she inhaled the scent of his body, and desire rippled through her.

He's dangerous, a voice whispered inside her head. *You're supposed to get the story on him.*

Get it any way you can, her boss would say.

But the story wasn't driving her now. Her own feminine need fed her inability to resist and push him away. And foolishly, the danger radiating from him only heightened her excitement.

Her pulse raced with anticipation as he lifted his hand, cupped her neck, and pushed her against the wall.

"What are you doing?" she whispered.

"The hell if I know." He leaned forward, his hard sex pressing against her thigh, his thick, dark coarse chest hair brushing her nipples through the thin satin fabric of her gown.

Her legs buckled, her stomach fluttering. His muscles were corded and thick, his shoulders broad, his voice a mixture of sensuality and gruff male as he whispered her name. Terror shot through her, but also a surge of something else she didn't want to feel.

Potent desire.

"I've fantasized about tasting your skin," he murmured. Then he pushed her hands above her, pinning her against the wall. His eyes darkened, and he dipped his head and traced his tongue along her lips. His heady smell enveloped her, erotic and taunting.

She sucked in a breath, stifling a wail of panic and a plea to him to take her.

A wave of heat passed between them as her gaze met his. Something so raw and primal that her own wicked fantasies surfaced.

He dropped his dark gaze to her mouth and muttered an obscenity as if he was battling his attraction to her.

Maybe he did have a conscience.

She parted her lips on a soft sigh, imagining his large strong fingers working magic on her body.

Growling low and throaty, he slid his knee between her legs, stroking, the friction igniting a seed of longing that made her moan. Warmth spread throughout her lower body, desire flickering to life like a fire that needed stoking.

"Dammit, Annabelle," he murmured. "I didn't ask for this." But he didn't back away.

Instead, he tightened his grip on her chin, then lowered his head and fused his mouth with hers.

Quinton couldn't believe the turn of events. He had been ordered to kill Annabelle, yet now he'd teamed up with her and was protecting her. And kissing her to boot.

Had he lost his mind?

Hell, maybe so. But she wanted him, and any semblance of control snapped.

He needed sex like an animal needed food. He had to have her body.

Annabelle moaned as he nibbled at her lower lip, then plunged his tongue into her mouth. She tasted like a decadent piece of exotic fruit, sweet and tangy and . . . ripe.

And with just enough bite to make his mouth water for more.

She lifted one hand and pressed against his chest as if to push him away, and he stilled. If she wanted him to stop, he would. Although his heart was hammering away, his body hard and aching, his hands itching to strip that nothing of a gown from her, throw her down, and take her on the floor.

"I want you, Quinton." Then she threaded her fingers in his hair, pulling him closer, urging him to deepen the kiss, awakening his darkest, most wicked fantasies.

Fire heated his loins, and he ravaged her mouth as he wanted to do the rest of her luscious body. His fingers trailed down her shoulder, over her arms, then over one plump breast.

Her quick intake of breath was steeped with arousal, and she threw her head back and clung to him as he lowered his mouth and dropped kisses along her neck and throat. His hand moved, cupping her breast, his thumb flicking her nipple through the silky fabric. The soft bud stiffened beneath his touch and his cock hardened.

Desperate to be inside her, he rubbed his length against her as he dragged his mouth downward, licking her salty skin. Need surged through him, and he slid open the edges of the robe, then pushed it off her shoulders until it fell in a puddle at their feet. He slowly unbuttoned the top buttons of her gown, and pushed the satin aside until her breasts spilled into his hands and he closed his mouth over one pebbled tip.

She moaned and arched her back, and he suckled her greedily, then slid his other hand down to stroke her inner thighs. She quivered, then his finger found the place where he'd seen the tattoo.

"I want to see that tattoo," he whispered against her skin.

She suddenly froze, and he squeezed his eyes closed, realizing he'd just made a mistake.

Another first. He never made mistakes. *Never* lost control.

Never let anything stand in the way of his job.

She wrenched herself away and swiped at her mouth, frantically pulling her gown back together. Her blue eyes glinted with emotions that sucker punched him. Horror, disgust...hurt.

Dammit. A twinge of guilt pinched his gut.

"How did you know I have a tattoo?"

He crossed his arms, his body still hinged with tension, wanting her, craving more of her. "I saw you dress in the hospital."

Her breathing was erratic, pounding with tension and anger. "You're lying. I had on underwear then. You couldn't have seen it there."

He swallowed, reaching for her, determined to sidetrack her.

But she held up her hands. "Tell me the truth. You've been watching me, haven't you, Quinton?"

He shrugged at her accusation. "It was part of the job. You asked for it when you broke into my house and threatened to expose me."

She paced to the window and stared out, then turned to him, cold fury evident in the tight set of her lips. A sensuous mouth he'd been kissing moments earlier.

One he craved the taste of again.

Judging from the contempt in her eyes, that would never happen.

"I didn't ask to be violated."

"You probed into my life," he said in a gruff voice. "You broke into my place and rifled through my things."

"Because you're a killer."

A long tense second passed, then he replied. "I thought we'd gotten past that."

He squared his shoulders, for once wanting someone to understand. "I'm a soldier, Annabelle. Soldiers do the dirty work that pretty girls like you don't want to know about."

She crossed her arms, then glanced around the room. "Where are they?"

"Where are what?"

"The cameras," she snapped.

"The cameras I installed to protect you in case someone came after you?"

But she didn't buy it. "The cameras you used to watch me like some damn voyeur."

"I do like to watch," he admitted, her spunky temper spiking his hunger. "And you were a treat, darlin'."

"Either remove the cameras," she snarled, "or change rooms with me now."

A sardonic smile curved his lips. "Then we'll change rooms. I don't mind you watching me get naked." He leaned closer, taunting her again. "And if I decide to take sex into my own hands tonight, know that I'll be picturing you in my mind when I come. I'll fantasize that my cock is inside you and that you're coming at the same time."

She swallowed hard, anger glittering in her eyes, then grabbed her things and stalked to the other room.

He stared at the closed door, trying to probe her mind, but all he read was her disdain for him. The regret that she'd dropped her defenses, that she'd let him kiss her.

That she'd die before she'd let him touch her again.

He fisted his hands, hating this war inside his head. Why the fuck should it matter to him if she hated him?

But for some reason it did. It bothered the hell out of him.

Annabelle retreated to the other bedroom, her body riddled with fury and tension. Tension that she wanted Quinton to relieve.

Good God, she was such a fool. He was playing games with her. Toying with her. Making her crazy with lusty thoughts.

Making her forget that she was here for a story. To get the scoop on what made him tick. And to stop this killer.

Human or supernatural? That mystery intrigued her.

But she'd never bargained on wanting the damn man so much. Or actually having compassion and admiration for him.

You can't fall for him. He'll only hurt you.

Besides, she was a by-the-book reporter. She printed the truth. Needed concrete proof. Everything in black and white.

And Quinton was as gray as it got.

For heaven's sake, he might be involved with demons. An entire world that she wasn't certain she even believed in. And certainly not one she wanted to become involved with.

No, it was too dangerous.

And so was Quinton.

She had to keep her distance. Had to protect herself, not only her life but her heart.

Her own father had deserted her. There was no way Quinton Valtrez would ever stay around for the long haul.

And Annabelle wanted it all.

Exhausted, she crawled into bed, but her gaze strayed

to the computer monitor. Quinton had sprawled on top of the covers, totally naked.

Her breath stuttered in her chest at the glorious sight of his masculine body. He was big...everywhere. Big chest, muscular arms and thighs, and his sex...

It was engorged and standing at full attention. He propped on one elbow and stared at the camera with a devilish smile, lowered his free hand to his cock, and began to stroke it.

She ordered herself to roll over and put a pillow over her head, to tear her gaze away, but she was mesmerized by the sight.

His hand closed around his member, stroking from the base to the top of his shaft, where moisture glistened on the tip. Automatically, her tongue shot out as if to lick it off.

Up and down he stroked, his long legs stretched out as if to purposely give her a full frontal view. His eyes became more hooded, dark orbs of hunger glowing in the dimly lit room as he worked his fingers up and down. She moaned in frustration as she remembered his words.

I'll be picturing you in my mind when I come. I'll fantasize that my cock is inside you and that you're coming at the same time.

Damn the smug son of a bitch.

She slid her hand beneath the covers and found her own sex slick and swollen with need. He couldn't do this without her. It wasn't fair.

No, she wouldn't suffer because of him.

She parted her legs, then slowly began to stroke herself, her gaze locked with his as he brought himself to the brink.

"Are you with me, baby?" he growled into the camera.

"Yes," she whispered.

She imagined his cock filling her, stretching her, hammering into her, and lifted her hips at the same time he did. As his release came, so did hers, swift and fierce.

From the other side of the wall, she heard him moan, and she twisted the sheets between her fingers, desperately wishing he was inside her.

She came with a vengeance, then rolled to her side and hugged her pillow to her chest, feeling empty and still wanting him.

The vultures soared and dipped in the early morning sky, picking pieces of carrion off their talons and feathers, rejoicing in the feast they'd had earlier that night. The new leader was feeding them well. Rooting out crops of the dead for their fodder. Charging ahead to make certain their endangered species didn't dwindle to nothing from starvation.

The Death Angel screeched out the call, and they chattered among themselves, spreading the news that more deaths were imminent.

It would mean traveling again. Off to a new city.

But the rewards would be worth it. More bodies, bones, carnage . . .

A feast and another celebration.

They congregated to form a flight pattern, paying homage to the great Zion, who had opened the portals for the demons to enter the mortal world and attack.

Zion would ensure they never died out. And one day they would rid the world of the humans.

Chapter Sixteen

Quinton had learned long ago to do without sleep. When he lived with the monks he used to lie on the cot, alone in the darkness and fighting his fears of the monsters and demons. Determined to banish the memory of the encounters he'd had.

Once the demon Mephguour had taken him. He hadn't slept for the entire six days he'd been held captive. Although he had reddish skin, Mephguour had appeared in human form. Dressed in one of the monk's earth garbs, he had led Quinton into a trap. Mephguour had been summoned by a dark sorcerer to lure Quinton to the army of the undead warriors.

But Quinton had meditated as the monks had taught him, had called upon his chi, and for the first time had unleashed his power and vanquished the demon.

He cursed as he paced the room.

Now he was more afraid of his growing feelings for Annabelle Armstrong than he was of the demons.

Death would come. It was the natural order. As long as he had no one to care about, no one attached to him or whom he was attached to, the end didn't matter.

Dammit. If she was a casualty for the cause, he'd deal with it. He always had before.

He'd been an island unto himself, and he liked it that way.

Now . . . now he had a brother he'd met but didn't know and another he didn't even remember. Yet curiosity and something deeper, maybe the blood connection, made him want to give Vincent a chance.

But how could he and Vincent ever have a normal relationship when they were demonborn?

When he'd never be able to trust Vincent completely because their father and the dark side might win him over at any minute?

Although Vincent was his brother and he couldn't screw him over—he had to help him.

Next door, footsteps sounded and the bathroom door squeaked open. He stiffened. Annabelle was awake. He'd heard her tossing and turning during the past few hours and knew she hadn't rested well.

Not even after their sexual interlude.

A smile broadened his face. Hell, he would have liked it far better if he'd actually been inside her, fucking her senseless, until he obliterated thoughts of any other man's touch from her mind.

He'd barely resisted storming into the room and giving her what she'd fantasized about—his cock inside her, hammering away, filling her with himself until she'd ache for him again.

He'd ordered a big pot of coffee to the room, so he poured her a cup, then knocked and entered without waiting on a response. If she thought she would thwart him now, after last night, she was wrong.

He would have her.

It was only a matter of time.

She shoved a mass of tangled hair from her face, and

yanked at her gown, which had fallen off one shoulder, giving him a glimpse of her cleavage.

"I didn't say you could come in," she said irritably.

He chuckled. "I know, but I brought coffee." He crossed the room to her and waved the cup beneath her nose.

She grabbed it greedily. "I feel like I got run over by a Mack truck," she said as she took a sip.

"You look sexy as hell."

She glared at him. "Don't start."

He threw his head back and laughed, really laughed. God, when had he last done that?

Ever?

No.

His life had been full of pain, torture, death, and preparing for the battle he now faced.

"Did you enjoy yourself last night?" he asked anyway.

She bit her lip. "You are cruel."

"No, it's cruel that you denied us being together." He leaned forward and brushed his lips against her cheek. "You know I'm going to have you," he said simply.

She gave him a sardonic smile with an eyebrow lift thrown in. "Maybe I'll have you."

He stretched his arms wide, offering himself up. "Do as you will."

She rolled her eyes but broke down and laughed. "You are incorrigible, egotistical, and—"

"Sexy as hell?"

She shook her head. "The devil in disguise."

He sobered slightly at that barb. His father was a spawn of Satan. He couldn't deny that.

As if he'd already gotten too close and she realized

she'd let down her guard, her expression tightened. "Have you heard anything from the police or FBI?"

"No."

"I was thinking," she said, and he smiled as her eyes brightened.

Did she have to be so damn smart?

"That we should check online communities for support groups for PTS sufferers. With cyber crime, it would be an easy source for a predator to find victims."

"Good point." Were demons computer-savvy?

Maybe in human form.

He snapped his fingers. "Let's get to work."

"I need a quick shower," she said and headed to the bathroom.

He arched a brow. "Need some help?"

She slammed the door in his face with a resounding no. He laughed again, but his mouth watered. He knew what lay beneath that satin gown.

And the sound of her moans was imprinted in his brain.

Before they parted ways, he would feel her writhing in his hands and calling his name while they both fed their hungers.

Annabelle quickly showered, trying to banish fantasies of Quinton from her mind. She had a job to do, and they both needed to focus.

She flipped on the TV set, but the news of the devastation the night before filled the screen.

Would there be another attack? And where would it be this time?

She checked her phone but had no messages. Damn.

She wanted the killer to contact her again, to give her a clue as to how to find him.

But he was obviously enjoying taunting her, making her wait and wonder...

She hurriedly dressed in jeans and a T-shirt and pulled her hair back into a ponytail, certain the look would deter any more sexual innuendos from Quinton.

Quinton had ordered food for them, and she realized she was starving. Her head felt clearer now, and although she was still slightly stiff, coffee and a sandwich worked wonders.

"There are several online support groups for PTS sufferers," Quinton said. "Trouble will be finding the identities of the posters. Most use screen names for anonymity." He sipped his coffee, then unpocketed his phone. "I'll call Homeland and see if they can put a tech on it."

Annabelle nodded, then began to skim the posts herself. He was right.

Several referred to a Dr. G. who had visited local hospitals to lead groups. Was that Dr. Gryphon?

He still hadn't returned her call, so she tried the number again, but once more received his voice mail. This time she left a message claiming that her father was a PTS sufferer and that she was seeking help for him.

Quinton was watching her when she hung up. "Is it true?" Quinton asked. "You father is suffering from PTS?"

She shook her head. "No, but something happened to him when my mother died. As I told you, the day of the funeral, he just walked away and never came home."

He nodded but didn't comment, then stepped into the other room to make his phone call. She made a quick call to the social worker she'd met in Savannah and learned that both Reverend Narius and Dr. Gryphon had met with some of their residents.

She googled the reverend's name and browsed through his Web site until she located his schedule.

He had been traveling across the country, preaching in different cities, appearing on local television spots and at churches and revivals. He was supposed to be in New Orleans next.

Was it possible that he wasn't saving souls but ending lives instead?

So far, he was their only connection to the two bombers. And there had to be a connection.

Her cell phone vibrated from the desk, and she checked the number. Dr. Gryphon.

She quickly connected the call.

"Miss Armstrong," he said, "I received your message. What can I do for you?"

"I'm interested in your work with PTS sufferers. My father is suffering from the disorder." She explained about her mother's death, then fabricated that her father had been questioned in her death. "The police believe that he snapped. That something that day triggered a flashback, and that he thought she was the enemy."

"And you don't believe that's possible?" Dr. Gryphon asked.

Annabelle hesitated. "I don't know. He had . . . episodes. Flashbacks. He'd become disoriented and behaved strangely, but he'd never been violent before. And he loved my mother."

"Mental disease or trauma can change a person," he said. "Sometimes the mind just shuts down, and the person isn't even aware of their actions. During a flashback, the person becomes immersed in the moment, actually living out the scenario again. What do you think triggered the flashback this time?"

"I don't know," Annabelle said. "I wish I did."

"So how can I help you?"

"Tell me about your treatment program. Maybe I can convince him to join."

"Treatment is on an individual basis, although we do have support groups. Meeting with others who understand can be very encouraging."

"How about hypnosis? Drug therapy?"

"Yes, sometimes. Again, it depends on the patient. I'd have to meet with your father individually to assess his condition, then formulate a plan of treatment."

"Let me ask you another question," Annabelle said. "Do you think it's possible for an individual to exert mind control over another person?"

Dr. Gryphon sighed. "You're talking about brainwashing techniques?"

"Yes."

"The military has used them. Of course they don't talk about it. Why? Do you think your father was a victim of a brainwashing technique or torture?"

Annabelle hesitated over confiding her theory. But she wanted his reaction. "I'm investigating the recent bombings, Doctor. So far, the two suicide bombers were both homeless men. The first suffered from PTS, the second, I'm still waiting to find out. But I'm trying to make a connection, possibly explain their motives."

"Maybe someone paid them or offered to pay their families," Dr. Gryphon suggested.

"It's possible, I suppose."

Quinton appeared and passed her a slip of paper with a message on it: "Both Warren Ames and the latest suicide bomber, B. J. Rutherford, participated in online support chats where Dr. Gryphon posted."

Her stomach knotted. "By the way, Dr. Gryphon, I just learned that both bombers participated in online chats with you."

A tense second passed. "Just what are you implying, Miss Armstrong?"

"I'm just making an observation. Do you remember conversing with them?"

"I believe this conversation is over." The phone went dead in her ear.

"What did he say?" Quinton asked.

"He hung up on me." Her phone vibrated again, and she checked it. Another text message.

She swallowed hard as she read it:

Midnight tomorrow. Another city. Watch them die.

The stench of decomposing flesh and blood in the morgue swirled like an aphrodisiac around Dr. Sam Wynn. He inhaled, using his gloved hand to pick a piece of metal from a man's mangled eyeball.

This was the man who'd bombed the Charleston coliseum.

He'd already matched DNA, skin and tissue samples, and pieced a few tiny parts of the man back together. Not enough for a coffin but just enough to make an ID. He'd also recovered a piece of bomb material from the man's finger, and the lab had discovered a swatch of his coat with powder burns from the bomb on the fabric.

He could now confirm the authorities' suspicions, that the man they'd seen in the security cameras was this man, B. J. Rutherford.

He picked up the phone to report the match. Then he had more bodies to identify. More bones and flesh and blood. More erotic smells and mangled faces.

More wide eyes staring at him in death.

With a smile, he plucked a piece of splintered bone from the man's ribs to add to his wall of bones.

THE UNDERWORLD

Zion itched to go aboveground to earth, enter the mortal realm himself, and seek out his sons. As much as he enjoyed the power of doling out orders and having his minions do the dirty work for him, the urge to wreak his own brand of havoc and justice gripped him.

Profoundly blissful memories of torturing Vincent, of taking a woman savagely into his bed, resurfaced, taunting him that with his rising, he was no longer chained in hell.

That he could travel in both worlds now and visit the earth in human form.

He had not yet done so because ruling his kingdom had occupied his full attention. The swearing in of the demons, the hundreds of new souls the Collectors had brought to him that had to be assigned to their places in the underworld, their duties and punishments metered out.

But one day soon he would travel through the portal

to claim what belonged to him and reap the sweet taste of mortal flesh.

For a brief second, his earthly wife's image flashed in his head, the memory of her lithe body beneath his making him hard and achy. And reminding him of what he'd once had before the darkness consumed him.

But he could have no regrets.

He was born to be a leader, and he had taken his rightful place just as his father had ordained.

Firelight slashed yellow and orange lines across the black rock. He strode to the Seer's side and looked into the burning embers, wishing he could see through her eyes. White glassy eyes that saw things no human could.

Eyes with the foresight of the vulture.

"Tell me what you see," he commanded.

Her red cape billowed around her as she waved a hand across the top of the flames, allowing him a glimpse into her visions.

"The Death Angel claimed another victory in the town the mortals call Charleston. The Soul Collectors are celebrating, although there are many souls still lingering," the Seer said. "Their spirits float above the town in limbo, while others guard the humans and battle the Soul Collectors."

Zion roared his disgust. More angels. Hell! Evil had to win and outnumber them.

"And my sons? I want to see them."

She blinked, her white eyes wide as she nodded. With another wave of her nimble black hand and a chant from ancient times, the image of his oldest son, Vincent, glowed in the flames.

He had tried to turn Vincent so many times, but he had the strength of . . . Satan. And that damn woman he'd mated with fucked him daily and kept his darkness in check.

Now Vincent was at a place where they stored blood vials. Some of the vials had been stolen. The vials containing his son's blood were among them.

Zion grinned. One of his minions had taken the blood to serve him. The minion would follow Zion's commands and use the blood to create more demons and spread evil.

She waved her fingers again, and an image of the twins his wife had given away and hidden from him appeared, an image from long ago but one that incited his wrath. Two infants, almost identical. Both with powers that needed developing.

Then he saw one of them, Quinton, as an adult, with a blonde-haired angel of a woman.

His sons were all meant to follow him one day, as all the Valtrez men had been destined to be leaders of the dark forces.

He should never have been deprived of them. And this woman, Annabelle Armstrong, was destroying Quinton's urge to follow his destiny.

Rage shot through Zion, rallying his temper, and he roared his fury across the black cave, making the walls tremble and sending tremors through the ground to rock the earth.

His sons' bodies, like his own, carried an insatiable hunger for a woman's flesh that needed to be fed daily.

"She is his soul mate," the Seer said. "But he has not had her yet."

Zion cursed, disappointed and relieved at the same time. If Quinton wanted the woman, why hadn't he had her? Because his dark side was weakening in her presence?

Yet knowing he hadn't tasted her flesh gave them time to turn him.

"She must be eliminated," Zion roared. He stalked to his throne and summoned the Death Angel. "She's searching for her father. Use him to destroy the bond between her and my son."

The Death Angel nodded, flapped his wings, and soared toward the portal to earth to do as Zion commanded.

Chapter Seventeen

Quinton read the text and cursed. "Fuck. I'm sick of being led around like a puppet on a string."

Annabelle's face paled. "Where do you think they'll strike next?"

"I don't know. But I'll phone Homeland and alert them to the fact that you received another message."

She clenched the phone with trembling fingers. "Do you think it's a coincidence that I received another warning after speaking to Dr. Gryphon?"

"It is suspicious. I'll have one of our agents check him out."

Annabelle paced to the window and stared out. Quinton started to phone the agency but decided to call Vincent first. He hesitated, remembering Father Robard's comment—he didn't believe that Vincent had turned yet.

Would Quinton be able to tell if he had?

He shoved a hand through his hair, debating. What choice did he have? He certainly hadn't stopped this demon on his own.

Vincent answered on the third ring. "Special Agent Valtrez."

"It's Quinton. I'm in Charleston."

"I saw the news," Vincent said. "You almost caught him."

"Almost was too fucking late." He wiped a drop of sweat from his brow. "And it's not over. Annabelle just received another text. Midnight tomorrow he strikes again."

"Any idea where?"

"No, not yet. I was hoping that Clarissa might have some insight."

Vincent sighed. "I'm afraid her gift doesn't work that way. She doesn't see the future, only the spirits in distress. And she's having a hard time now."

"Dig up everything you can find on a psychiatrist named Gryphon."

"Sure. Just give me some time."

Annabelle tapped on his arm and gestured toward the TV.

"Reports are coming in that vultures are now flooding New Orleans. In light of the sightings in Charleston and Savannah and the recent bombings, citizens are nervous."

"Shit. Vincent," Quinton muttered, "the vultures have moved to New Orleans. I'm on my way there now."

"Keep in touch," Vincent said, then hung up.

Annabelle hastily packed while Quinton phoned Homeland Security to alert them of the threat, throwing together his own duffel bag as they talked. When he hung up, Annabelle slung her computer bag over her shoulder.

"Reverend Narius is going to be in New Orleans tomorrow, but he's still here tonight," she said.

He grabbed his computer bag as well and gestured toward the door. "Then let's pay him a visit before we head to New Orleans."

*   *   *

When they arrived at the cemetery, mourners had lit candles to hold a vigil as Reverend Narius finished his sermon.

Quinton brushed his hand over a tombstone, had a vision of someone putting flowers on the grave, and jerked his hand free.

Nothing helpful there.

Annabelle sniffed beside him, and Quinton steeled himself to the stark look of grief on her face.

The damn woman felt too much. Probed too much. Was getting into his head and making him wish he hadn't lost his soul a long time ago.

"We've come together today to say good-bye to these young people whose lives were lost so tragically to violence and evil," Reverend Narius said. "At these times, we ask ourselves why.

"But we need to ask ourselves if we're right with God, if there are sins we need to atone for. If we're ready to turn our souls over and follow the righteous path so that we may reunite with our loved ones on the other side."

Quinton searched the faces of the attendees, noting the way Narius's followers hung on his every calculated word. Narius struck when the people were grief-stricken, preying on them, sinking his claws into their minds when they were the most vulnerable emotionally.

A perfect plan.

The fall wind swirled dead leaves across the parched grass, the scent of despair and fear heavy as mourners clung to one another and began to file out. Some lingered to speak to the reverend, to drop flowers on the graves interspersed across the cemetery, and to console one another.

Quinton imagined the spirits lingering in shock, wondered if demons haunted the graveyard now.

Finally, the crowd dwindled as night stole the last vestiges of light, and he and Annabelle approached Narius.

Quinton held back, knowing the reverend would probably welcome the publicity Annabelle could give him, and probing his mind to determine if he might be a demon in disguise.

Annabelle pasted on a smooth, charming smile. One Quinton had seen on TV but not one she'd graced him with.

"Reverend, my name is Annabelle Armstrong, CNN News."

His too-polished face lit up with a grin. "Yes, I recognize you from TV. It's a pleasure to meet you."

Quinton identified himself, and the reverend gave him a wary look.

"Such a tragedy," Reverend Narius said. "The Lord works in mysterious ways." He straightened his tie. "Did you want a photo, Miss Armstrong? Or did you take some of the service?"

"I'm not after a photo."

"You spoke to the homeless shelters in both Savannah and Charleston," Quinton cut in. "What do you know about the bombers, Warren Ames and B. J. Rutherford?"

The age lines around the reverend's mouth stretched with his frown, making him look older than he appeared on TV. "I see and speak to hundreds when I visit each town," he said. "Nothing about either one rings a bell."

Annabelle removed two photos from her purse. "This is Mr. Ames. And here's a picture of B. J. Rutherford. They were both veterans."

"Many of the men I meet are," Reverend Narius said. "And many are suffering from illness—mental, physical, spiritual. I do what I can."

Quinton studied Narius. "We think these men might have been hypnotized or brainwashed as part of a larger plan."

Narius pursed his lips. "Brainwashing? That sounds preposterous."

"It could be possible with drugs," Annabelle said.

Reverend Narius narrowed his eyes. "Or maybe there's another reason. Perhaps the devil got to them."

"You know the devil personally?" Quinton asked.

Reverend Narius clutched his Bible. "I recognize him at work."

Quinton grunted. "We all know cults have brainwashed people before," Quinton said. "There are documented cases of suicide pacts that prove it."

Reverend Narius jerked his gaze toward Quinton. "That may be true. And if that is the case with the bombings, I'll pray for the lost souls." The wind ruffled his lacquered hair, and he patted the strands back in place, then started walking, his movements stilted. "I need to go now. I have a flight to catch."

"Where are you off to now?" Annabelle called.

He gave her an odd look. "To New Orleans. I heard that the vultures have descended on the town. I want to be there in case there's trouble."

Quinton twisted his mouth sideways. "You're expecting there to be?"

"We all know the meaning of those vultures," Narius said.

And then he was gone.

"What do you think about the reverend?" Annabelle asked as they settled back into the SUV.

Quinton grunted. "The jury is still out."

She nodded. "I'd hate to accuse an innocent person, especially a well-known preacher, of murder. But I don't trust him."

"Neither do I."

She gripped her bag, the silence ominous as he drove toward the airport. Her head began to throb again, and she reached inside her bag for painkillers, then popped two from the bottle and swallowed them dry.

"You want to rest tonight, then fly out in the morning?" he asked.

"No. Let's go. Time is running out."

He nodded, then punched in the number for the airlines to book them a flight.

Two hours later, they boarded the last flight of the night. Quinton gripped the seat edge, his body wound tight. But there was nothing he could do at the moment but try to get some rest. He couldn't have sex with Annabelle.

Well, he could, but he didn't want a quickie in the bathroom stall. He wanted long and slow and languid. Hell, he wanted fast and furious and wild.

This dark, endless hunger was driving him insane.

Annabelle glanced up at him as if she'd read his mind, and his mouth thinned. He didn't like what she was doing to him.

Didn't like that he was worried the demon might be after her now.

"You should rest," she said softly.

"So should you." He picked up her hand and pressed

it against his cheek. The sound of his beard stubble raking across her tender skin sent his senses into overdrive, and he leaned his head sideways, pressed his lips into her palm, and kissed her hand.

Surprise flashed in her eyes at the tender gesture. Then a shuttered look crossed her face, and she turned away and pulled her hand to her lap.

Needing the physical contact, he clasped her hand back in his. Her gaze dropped to the bulge in his jeans and desire flickered in her eyes. But wariness quickly stomped it.

"You are wicked," she said. *But I want you anyway.*

Suddenly a vision filled his head. Annabelle tied up, a demon breathing down her neck.

He shuddered, tightening his grip. His heart pounded as he blinked her back into focus. He had to stop this demon before he hurt Annabelle.

"I'm dangerous to you," he said.

"I know." She closed her eyes, but she didn't pull her hand away, and he held it to his chest, savoring the contact.

That was one vision he wouldn't allow to come true.

Forcing himself to reserve his energy for the battle they faced, he finally fell asleep. But the darkness sucked at him, clawed at him with a choking grip, and no matter how much he fought, it won.

He was entombed in it.

Trapped in the underworld with monsters and demons, huge hulking dark shadows, twisted inhuman creatures, shape-shifters and vampires and serpents hissing at his feet, ready to strike.

Then his father appeared, a reincarnation of Satan.

"Kill for me and we'll rule the world," his father ordered. "Follow your destiny, succumb to the darkness, and you will walk by my side as a fearless commander."

The vulture screeched and flapped his black wings, a blazing fire lit the cave, and his father waved his hands and breathed fire from his fingertips.

Then he spotted Annabelle. His father had tied her to a post and strapped a bomb to her.

Quinton jerked awake, sweating and hating what he was—a demon. Hated that he couldn't have a normal life or a woman by his side.

Because being with him would get anyone he loved killed.

Apprehension rippled through the air as Quinton drove them toward downtown New Orleans. For a moment on the plane, Annabelle had felt a connection with him, as if he might actually care for her.

But when she'd awakened, he'd had a fierce look on his face and had shut down. Would she ever see the real man beneath that tough facade?

A vulture soared above them as if following them, and she switched her attention back to the job at hand. They were here to stop a bomber, not for her to become more involved with Quinton.

The French Quarter stretched ahead with its ancient culture, detailed ironwork, and impressive architecture. Colorful flags and banners announced the Swamp Festival and a smaller jazz festival, welcoming guests.

Vultures were perched everywhere—on light posts, awnings, the tops of buildings, window flowerboxes—and the aboveground cemeteries were swarming with the vile-looking creatures.

The screaming sounds that erupted from the black-winged predators as they swooped and soared above Bourbon Street terrorizing people made her break into a cold sweat.

Quinton pulled into a hotel parking lot in town, and they went inside. "Adjoining rooms," Quinton said matter-of-factly.

She ignored the clerk's curious look, then followed him to the elevator in silence. As soon as they entered the second-floor suite Quinton stalked inside and opened the door connecting the two rooms.

She folded her arms, watching him, remembering the cameras he'd installed in the hotel in Charleston. His gaze met hers, intense, sultry, suggestive—as if he remembered as well. It took every ounce of her courage not to blush.

Instead, she lifted her suitcase to put it on the foldout luggage rack, but he took it from her. Odd, a killer who possessed a sliver of chivalry.

"You look exhausted," he said. "Do you need to rest a while?"

"No."

He nodded, but instead of retreating to his room, he stepped closer, his gaze raking over her, his scent drawing her into his seductive web.

She arched a brow. "No cameras this time?"

A wicked grin lit his face. "I don't need them now. I have a permanent picture in my mind." He lifted a strand of her hair between his fingers. "One I won't forget."

Anger flared inside, but her body tingled with desire at his gruff tone. So he had liked what he'd seen.

She forced a breath through her lungs. "Nothing is going to happen between us, Quinton."

"If you say so," he said in a gruff voice, although he stroked her cheek with the pad of his thumb so tenderly that her heart squeezed, and she had to struggle not to succumb to his alluring power.

He glanced at the open bathroom door, his tone low and husky. "I'm sure you're still sore. You might need some help in there."

A nervous laugh bubbled in her throat. Yet her nipples budded with excitement at the thought of him touching her. "I'll manage," she said softly.

She backed toward the door, knowing she had to escape before she relented and kissed him again.

One more kiss and she wouldn't stop. She'd let him have her completely.

But giving him her heart would be foolish. She had to protect herself, or he would destroy her.

Chapter Eighteen

Quinton retreated to the other bedroom, his body rock-hard and aching. He might be half demon, but his human side had surfaced, and he let her go.

He'd have to bide his time. But he would have her, and she would love it. And he'd have her more than once.

But not now.

He stripped and jumped into the shower, letting the cold water calm his raging libido and revive him.

After scrubbing himself, he rinsed off, then stood naked in front of the mirror, wondering what Annabelle would say about the numerous scars on his body. Had she noticed them when she'd watched him through the camera?

Knife wounds crisscrossed his back, a deep scar from a gunshot wound marred his right thigh, and burn and whip marks reddened the flesh on his back and chest.

The angel amulet seemed ironic against his scars; the serpent-shaped birthmark on his upper shoulder mocked him, reminding him of the endless evil running through his blood. The profound emptiness that he'd lived with for so long. The cold reality that he wasn't completely human.

Maybe he should make love to her in the dark.

Make love?

He choked on the thought. He'd never made love to a woman. So why had he thought that now? Making love implied feelings, emotions. He didn't indulge in anything more than carnal pleasure.

Not even with Annabelle.

Body riddled with anxiety, he grabbed a shirt and tugged it on, then boxers and jeans, socks and boots, then unpacked his computer and set it up on the desk and removed the book *Deadly Demons*.

He flipped through the pages, studying the sketches of All Hallows' Eve along with the history of the holiday and read the description he'd written based on the monks' teachings:

All Hallows' Eve began as a pre-Christian Celtic festival of the dead. The Celtic calendar divided the year into four holidays. November 1 marked the beginning of winter and signaled the ending and beginning of an eternal cycle. At that time the festival was called Samhain (sah-ween) and was the biggest holiday of the year.

The Celtics believed that the souls of those who had died during the year traveled into the other-world on Samhain. Later, Christian missionaries tried to change the Celtics' religious practices.

Thinking the Celtics' version of religion pagan, the Christians branded the holiday as evil, associating it with the devil. Although people continued to celebrate All Hallows' Eve, they began to set out food to propitiate the evil spirits.

"Quinton?"

He was so lost in the legend that he hadn't heard Annabelle approach, didn't realize she was standing behind him looking over his shoulder. Not a good sign.

His instincts were off.

Letting that happen again could get them killed.

"What is that?" she asked, gesturing toward the book. Then her eyes flickered with the realization of what he'd been reading. "You think this killer is some kind of supernatural creature?"

He shifted. "Are you still looking for a story?"

"That and the truth," Annabelle said.

He flipped the book closed. "You don't want to know what I think."

"Yes, I do. You believe in the supernatural, in those demons in that book?"

"There are dark evil forces at work here, ones you couldn't even imagine."

Her gaze met his, and he knew he'd frightened her. Good. She should be scared.

Because this demon wanted to spread death. And if he was contacting Annabelle, then she was on his wish list.

"What about you?" he asked. "Do you believe in them?"

She hesitated. "I believe that years ago people spoke of demons, but that usually those people were mentally ill. Other demon legends were created to explain things they didn't have answers for, but that science does."

He gave a clipped nod. "So you don't believe in angels or God either?"

She folded her arms. "I have faith," she said. "And yes, I believe in God."

"Then you have to believe in demons." He shifted slightly. "The Death Angel is here now," Quinton said. "The vultures are his sign."

Alarm darkened her eyes. "You really are scaring me now."

"You can walk away if you want. I won't blame you." He stroked her arm. "In fact, it would be safer for you if you did."

She shook her head. "No way. I came for a story, and I'm not running away from it."

He lifted his hand and brushed a strand of hair from her cheek. "No matter where it takes you?"

She sucked in a sharp breath. "No matter where it takes me."

He dropped the strand of hair and gritted his teeth. "Then you have to stick by me. It's the only way I can protect you."

She raised her chin. "I can take care of myself."

His sardonic chuckle bounced off the walls. "Not against a demon." He grabbed his wallet and phone, strapped on his weapon, and pulled on his jacket.

Then he leaned over and whispered against her ear. "And I don't want to lose your pretty ass before I get to sink myself into it at least one time."

Annabelle wished to hell Quinton would stop toying with her. Taunting her one minute with his sexuality. With comments and tawdry looks that triggered wild and wicked fantasies in her head.

Then withdrawing the next, as if she were a snake that had bitten him.

What in the world was wrong with her?

This intense attraction was just an adrenaline rush caused from the danger they were involved in.

Determined to ignore the sexual chemistry between them, she remained silent as they drove to the police station. The downtown area seemed eerily deserted for New Orleans at lunchtime, a ghost of a city compared to the usual hubbub of tourists and locals venturing through the narrow streets and marketplaces.

A stiff fall wind made Annabelle's skirt swirl around her ankles as she climbed out and hoisted her bag, complete with notepad, recorder, and laptop, over one shoulder. More vultures soared above, and she headed toward the building at a brisk pace, Quinton following close behind. Begrudgingly, she found it comforting to know that he was close to her, watching her back.

Though she still hadn't figured out the reason. He was a hired killer. Had practically admitted it to her face.

Yet he hadn't killed her and had saved her life.

Because he wanted to get laid?

No, he had a code—he'd told her that, and she believed him.

Besides, he could have any woman he wanted. All he had to do was use his potent masculine charm.

He opened the door for her, and after they cleared security, a receptionist behind a screened glass greeted them.

Quinton flashed his ID and introduced them. "We'd like to speak to one of the detectives in charge."

The heavyset woman scowled but drawled, "All right," then punched a button and five minutes later, a tall, brown-haired man with a warm tan appeared and ushered them to a small interrogation room. "I'm Detective DeLang," he said. "Miss Armstrong. It's a pleasure to meet you. I've seen you on TV." He scowled as he turned to Quinton. "And you're the Homeland Security Agent who called?"

"Yes. Quinton Valtrez."

The detective stiffened and gestured for them to sit down. "What's going on?"

Quinton cleared his throat. "We have reason to believe that your city is the next target of the suicide bomber."

New Orleans, the city of the dead—and more death was on its way.

The devil had spoken to him and told him his plan.

The vultures had already converged, the hint of panic and smell of blood and mangled flesh hanging heavy in the moss-covered trees and backwaters of the marshy bayou.

Reverend Narius had arrived in the devil's city to gather more worshippers and lost souls.

So many lost here, just as in Charleston.

New Orleans posed a challenge. When the deadly storms had struck, he'd swooped in and gained numerous souls for his cause. The vile humans with crime on their evil minds, the once-chaste women and men now wanton with their sinful lusts and greedy acts. They had prayed and he had come to their rescue.

But there were so many more who needed him.

And there would be mass devastation again.

Such trying times. Such humbled, pathetic weak minds.

He could already smell the murky odor of sin and debauchery just as he had after the hurricane when bodies had floated through the streets in the vile floodwaters.

Oh, he understood the sinner's mind because he had sinned as well.

But thankfully, no one knew his secrets.

———

The detective called his men together, and Quinton explained that they'd come to help.

"We need to pinpoint possible target areas," Quinton said.

The detective nodded, then pulled up information regarding all the functions scheduled that day and evening on his laptop.

A sense of helplessness nagged at Annabelle. How could they prevent more deaths if they had no idea who was behind them? Especially if Homeland Security and the Feds were stumped?

"The Swamp Festival is this weekend," Detective DeLang said. "The bulk of the celebration is at the Audubon Zoo. There was a five-k run this morning to raise money for the zoo, along with a parade and an arts festival. And tonight the zoo and several bars in town are featuring blues and zydeco music."

"Sounds like there will be a lot of people on the streets," Annabelle said worriedly.

"It's surprising that more people aren't staying home because of the Savannah and Charleston crimes." He shook his head. "Holy mother of God, haven't the people of New Orleans suffered enough?"

"I know, it's true," Annabelle said. "That's why we're here."

He turned to Quinton. "Do you have any concrete

information to help us nail down where this bomber might attack?"

"I'm afraid not," Quinton said. "Now, what other major events are in town?"

"Tonight? No ball games, thank God. But Reverend Narius draws a big crowd and will be at the festival, and tonight he's speaking in town. There's also a big fund-raiser planned for the local charities. And a jazz festival at Woldenberg Park."

Quinton nodded. "Then we focus on those events. Beef up security all over town, and install cameras everywhere possible."

Quinton and the detective outlined a plan, and while the detective briefed his men, Quinton coordinated with the governor, Homeland Security, and the FBI.

But worry knotted his neck as the plan was put into motion.

What if he was wrong?

What if a different city was the target?

Quinton clenched his jaw. He couldn't second-guess himself. The vultures were a sign.

Tonight there would be another bombing—and more deaths if they didn't figure out the target before midnight.

"Do you think we're on the right track?" Annabelle asked.

Quinton gritted his teeth. "I hope so. We have to beat him this time."

He scanned the area as they rushed to the car. Was the killer watching them?

Of course he was. He was playing a cat-and-mouse

game, laughing at them as they moved from city to city chasing him.

"You think he's here, don't you?" Annabelle asked. "Do you feel it, Quinton? Is that part of your power?"

He ignored her question. "I'm not taking any chances, not until this demon is caught." His jaw twitched as if he'd just realized his admission. "I mean, the person behind the bombs. After all, only a monster would destroy so many lives."

"You do think it's a demon?" she said.

"We've been over this before." He cut her a sharp look. "But you can't print that."

Annabelle sighed wearily. "If I did, no one would believe me. I'm still having trouble believing in the possibility myself."

He gave her a cold, dark look, pinning her to the seat. "You can't see the wind, but you feel it."

She reluctantly nodded. He was right. "You could give me proof."

He snorted. "Try naming me as a source, and I'll tell everyone you're crazy."

"I have a picture of you moving that beam."

"I can always say you rigged the photo."

She glared at him, then crossed her arms, resigned. They'd finish this, then she'd decide what to do with whatever she learned.

"The VA hospital was demolished in Katrina, wasn't it?" Annabelle asked.

He steered the car onto a side street. "Yes. There's plans for a new one, but right now there's no facility."

"So there's no way to find out if a local veteran might be involved." She ran a hand through her hair. "Let's stop by the largest homeless shelters, question the social workers, and see if Reverend Narius has visited. Then let's talk to the good preacher. Maybe you can feel out the crowd at the Swamp Festival. See if you sense a demon there."

He didn't comment, confirming her thoughts.

And intensifying her fears. The authorities would eventually find the mastermind behind these bombings—if he was human.

But if a demon was involved, how would they identify him?

Only another demon could.

One more reason she needed to fear Quinton and keep her distance.

———

The screams of the dead and dying reverberated through the cavernous walls. Music to the Death Angel's ears.

They belonged to him now.

His to do with as he pleased. Their pitiful lives as mortals were extinguished as they turned themselves over to him. Their souls would be in limbo until they completed his mission.

One touch, and he had easily put their feeble minds to bed for eternity. Then their bodies had fried from the inside out.

He had offered them redemption and a chance to walk the earth one more time in exchange for immortality.

Tonight at midnight he would watch another kill in the name of his glory. And this time the Armstrong woman would lie in the rubble.

More bones to clean. More flesh to feed on.

The screech of his fellow vultures echoed to him, the anticipation of the feast to come stirring the air with the scents of death and blood—and soon, the end of humanity, as chaos and evil reigned.

Chapter Nineteen

The knowledge of the daunting task they faced today gnawed at Quinton as he drove to the Loving Arms shelter. He'd almost stopped the bomber in Charleston but failed.

He hated failure.

He parked in front of the concrete facility, a former office building that had been flooded during Katrina. Thanks to donations and government funding, the much-needed shelter now occupied the space.

As they climbed out, Quinton scanned the perimeter for a possible suspect. The area was on the outskirts of town, not in the best section of New Orleans, with other dilapidated and deserted buildings nearby.

A half dozen patrons loitered outside, huddling together to battle the heavy fall winds that threatened rain and brought the stench of the bayou and garbage swirling around them. Two women wearing worn housedresses glanced up at them suspiciously, while a white-haired man with a shaggy beard grinned, revealing a lack of teeth. Annabelle smiled and spoke to each of them, then rushed inside.

Quinton followed her silently, his senses honed, hunting for the smell he'd detected in Savannah, for the glassy eyes of a lost soul, the vacant mind of someone who'd been possessed by the demon.

Inside, a tall, exotically beautiful black woman with waist-length hair greeted them. "I'm Shayla Larue. How can I help you?"

Quinton introduced them both, then explained the reason for their visit.

Shayla's gold tooth glittered as she smiled. "Yes. I've been expecting you."

Quinton frowned. "You have?"

She gestured for them to follow her into her office, a cubicle off to the side of a large kitchen, where a plate of beignets sat the counter. "I have bad feeling. Especially when the vultures arrive," she said, her Cajun accent heavy.

"Have you noticed anything strange lately?" Quinton asked.

Annabelle cleared her throat. "Anyone who seems suicidal? Maybe someone who talked of death or heaven or hell?"

Shayla smiled. "It not unusual for our visitors to speak of death and the future. Many are depressed or have failing health. As we age, we look at life differently."

"How about veterans?" Quinton asked.

She pursed her mouth in thought. "Yesterday a man came through who seemed disoriented and lost. But again, that not normal."

Quinton folded his arms. "Has a doctor named Gryphon visited the center?"

Shayla nodded "He come by early this morning. He say he trying to help. He talk about his experiments with memory problems and PTS. He say he get results with subjects."

"He's been honored for his work in helping the homeless and indigent," Annabelle said.

"So nice, he was," Shayla said, "when so many others trying to take advantage of these people."

"Did he talk to anyone here?" Annabelle asked.

She frowned. "He do routine health checks. Then say he be back."

Quinton cleared his throat. "What about Reverend Narius? Has he visited?"

"No, not yet. But he supposed to stop by sometime." She paused, rubbing her hands up and down her arms. "I worry that he be too late."

Her words made the hair on the nape of Quinton's neck rise, and he studied her. Did she have some kind of power or second sense?

"My grandmother a voodoo priestess," she said, as if she'd read his thoughts.

An unnerving idea. "I have her gift of the visions," she said quietly.

"So what have you seen?" Quinton asked.

"Death. Satan. That you here to find the demon come to N'awlins. I try to put protective spell around the city."

He searched her face. "What do you mean, you know who I am?"

"Those in the magic community know of your father's power. That you and your brothers are Dark Lords."

He tried to telepath for her to be quiet, that Annabelle didn't know his story. But she gave him a sad look, and he read her silent message. She thought Annabelle deserved to know the truth, that she could handle it. That she could even help him.

"You believe in demons?" Annabelle asked.

"I am born of a family of voodoo priestess," she said, her odd-colored eyes flickering with shadows. "A demon-slayer as well."

"Then tell me how to recognize a demon," Quinton said.

"Utilize your sense of smell," Shayla murmured. "And your other senses. When you begin to use them more, your powers will grow. Although some demons are better at covering their odor than others."

For a brief moment, Quinton frowned. He already knew this but had hoped for more and glimpsed into Shayla Larue's mind. He saw her creating magic potions and spells, battling evil ones and walking through the cemetery with the dead.

"You must protect the woman," she said, a low, ominous hint to her voice as she gestured toward Annabelle. "She is in great danger. They will use her to get to you."

Annabelle bit down on her lip but refrained from commenting.

"The ancients say the Death Angel turn people into the Walking Dead," Shayla continued. "They die but they come back from grave. They gots a gray color and carry the smell of death on they skin. They be brought back by the devil to do harm."

A dark aura engulfed her, her eyes glowing in the dim lights of the shelter. "Who's doing this?" he asked.

Her dreads swung as she shook her head. "I can't say who the bomber is, but the Death Angel has possessed him. There are many demons among us now, walking in the shadows. I met two vampires just last week, and a shape-shifter with the power to change into human form at will. This demon is for you to find. The vultures mean death, and they here to stay."

Annabelle shivered as she fought the wind on her way back to the car, Shayla's warning echoing in her head.

She is in great danger. They will use her to get to you.

Quinton climbed into the driver's seat, his face a wall of granite, then steered the vehicle onto the highway toward the Audubon Zoo, where the Swamp Festival was to be held. Annabelle folded her arms, the gray cast to the sky adding to her dismal mood. A thick fog blanketed the bayou, the gnarled and twisted branches of the giant live oaks sweeping the ground with their spidery gray moss, the crocodiles and snakes slithering through the muddy Mississippi, their beady eyes piercing the darkness like silent stalkers ready to pounce.

The vultures normally didn't like woods, but they hovered there now, ready to feed off the smaller animals seeking refuge inside.

The air felt oppressive, the stench of death and blood wafting from the depths of the backwoods, the local legends and folklore of the gators, of voodoo, and of satanic rituals rolling through her head.

Annabelle had seen the book *Deadly Demons*, had even witnessed Quinton use his power. But to have this woman confirm what she suspected and speak of the demons' being after her made her stomach cramp.

What other demons were walking the earth? Shayla had said there were shape-shifters and vampires...

She'd read about them in books, but were they real?

And what if they couldn't stop this demon? What if he continued to wreak death and destruction?

*   *   *

Vincent Valtrez plugged into the FBI databases to search other possibilities for the bomber while he waited for Agent Blackwell to join him at the local office near Blood-Core to discuss the stolen blood vials.

He searched for connections between the bombings, along with the homeless shelters, looking for anyone who might have donated to all the shelters. Insurance agents, charities, politicians...the list was endless. He also plugged in the names of social workers, medical personnel, neighboring hospitals, then police and investigators who might have worked more than one scene.

McLaughlin had been assigned to the Charleston case, while another agent, Davis, was sent to Savannah. Reverend Narius's name popped up, along with various charities and churches he was affiliated with.

Then Dr. Sam Wynn's name—the Bureau's resident specialist in forensics and identifying bones. He was working all the bombings.

Vincent scratched his forehead in thought. Was it possible?

Agent Blackwell rapped on the door then poked his head inside the room. "Valtrez?"

"Yeah. Any news?"

Blackwell shook his head. "No concrete terrorist cells. We're watching a couple of small cells, but we haven't found any conclusive evidence that connects them to the bombers."

Vincent gritted his teeth. He wished to hell they had, that he was wrong and it wasn't demonic. "What about the missing blood vials?"

"Other than the lab techs and doctor, the only finger-print we found in the research facility belongs to a dead man." Agent Blackwell massaged the back of his neck with one hand.

Vincent's mind spun with questions. "Who did the print belong to?"

"A man named Jerome Huntington. He was a sadistic man who drank blood from his victims."

"Jesus. Where is he now?"

"He was given a lethal injection on death row last year."

Holy shit. What if he had gained immortality as a demon or a vampire and had stolen the blood to feed his bloodlust? They needed to check the grave, see if his body was still there.

"There's something else," Blackwell said.

"What?"

"According to our information, Reverend Narius didn't exist until three years ago."

Vincent punched in Quinton's number to relay the news. Maybe they'd caught a break.

Narius just might be their demon.

Quinton contemplated the odd aura he'd detected around Shayla Larue as he drove toward the zoo. His cell phone rang and he saw it was Vincent so he answered.

"Listen, Quinton, I found something interesting. Rev-erend Narius didn't exist until three years ago."

"What?"

"I'm trying to find out more about him, but you should check him out."

"We're on our way to do that now." He hung up, and rubbed his hand over his mouth. The monks had taught him to trust in spirituality. Was Narius taking advantage of believers and faith seekers in order to steal souls for the dark side?

Traffic thickened as they neared the zoo, and a flock of vultures lingered overhead, black monsters barely visible through the heavy fog. Surprisingly, they hadn't frightened off the crowds of locals and tourists rushing to see the exhibits. The zoo housed more than thirteen hundred animals, everything from exotic white tigers to albino alligators.

The wind tossed dry leaves around their feet as they walked to the gate, bought tickets and a program, then strolled through the zoo, looking for anyone suspicious and heading toward the tent where Narius was scheduled to speak.

Children tackled the climbing wall and raced to ride the Endangered Species Carousel and the Swamp Train, while teens and adults alike lined up for the Safari Simulator. A special presentation with live alligators had drawn dozens of visitors. A voodoo priestess sat in the center of a stage not far away, surrounded by a display of various voodoo dolls and mojos, spinning tales of local legends and folklore.

Vendors peddled treats—alligator on a stick, beignets, and heaping bowls of gumbo and Jambalaya—while crafters and souvenir vendors sold replicas of the animals in the zoo, T-shirts, hats, voodoo dolls and kits, along with Mardi Gras masks, beads, and books on ghosts and other mysterious creatures rumored to inhabit the swamp, especially the infamous loup-garou.

Excitement from the festivities hummed through the crisp fall air, yet Quinton couldn't shake the feeling of impending death.

Tonight at midnight.

At least most of these women and kids would be home by then.

But where would the bomber attack? With the town's festivities, any number of places could be targeted.

Narius was supposed to speak at three at the zoo for the Swamp Festival. He planned to visit several hospitals, including a children's ward, and he was to attend a charity fund-raiser in the evening, to help raise money to rebuild homes for the needy, which was scheduled to last until midnight. The shelters weren't listed on his agenda, and with his packed schedule, Quinton didn't see how he'd fit them in.

He would follow him anyway, and if he was behind the bombings, he'd kill the SOB.

They grabbed po'boys and took a seat at a picnic table across from the stage while the reverend spoke to the crowd.

While he ate, Quinton thumbed through the program. "This is interesting. Dr. Wynn, the chief medical examiner from the Bureau, is here, too. It says that he grew up in New Orleans and contributed time and money to help the locals recoup after the hurricane."

Reverend Narius raised his hand, gesturing across the crowd. "Let's turn to John 8:7: 'He who is without sin among you, let him be the first to throw a stone at her.'"

"Amen!" several people shouted.

"Praise the Lord."

"Yes, we're all sinners," Reverend Narius said. "I, too,

have walked on the side of sin. I, too, have given in to temptation with impure thoughts and actions." His voice rose to a fever pitch. "But God sent Jesus to die on the cross so that we might receive forgiveness for our sins. I command you now to turn your life over to the Lord. Do so, and you will find redemption and walk into the land of immortality."

Quinton frowned, wondering what kind of immortality the reverend promised behind closed doors. Narius offered the benediction, then crossed the stage and descended the steps as applause rang out.

Quinton and Annabelle waited until he'd woven through the throng, shaking hands and accepting praise, then approached. Why couldn't people see his lack of sincerity?

Narius's smile faded. "Are you two following me?"

"As a matter of fact, we did come to talk to you," Annabelle said.

Quinton cleared his throat. "Yes, Reverend. Mind telling us why you didn't exist until three years ago?"

Anger flared in Narius's eyes, replacing his practiced smile, and he gestured for them to step aside behind the tent. "Where did you hear that?"

"I have sources," Quinton stated. "Very reliable sources."

The reverend leaned closer to them, his calm facade slipping. "Have you ever done something that you've regretted?" he asked in a low voice.

Hell, yeah. Getting involved with Annabelle.

But killing? No. The ones he'd eliminated deserved to suffer.

"Well, I did," he admitted quietly. "But three years

ago, I was saved, and when I was reborn, I saw a chance to make a new life and help others. To do so, I needed to kill the person I was before." His tone sounded grim. "That meant assuming a new name."

"Is that the only person you killed?" Quinton asked.

Narius's eyes narrowed in cold fury.

"What did you do that was so bad?" Annabelle asked.

"That's between me and my Savior," he said quietly. Then he turned and stalked away.

Chapter Twenty

Anger suffused Annabelle. Didn't the reverend know that his secret only spiked her curiosity? That she wouldn't stop until she discovered the truth?

Just as she hadn't backed down from Quinton in the beginning.

Then everything had changed...

But she wasn't backing down from this bomber.

"I'm surprised by the crowd at the festival," Quinton said. "With the press alerting everyone about the bomber's pattern, I expected more people to stay home."

"I guess they refuse to let terrorists frighten them into not living their lives. Besides," she added, "we haven't publicized the fact that New Orleans might be attacked tonight."

She watched a family of four strolling along, the father hoisting the toddler onto his shoulders, and her chest clenched as she recalled her own father doing the same.

"Maybe we should issue some kind of warning tonight."

"That would only create panic. And if we're wrong?"

"We weren't wrong about Charleston."

He sighed, looking weary.

She gestured toward Narius, who was still shaking hands. "Shall we stay with the reverend?"

"We have no other suspects," he said through gritted teeth.

And it was only a few hours until midnight.

Somber, they headed to the car, and they trailed his limo to the children's hospital while Annabelle checked the schedule of the day's events.

"The bars are all possibilities as targets, since they're hosting celebrations. Or perhaps the jazz festival."

"We'll stop by there and check it out," Quinton said.

Annabelle nodded. "My guess is that they'll hit the big reception for the fund-raiser. It looks as if the reverend will be there. In fact, he's being honored. And Dr. Wynn is attending, too." She frowned. "Along with the governor, Dr. Gryphon, several wealthy donors, volunteers, social workers for the state, and some of the FEMA staff."

"You're right, that may be the target," Quinton said. "And if Narius is involved, he might have set it up so he'll be present to watch. That's not uncommon for serial killers."

He phoned Detective DeLang, and Annabelle listened while he discussed the security measures they'd implemented in the city for the night.

Then he called the tech at Homeland Security. "Check that online support group for veterans again. See if you find anyone posting from New Orleans."

"I'll get on it, but it'll take time," the tech said.

Quinton gritted his teeth. "Work as fast as you can. It could mean life or death."

When Quinton disconnected the call, they'd reached Woldenberg Park, where the jazz festival was being held. Vendors were in full swing offering local Cajun foods and beer. Already people were spread out on blankets, and the park was packed as the musicians began to play.

Uniforms and plainclothes policemen were interspersed among the guests. Quinton struggled to read thoughts as they combed through the crowd.

The scent of garbage rolled off one man, and Quinton paused by a park bench, but the minute he tapped into the man's thoughts, he realized he was an undercover cop.

"This place is covered. Let's check out Bourbon Street and go into some of the clubs."

She nodded, and they returned to the car, the clock ticking.

"We'll need dress clothes for tonight," she said quietly.

A muscle ticked in his jaw. "Right."

Before they stopped to shop, they visited several landmarks, including the House of Blues, the riverfront shops, and the French Market.

Frustration nagged at Quinton as the time passed. At least in Charleston they'd had a name.

Here, they had nothing.

They stopped at a boutique in the shopping district where he purchased a suit, and she bought a little black dress and strappy sandals.

Quinton drew inward, resorting to his professional persona. Shayla's threat hung over him like a black cloud of doom.

He phoned the tech again. "Do you have an update?"

"Not yet."

"Can you check something else? Pull a list of all the people invited to this awards ceremony tonight, and see if anyone there is a veteran."

"Sure. I'll get back to you."

He thanked him and hung up, then parked at the hotel, and they climbed out. In spite of logic telling him to keep his distance, that he needed to be clearheaded and focused tonight in order to ferret out this demon, Annabelle's scent drove him crazy as they hurried to their rooms.

He needed to expel the tension in his body so he would be free to focus.

But the only way to do that was to have her. To touch her, taste her, work out his hunger for her.

"I'll go get dressed," Annabelle said. She gave him a weary look, then hurried to the shower.

As he heard the water start to run, thoughts of her naked body consumed him. He paced the room, trying to banish them, but when she emerged wearing that low-cut dress with the slit up her thigh, his cock hardened and desire shot through his balls.

What if a demon did show tonight? What if the demon hurt Annabelle, and he failed to protect her?

His blood turned hot, dark thoughts flowing through his mind, and he felt his evil side emerging.

On the heels of that darkness, panic tore at him. He wouldn't fail.

He *couldn't.*

"Quinton, aren't you going to change?" Annabelle asked.

His gaze met hers, and he recognized the same fears he was feeling. She was anxious, wired, dreading the next few hours.

Wondering if they'd survive.

His body smoldered with lust, and her eyes flickered with heat, her breath raspy as he walked toward her. When he was only an inch away, he inhaled her sweet body, the slight hint of perfume she'd dotted on her neck, and his mouth watered.

Wanting to soothe her nerves, he rubbed her arms with his hands, then leaned close to her ear and dragged in a breath. "I know how we could relieve some tension."

"How? Did you see a gym downstairs?" she said sweetly.

He chuckled. Dammit, they might die tonight. He wanted her first.

And it was just sex.

He had his own agenda, and it didn't involve having a personal long-term relationship with her.

All physical. No commitment.

She turned her back to him as if to dismiss him, but he brushed her hair back from her neck. Then he pressed his lips to her tender skin. "I want you, Annabelle, and I know you want me, too. I can feel it in the heat radiating off you."

"We can't do this," she whispered.

"Why not?"

"Because we have to concentrate."

"You're distracting me from work. I can concentrate better when my mind isn't full of wanting you." He nipped at her earlobe, then placed his hands on her shoulders and kneaded the tightness from her muscles. She moaned as his fingers worked magic.

"Why are you doing this?" she asked hoarsely.

"You know why, Annabelle. You feel the heat blazing between us just as I do." He raked his fingers lower to her waist, then gripped her and slid his thigh between her legs, stroking her as he pulled her ass against his rock-hard body.

"God, Quinton," she said in a pained voice, tinged with longing.

He flipped her around and cupped her face between his big hands. His heart raced, his body aching.

But fear seized him.

Not only fear of losing her to this demon.

But fear that if he did take her, he wouldn't be able to walk away when it was over.

The thought made him take a step back and release her.

Annabelle swayed, dizzy with desire.

But suddenly he pulled away. "You're right. I should get ready."

A tormented look crossed his face, then he turned and went into the shower.

She stood in stunned surprise, her body quivering with want, need, and unsated desire.

She wanted Quinton. Had teetered on the edge of letting him have his way with her. Because her hunger for him was so strong she could no longer deny it.

But having sex with him would only sate part of her.

She wanted more. Something he couldn't give her.

Love.

And that was the reason she couldn't go to him.

Besides, he had supernatural powers...

She paced across the room, listening to the shower water run. To the sound of the wind outside.

Her nerves on edge, she moved the curtain aside and looked out into the night, searching. Streetlights dotted the distant horizon; the sounds of Bourbon Street, traffic, jazz music, and partygoers filled the air. Moonlight bathed the street; stars glittered in the clear sky. It was a beautiful night.

Too beautiful to die.

But reality clawed at her. A monster—human or demon?—was preying on unsuspecting innocents, ready to kill more people. And she might be on his hit list.

What if she died and never slept with Quinton?

They'd been working for days to stop this killer, barely sleeping or eating or living themselves.

What if she never felt his lips teasing her, kissing her, his fingers stroking her secret places. Secret places that begged for his hands and mouth.

What if she never felt the power of his big body above her, filling her, holding her, making love to her?

She closed her eyes, willing her rational side to return, to hold her libido in check, but instead, images of him lying naked on the bed pleasuring himself drifted to her, tormenting her. What if he was taking his own pleasure now in the shower?

No...it wasn't fair. He couldn't get her all stirred up and achy, then leave her like this.

Her body thrumming with tension, she opened the bathroom door. He had just stepped from the shower, and he stood naked and dripping wet, his corded muscles slick, his sex jutting forward, thick and heavy and pulsing with need.

"I thought..."

A slow smile curved his mouth. "That I took care of things?" He chuckled and gestured to his rigid cock. "No. I was hoping a cold shower would work. But nothing seems to work around you."

"Good." Courage suddenly bolstered her, then she

lifted her hands, unfastened the cocktail dress, and let it slide to the floor so she stood wearing only a pair of black lace thong panties.

The stark need in Quinton's sigh flamed her hunger.

"You know I'm bad for you," he said in a gruff voice. "That I'm not a good guy."

Defiance made her lift her chin. "I don't care. We might die tonight."

"And?"

"And I want to be with you," she whispered. "I want you to make me feel alive."

Chapter Twenty-one

Her gaze met his, and something hot and intense passed between them, a draw that she couldn't deny any more than she could deny that she needed air to breathe.

"I wanted to join you in the shower earlier," he said in a gruff voice. "I can't get you out of my head. The picture of you naked..."

"I can't erase the picture of you from my mind either," she whispered.

He lifted an eyebrow. "So you did watch?"

A flush crept up her neck at the excited look in his eyes.

Spurned by that thought, she lowered her gaze, perusing his body.

Instant heat pulsed through her. He was the most gorgeous, virile man she'd ever met. A bad boy in every sense of the word.

His gaze fell to her breasts, and her breath heaved in and out. "Touch yourself," he said in a low, gruff voice that made her heat grow wet with need.

She couldn't resist his command. She had to obey.

Her heart pounded as she lifted her hands and cupped her breasts. At the first touch, his breath hissed out. "More."

A tiny thrill raced through her, and she licked her finger, then circled her areole with it, stroking her nipple between her damp fingers. Her nipple budded to a stiff peak, and she imagined him closing his mouth over it, tugging the tip. Warm erotic sensations splintered through her, and she slid her other hand downward over her body, then between her thighs, teasing her clit. Desire surged through her.

"Enough." Hissing between his teeth, he suddenly shoved her hands away and cupped her breasts in his big hands, kneading them as he blatantly stared at her stiffening nipples.

"God, you're magnificent," he murmured.

Her chest rose and fell beneath his hands, her body craving more, aching for him as she never had for a man, her mind racing with unfulfilled fantasies. Erotic fantasies that she'd never considered before. Fantasies of him taking her against the wall, outside on the park bench. Of him tying her to his bed and making love to her until she thought she'd die from the torture.

He plunged his hands into her hair and drew her to him, nipping at her lips until she opened for him, and he thrust his tongue inside, ravaging her mouth.

She slid her hands up his chest as if to push him away, but pulled him closer, clinging to his arms as he deepened the kiss. His mouth was sensuous, his throaty sounds prodding her to kiss him again and again, to whisper his name and cling to his muscled shoulders.

To beg him to make love to her.

He trailed tongue lashes along her throat and neck, then along the curve of her breasts, and she pressed her knee between his thighs and stroked him. His cock surged to life, hard and pushing against her abdomen. She wanted him between her thighs, filling her, making her feel whole, reminding her that she was alive and worth loving.

Even if it was just for the moment.

He moaned her name, a throaty sound that was so erotic it almost sent her over the edge, then he sucked one nipple into his mouth and she threw her head back in wild abandon.

He gripped her hips, then led her to the bed where he gently pushed her down, lowering himself over her as he greedily suckled one breast then the other. She threaded her fingers into his hair, panting as he trailed kisses down her abdomen, then shoved her legs apart and tasted her wetness.

Another groan from him made her buck and try to push him away, but instead, he flicked his tongue against her clit, taunting her. A million delicious sensations spiraled through her, then he closed his lips around her clit, gently sucking the sweet nub, and she cried out as her orgasm rocked through her.

Quinton had never tasted anything so sweet and hypnotic as Annabelle. Her honeyed release filled his mouth with a craving for more, and fucking her once wouldn't sate him.

He'd never be sated without her.

The realization nearly splintered his sanity. If he took her now, he might never let her go.

He was a loner. He had to be in order to keep her safe.

Still, his body surged with need, and he was beyond stopping himself.

Annabelle jammed her hands in his hair as he rose above her and looked into her eyes. He'd wanted her for months, had denied that desire and hunger to protect her and himself—but she was right.

They might die tonight. He might not win against this demon.

And his dark hunger had to be sated.

She pulled his head down and fused her mouth with his, thrusting her tongue into his mouth and arching her hips to cradle his thick, throbbing erection between her thighs. He moaned, then stroked his cock against her wet damp flesh.

He kneed her legs wider apart, trailed kisses down her neck to her nipple, then bit the tip hungrily and thrust his length into her, ramming deep inside her.

She whimpered his name, then undulated her hips in silent invitation, and he buried himself deeper, then pulled out, teasing her clit. She cried out and begged him to fill her again, and he complied.

His breathing panted out as he thrust in and out, building a rhythm and sinking himself deeper each time, until her body began to spasm around him, milking his length.

Dark thoughts tried to destroy this pleasure. The devil called his name, whispering that he'd put one foot in the door when he'd joined the Ghost team. Taunting that he could take her again and again, irregardless of whether she wanted him.

But having learned to school his emotions, he banished the evil voice.

Still, a sharp noise cut through the bliss as he pounded himself home and relief came.

Reality intruded as he realized the noise was the

phone. The sharp ring jarred him from bliss to the danger they faced.

Annabelle sighed and curled into him as he rolled over and reached for the phone.

But Quinton pulled away and stood, knowing they had to get dressed. As much as he'd like to pretend that staying in bed would cure all, he knew otherwise.

He glanced at the clock and connected the call. The FBI. "This is Agent Horton, I was called by the local police to assist. We need your help."

"I'll be there in five minutes," Quinton said stiffly. "Did Detective DeLang send over that list of guests?"

"Yes, I have it. And he's pinpointed at least six veterans. We're going to pull them aside at the door and question them."

"Good. I'll be right there." He disconnected the call and rushed to get dressed. Time to face the demon.

And hope he recognized him and could stop him before anyone else died.

Anxiety knotted Annabelle's shoulders as the next two hours passed.

The ballroom at the country club where the charity event was being held overflowed with guests. Waiters served appetizers and champagne throughout the festive room filled with white-linen-covered tables. A buffet overflowed with fruit and Cajun cuisine, and sinful desserts filled another table, a chocolate fountain serving as a centerpiece.

The enormous ballroom was packed, decorated with flags that boasted of Mardi Gras and honored patrons of the renowned city. Other displays included statues and photographs of contributors as well as legendary figures in the town; a separate wall had been dedicated to musical artists, folklore and legends, and artists who kept the culture alive.

But even with the hundreds of people surrounding her, Annabelle had never felt more alone in her life.

As soon as the phone call from the FBI had come in the hotel room, Quinton had distanced himself from her as if he'd clicked a button and ended any connection they'd shared.

She forced herself to make polite conversation, to make contacts and accept business cards for future stories, while he met Detective DeLang in a neighboring room to question the veterans who'd shown.

But she'd seen Quinton's expression as he'd touched each one of them. He'd shaken his head at her each time, indicating he didn't think any one of them was their man.

So where was the bomber? Was he here now?

The scent of danger and desperation floated through the air as if the devil had truly made his entrance into town. The hurricanes had brought enough devastation to the people, the economy, the psyche, but the sight of the vultures had heightened panic and a sense of doom, hinting that the city of death was indeed steeped with ghosts.

And that more deaths would come.

Quinton finally joined her just as the speeches began. The governor took the stage, complimenting the joint efforts of the volunteers and donors as well as the social workers. She searched the crowd for Dr. Gryphon, and finally spotted him in the back corner talking to another man.

The governor announced the awards, giving several to local charities for donations, one to a private sponsor, and one to Dr. Gryphon for his help in offering free medical services to the needy.

"Thank you," Dr. Gryphon said as he stepped in front of the microphone onstage. "It is up to the people of every city to take care of their own, to embrace the soldiers who have fought for us, to honor the heroes of the natural disasters our nation has faced, and to care for our aging."

Applause broke out as everyone cheered.

Quinton remained silent, his gaze tracking the room, monitoring the doorways as people entered and left. So far, no one suspicious had arrived.

Was the person behind the bombings here watching in anticipation? Preparing to gloat over more deaths?

Or was he at one of the other possible target locations?

The governor called Reverend Narius up to the stage. The hair on the back of Annabelle's neck rose, and she suddenly spotted a waiter toward the front who looked familiar. The tilt of his head, his slight limp, his wiry graying hair, his profile . . .

Dear God. It was her father.

She staggered and reached for Quinton's arm to steady herself. She had to be seeing things. Had to be wrong. "Quinton . . ."

"What?"

"That waiter. He's my dad." Hope suffused her as she hurried toward the front. She couldn't believe he was here, especially working as a waiter. He was a scientist.

Tears blurred her eyes, but she blinked them back as she shoved through the people. But her father kept moving toward the stage, his movements rigid and awkward.

Something was wrong.

Frustration and anger coursed through her. She was so close. Why was he ignoring her?

Quinton caught up with her, his expression tight. "Wait, Annabelle. Something's not right."

She ignored him and pulled away. "Daddy, stop, it's me, Annabelle!" She ran forward and grabbed his arm, but he felt stiff and cold to the touch.

And when he turned around, he stared at her with an empty look as if he didn't recognize her.

"Daddy," she whispered. "It's me, Annabelle. What's wrong?"

He shook off her arm with a strength that belied the seeming frailness of his body. Her stomach clenched. Her father had never been violent or physical before. But he'd been gone for months. Had he really changed that much?

He certainly looked different. His pallor was a chalky gray, and an odd odor radiated off him as if his flesh had been charred. Then his jacket fell open and Annabelle froze.

Inside the jacket, a bomb was strapped to his chest.

Chapter Twenty-two

Quinton gritted his teeth. Good God almighty. Her father was wearing a bomb.

Dammit to hell and back, he had to get Annabelle away from him. Had to stop him from triggering the explosive device.

He spoke into the miniature mike attached to his lapel, alerting security to evacuate the room and call the bomb squad.

Then someone screamed. "Bomb! He's got a bomb!"

Pandemonium erupted. "Run!"

"Help!"

People began to stampede the room while Annabelle tried to pull her father away to talk to him. But he shoved her backward with one hand, and she fell against the wall. Then he mounted the steps to the stage and grabbed Reverend Narius.

Even from the middle of the ballroom, Quinton smelled the stench of death and fried flesh radiating from the man.

Chaos reigned as guests screamed and raced from the room. Security guards hustled the governor off the stage, while others rushed to clear doorways and evacuate, bumping food trays and tables in their haste. Dishes and glassware rattled and fell to the floor, shattering.

Quinton wrapped his hands around Annabelle and pushed her behind him as he reached for his gun. Then he channeled his energy toward Annabelle's father.

"Stop, Mr. Armstrong," he said in a low voice.

Annabelle tried to jerk from his grasp, but he held her behind him with a firm grip. "Let me handle it, Annabelle," he murmured.

"Daddy, don't do this!" Annabelle cried. "Please, you don't want to hurt these people."

He ignored her and reached for the triggering mechanism to the bomb.

The reverend's eyes widened in terror. "Mister, think of the Lord. Remember the Ten Commandments..."

"Mr. Armstrong, stop." Quinton again channeled his thoughts toward the older man in an attempt to freeze his movements. "Please, release the reverend. No one needs to get hurt."

Instead of reacting, the old man looked at him with vacant eyes, and Quinton realized his mind had been possessed.

He clenched his hands and focused all his energy on entering the old man's head. On erasing the orders the demon had issued.

Fight the demon, he telepathed mentally. *Release the reverend, and you can be with your daughter.*

Several tense seconds passed, then Armstrong turned and stared straight into his eyes.

Fight the demon, Quinton said again silently. *He's telling you to do this, but you don't want to kill this man.*

A flicker of awareness brightened the old man's

bloodshot, glazed eyes. Quinton felt him wavering, literally felt the brain waves churn in his mind as if life were seeping back into a dead corpse.

Annabelle trembled next to him, her fear palpable. Behind Armstrong, two officers approached with weapons drawn, and a SWAT team moved into position. Inching closer and closer, they relied on Quinton as a distraction.

"Please, don't let them kill him," Annabelle whispered. "Please..."

Quinton signaled for them to hold off the gunfire.

Then Armstrong lifted a hand to his chest—to pull the triggering mechanism or submit, Quinton wasn't sure.

The SWAT team inched forward, but Quinton exerted his mental force to physically hold the team in place.

Then he walked toward Armstrong, mentally connecting once again.

As if the demon's spirit had left Armstrong's body, the man collapsed onto the floor, limp and unconscious.

Quinton released his mental hold on the police, then waved the bomb squad over to remove the bomb from the room. As usual when he used his power, his head was starting to throb, his energy waning.

Narius knelt to pray beside Armstrong. "Father, forgive this man, for he knows not what he does."

Annabelle raced over and dropped to her knees, then pulled her father's hand into hers. "Daddy, it's me. I'm here now. It's going to be all right."

"Get an ambulance," Quinton shouted.

"I'm on it," an officer yelled.

Annabelle's teary gaze met his, and his gut squeezed. Was Armstrong too depleted from the demon's possession to survive?

Then a movement caught his eyes. A black shadow with a cape billowing around it raced from behind the stage, a black shadow that morphed into a vulture in front of his eyes and flew toward the ceiling.

Quinton raised his gun and fired a round, aiming for the vulture.

The SWAT team pivoted to fire, but the vulture was too fast. It flapped its wings, swept across the room with a shrill cry, then dove out the door.

Annabelle clutched her father's hand, pleading with him not to die. But he lay stiff and cold, a shell of the man she'd once known, his eyes listless as he stared into empty space.

Rescue workers raced onto the scene, and a team of firefighters stormed in to check the premises. A paramedic hurried to her, knelt, and began to take her father's vitals.

"What happened?" the medic asked.

"He had a bomb," Quinton said, "but we disarmed it, and he collapsed."

The medic checked her father's pupils. "Was he taking drugs of any kind?"

"I don't know," Annabelle said. "I haven't seen him in months." Panic tore at her. "Is he going to be all right?"

"His pulse is weak and thready; he's nonresponsive, but he is breathing," the medic said into his radio mike.

"Please save him," Annabelle whispered.

"We'll do everything we can, miss." The medic waved for his partner to bring the stretcher.

Agent Horton and a man from the SWAT team approached Quinton, and he stepped aside to consult with them, while other officers canvassed the outside, questioning attendees.

Annabelle heaved a breath. All she could do was watch the scene in horror. She'd finally found her father, but he had turned out to be one of the suicide bombers. Was this some kind of pact the men had made? Had they known one another online?

Were they depressed, or had someone put them up to it, as she'd suspected?

"What happened?" Detective DeLang asked.

"I talked him down," Quinton said.

"They why did you open fire?" Agent Horton asked.

"I saw another man I thought might be behind the attack. He was fleeing toward the door."

Detective DeLang frowned. "What made you think that he was involved, not just a guest running away in fear?"

"All the guests had been cleared," Quinton said.

Agent Horton glanced at Annabelle with raised brows. "Miss Armstrong, do you know this man?"

She nodded. "He's my father."

The paramedics loaded Armstrong onto the stretcher, and Detective DeLang gestured toward the ambulance. "Well, he's under arrest now."

"He needs medical care," Annabelle said in a pained voice. "Something is terribly wrong with him. I called to him, but he didn't even recognize me."

"He'll receive medical care," DeLang said in a clipped tone. "But there will be a guard posted at his door at all times."

She nodded helplessly. "I have to go with him."

"I'll drive her," Quinton said.

Agent Horton caught Annabelle's arm. "You can't leave. We need to question you."

Quinton shoved the man's hand away. "You can talk to us both at the hospital. In fact, I intend to question Armstrong the moment he becomes coherent."

The agent reluctantly nodded, and Annabelle hurried behind the paramedic. "Sorry, ma'am," the medic said. "We can't let you ride with us." Instead an armed policeman climbed inside the ambulance.

People hovered outside watching, stunned and afraid, whispering and asking questions. Cameras flashed and a reporter raced toward her.

She shuddered and tried to shield her face, desperate to escape and get to the hospital. She usually got the story.

Now she was part of it.

"Leave her alone," Quinton growled at the reporter, then pulled her into the crook of his arms and ushered her through the crowd toward the rental car.

"I don't understand." Annabelle's throat clogged as she climbed into the car and he joined her. "That's my father and I don't even recognize him. He used to give me piggyback rides, help me decorate the Christmas tree, taught me to ride a bike, and planted flowers in the backyard. And I saw him about to kill all these people. If you hadn't stopped him..." She glanced up, searching his face. "How did you do that?"

He hesitated, his gaze dark. "It doesn't matter. Let's go to the hospital."

She grabbed his arm. "But I need to know."

"I tapped into his mind," he said in a low voice.

She wheezed a breath. "If you read his mind, then why did he do this?"

"I don't know," he said quietly. "His mind was empty, as if it had been erased."

She pressed her hand to her chest. "Erased?"

He nodded. "His only thought was that pulling that triggering mechanism was his mission. That he was supposed to kill the enemy."

"The enemy?" Her voice cracked. "But those were innocent people."

"I know. But I think our theory was right. Someone brainwashed him into thinking he was on a mission." He started the car and followed the ambulance. Annabelle twisted her hands together, then wiped at her tears.

Annabelle swallowed. "You said you saw the man behind the plan. Who was it?"

He cut his eyes toward her. "I didn't actually see his face, only a black cape billowing behind him."

She reached for him, wanting to shake him. "Why couldn't you stop *him* with your mind?"

He cleared his throat. "Because it was the Death Angel. He shape-shifted into a vulture and flew away before I could stop him."

Quinton's head reeled with questions. Armstrong had almost killed Narius along with himself. So if Narius wasn't responsible for the bombings and brainwashing, then whose body had the Death Angel possessed?

Dr. Gryphon had also attended the event, but he hadn't seen him when the chaos had erupted. Had he set the wheels in motion then stepped back to watch the explosion?

Quinton scowled. They needed to know more about the man's research.

But why would a noted doctor want to kill masses of people?

He's possessed, Quinton reminded himself. This demon, the Death Angel, had the power to rob a person of their mind—and soul—and bend it to his will. It was the only explanation. And who better to use than a renowned, award-winning, charitable doctor no one would suspect?

Annabelle wrapped her arms around her sides, as if holding herself together, and he frowned. He shouldn't have spilled his guts back there. He should have lied.

But this was personal to her. The potential bomber this time was her father, and he'd lost sight of that for a moment when her pain had suffused him.

Dammit, he didn't want to care about her.

Desperation and grief shadowed Annabelle's eyes. "You're scaring me," she finally said.

His hand tightened around the steering wheel. Good. She should be scared.

Of the demon and of him.

Dammit. He wanted to hold her, though, assure her that he'd make everything all right.

But he couldn't make promises he might not be able to keep.

He never should have had sex with her. Instead of sating him, it had only whetted his appetite.

And had connected him to her on an emotional level.

He had to break that connection; otherwise, how could he possibly do his job?

The ambulance careened up to the emergency room entrance, and medics unloaded her father, then rushed him inside. Quinton swung the car around to a space in the emergency room parking lot, then the two of them rushed inside and hurried to the front nurse's desk.

"My father was just brought in," Annabelle said, a tremor in her voice. "I'd like to be with him."

The security guard stepped in front of them. "I'm sorry, but Officer Carnes issued strict orders not to let anyone pass."

Quinton flashed his Homeland Security ID. "This man is a suspect and possible witness to the bombings in Savannah and Charleston. I need to question him."

The guard shook his head. "I have my orders."

"I can have them overridden," Quinton said sharply. "This is a matter of national security."

The guard stiffened. "I'll speak with the detective and inform him that you're here."

"Please, just let us know when he's conscious," Annabelle said. "I'm his next of kin."

He nodded and Quinton gestured toward the waiting room. Instead of sitting, Annabelle paced the length of the room. A man with a camera hurried in and flashed a press badge at the receptionist's desk. Quinton coaxed Annabelle into the corner.

The guard firmly ordered the reporter to leave, but he glanced around as if searching for them. Quinton shielded Annabelle from sight.

"I just can't believe this is happening," Annabelle whispered.

He pulled her up against his chest and held her. "I'm sorry, Annabelle. But at least he's alive."

She sighed against him. "My father...he used to be so gentle. He would never hurt a soul, not in his right mind."

Quinton stroked her back, trying to calm her. "He hurt you by walking out on you."

She nodded against his chest, her body trembling. "But he was depressed over losing my mother."

Quinton refused to let the man off that easily, just as he couldn't let his mother off so easily for sending him to live with the monks. "It still doesn't excuse him for abandoning his daughter."

"Why choose him?" Her voice broke. "Why send me warnings and then use my own father? Does this killer have something against me personally?"

Quinton clenched his jaw, the truth dawning. No, It was because of him.

The reason he would have to walk away from her when he vanquished this demon.

If Vincent's and Father Robard's predictions were correct, more demons would follow. And they'd use anyone he cared about to get to him.

⁓

The vulture picked the bones clean. But one lone, pitiful man did not fill his appetite. Not when he'd been expecting dozens of others.

His fellow vultures squealed in anger and circled the sky over New Orleans, hungry, preying, seeking sustenance.

Desperate to lick the blood juices, chomp on mangled flesh and charred skin.

Even though the human meat was old and brittle, his belly swelled with pleasure, and his mouth watered for more.

He would never get enough of death. Of the slaughter. Of circling the sky for the remains of animal and man. Of the feast that resulted as nature took its course and their bodies decomposed.

Now that he'd tasted humans, the craving for their flesh consumed him.

The Dark Lord had proven to be quite the adversary tonight. He'd even used his power against him.

He tore another tendon from the body and chewed it greedily, although rage that he'd lost the battle made him sink his sharp teeth into bone until it cracked and splintered.

The Dark Lord might have won a small victory tonight. But he would not win in the end.

Annabelle's ripe young body would taste so sweet and juicy.

Seeing the tortured look on the Dark Lord's face as he devoured her would be his ultimate offering to Zion. And would undoubtedly unleash the evil lurking within Quinton.

Chapter Twenty-three

It was the longest night of Annabelle's life.

She and Quinton both checked at the nurse's desk every few minutes for an update on her father, but the staff kept putting them off. Twice, reporters tried to trick their way inside, but Quinton and the guards kept them out.

Quinton had gone to get them a cup of coffee when Reverend Narius showed up with Dr. Gryphon right behind him.

"I will pray with you for your father's soul if you like," Reverend Narius asked.

"Thank you, but I just want to be alone," Annabelle said.

"I understand." The reverend clasped her hand. "I'll be in the chapel if you need me or decide to join me."

"How is your father?" Dr. Gryphon asked.

Annabelle studied him, searching for a sign that she should trust him.

"I don't know. The doctors won't tell me anything."

He offered her a small smile. "Perhaps I can talk to him, evaluate him. Help him in some way."

Quinton appeared behind the doctor. "I don't think Miss Armstrong wants your help," he said gruffly.

Dr. Gryphon pivoted and scowled at Quinton. "I am an

expert in my field. It appears to me that Mr. Armstrong has slipped into a catatonic state due to some traumatic event in the past. Perhaps with therapy we can discover what drove him to contemplate suicide."

"We will get to the bottom of what happened," Quinton said.

Annabelle cleared her throat. "In your work with PTS and the online group, did either of the two other bombers mention suicide?"

"No." He shook his head. "And after we spoke, I reexamined the posts just to make sure I hadn't missed any signs. But I saw nothing indicating suicidal thoughts. Depressed, yes. Irrational thoughts, yes. But not suicide."

"We'll have our own psychologist from the Bureau evaluate those posts," Quinton said. "We'll also bring them in to evaluate Mr. Armstrong."

"His recovery could be the key to discovering who's behind these bombings, correct?" Dr. Gryphon said.

"Exactly." Quinton narrowed his gaze at the doctor. "That's the reason we need our own people to handle it, not you."

That and the fact that they suspected he might be involved, Annabelle thought.

Then she remembered Quinton's theory of demons. Could Dr. Gryphon possibly be more than he seemed?

She'd witnessed Quinton's power. Did the doctor have a power himself?

Dr. Gryphon thrust his business card into her hand. "Very well. But please call me if you need me, Miss Armstrong. I very much want to help."

He left and Quinton gave her the coffee with a muttered curse. "I don't trust him."

Annabelle massaged her temple. "I don't know what to think." Not about Dr. Gryphon or her father.

Yet somehow she trusted Quinton now.

They lapsed into an awkward silence, and Quinton excused himself to make some phone calls as she paced the waiting room.

Finally her father's doctor appeared. "My name is Dr. Andradre." He extended his hand and Annabelle shook it.

"How is he?" she asked.

"He's stabilized, but nonresponsive. We want to run some tests, basic MRI, CAT scan, do a complete neurological workup, and have a psychologist evaluate him as well."

She nodded. "He is going to live, isn't he?"

"Everything indicates that. At least there are no visible physical injuries," he said. "But as I mentioned, we need to run additional tests to see if there are underlying medical issues causing his condition." He hesitated. "Can you give me his background? Was he taking any medications?"

"Not that I know of," Annabelle said. "But I haven't seen him in months. My mother died, and he just walked out and never came back."

"So he suffered emotional trauma and depression," Dr. Andradre said.

"Yes. But I don't know where he's been these past few months or what he's been doing."

"Before he left, did he exhibit signs of memory loss, confusion, dementia?"

She shook her head. "No. You don't understand. My

father was a scientist, a smart man in his field, not violent at all."

"Hopefully we can help him." He patted her shoulder. "But it may take time, Miss Armstrong."

She nodded. "My father was—is—a good man," Annabelle said. "He would never hurt anyone. I don't understand what drove him to do what he did tonight, but I think he may have been brainwashed."

His eyes narrowed as if he thought *she* might be demented. "Let's run some tests and see what we find. I'll keep you posted. And it'll be a while before we complete them, so if you want to go home and get some rest, just leave a number where you can be reached and we'll call you."

"Can I see him first?"

Compassion glimmered in his eyes. "I'm afraid he may not know you."

"I don't care," Annabelle said. "I need to see him before I leave."

He nodded solemnly, then led her through a set of double doors and into a triage room. The policeman at the door gave her a condemning look, but she ignored him and went inside.

The scent of antiseptic and alcohol filled her nostrils, the sounds of hospital machinery and voices whirring in the background. Quinton followed her, but he stood in the doorway as if to offer her some semblance of privacy.

Her father lay in bed in a hospital gown, his face still gaunt and chalky. His hair had thinned and grayed since her mother's death, she noticed now; he'd lost weight, and his skin was dry and cracked.

She placed her hand over his, shivering at the feel of his

ice-cold skin. "What happened to you, Dad? Where have you been? Why did you leave me?" Her voice choked. "You have to wake up, to get better so you can tell me who did this to you."

Grief and sadness welled inside her, but then she felt a tiny movement. His fingers inched around hers, and he squeezed her hand. It was only a small squeeze, barely discernible. But the movement gave her hope that her father was alive inside that shell.

And that one day he would come back to her.

Quinton popped two painkillers as he studied Annabelle and her father. He looked weak and frail, close to death. Even if Armstrong physically survived, would he be able to overcome the effects of the demon's possession?

While Dr. Gryphon had spoken with her, he'd probed the doctor's mind. Gryphon had delved into mind control for a government experiment. He had served in the military in the Gulf War and understood the trauma of combat firsthand. He'd consulted on research regarding dementia and replacing cognitive thoughts and memories through a combination of drugs and hypnosis, and was also experimenting with repairing memory through stem cell replacement.

In the military, the enemy had used brainwashing techniques on him. His own experience had prompted his obsession with that area of study.

Were the bombers a product of his experimentation? Were they his subjects?

Detective DeLang and Agent Horton met them in the waiting room.

"How is he?" Detective DeLang asked Annabelle.

"Still unconscious. But he did squeeze my hand slightly, so that's a good sign."

Quinton hoped to hell the man recovered. So far, he was the only witness who could prove that the suicide bombers hadn't been working of their own accord. If he could tell them who'd contacted him, how the mental suggestions had been planted in his head, Quinton could track down the perpetrator in human form and destroy him.

Agent Horton turned to Quinton. "So you haven't been able to question him?"

"Not yet. But as soon as he regains consciousness, I will. The doctors and nurses have strict orders to contact me immediately."

"Tell us about your father," Agent Horton said to Annabelle. "Did you know he was going to be at the charity event tonight?"

"No, I had no idea." She explained about her mother's death and her father's desertion. "I haven't seen him since."

"Did he ever exhibit violent tendencies?" Detective DeLang asked.

"Never." Annabelle massaged her temple. "He was a scientist, studying genetics. He was kindhearted, a hard worker. For goodness' sake, he didn't even like to hunt; he'd never hurt a fly."

"Yet he nearly killed himself and hundreds of others tonight," Agent Horton said.

She frowned, unable to argue.

"We found a connection between the first two bombers," Quinton interjected. "Both suffered from post-traumatic stress syndrome and had signed on to the same online support group."

"And Mr. Armstrong?" Horton asked.

"He didn't suffer from PTS," Annabelle said. "In fact, he was never in the military."

"So what were these guys saying online?" Agent Horton asked. "Were they forming some kind of cultlike vigilante group to get revenge on the world because they thought people had abandoned them?"

"Makes sense," Detective DeLang agreed. "Veterans often feel like they aren't appreciated, that they're forgotten once they return home. Especially if they've lost loved ones due to divorce, physical impairment, death, or if they're financially struggling."

"But for a group of them to plan a terrorist attack," Annabelle said. "That seems improbable."

"Sometimes when troubled people get together, they feed off each other's anger and bitterness," Agent Horton said.

"The mob mentality," Detective DeLang added with a worried frown.

"How about other motives?" Agent Horton asked. "You said these men were homeless. Could someone have paid them off or offered to send money to their families if they carried out the bombing?"

"So far, none of the men we've investigated had a history of violence. No big insurance policies or vendettas. Ames had no family," Quinton said. "And as far as masterminding the three attacks, none of them had the resources or presence of mind to orchestrate an intricate plan such as this."

But they had been easy marks for a demon to possess because they already suffered from some sort of dementia, substance abuse, or disease.

Quinton placed a hand at Annabelle's back. "I'm going to take Annabelle back to the hotel to rest."

"Just don't leave town, Miss Armstrong," Agent McLaughlin said.

Annabelle glared at him. "Don't worry. I intend to stay and help my father. And somehow I'll prove that someone else was behind what happened tonight."

Dr. Gryphon's name jumped to the top of Quinton's suspect list. In fact, some innocuous detail teased his brain, something from the monks' teachings. Hadn't old-world vultures descended from the griffin, the guardian of the mysteries of life and death?

He gritted his teeth.

Dammit. He couldn't share his theories—the truth—with the police or the FBI. They would think he was insane.

No, he had to figure out a way to work with them without divulging the truth. A way to stop this demon and explain what had happened.

A way to save Annabelle so his premonition didn't come true.

A way to leave her when it was over...

Exhaustion and a mixture of emotions left Annabelle drained as they exited the hospital and drove to the hotel.

Early morning shadows flickered across the city, the statuesque architecture looking almost garish in the darkness. The scent of death, evil, and fear permeated the air as they passed one of the aboveground cemeteries, the local legends of ghosts and the swamp devil echoing around her. The sight of the vultures circling above the mausoleums in search of human food sent a chill up her spine. Their angry screeching added to the desolate hopelessness she felt.

She wanted to shut down, tune out the world, the bombings, her feelings. Her contact with reality. Her own instincts when investigating a crime and unraveling a story.

All she wanted to do was crawl into bed and bury herself beneath the covers and cry.

And forget that she'd almost died tonight. That her mother was gone. Her father lost now.

Perhaps forever.

No, he would come back. She'd get him all the help he needed.

And she would expose whoever did this to him for all the world to see.

And Quinton...

God, he scared her. The power he'd wielded tonight without even touching her father or the police—he'd frozen them in place, literally held them back as if time had stopped. That was the only way she could explain what she'd seen.

He was a demon of some kind. Dangerous to her. He'd told her that himself.

But he'd saved hundreds of lives tonight, as well as hers and her father's.

She had to stay strong. To prove that her father hadn't acted of his own accord, that he'd been forced, brainwashed into committing a crime. The thought of him going to jail for the rest of his life for attempted murder or terrorism was more than she could bear.

But how would she prove his innocence? And how

could she print the truth if Quinton was right and the mastermind was demonic?

Quinton's gut tightened as he glanced at Annabelle's dejected face. Dammit, he wasn't supposed to let it get personal. Relationships interfered with the job and his objectivity.

But she'd somehow snuck past his defenses. And it was painful to see her this way, beaten down when she was such a fighter.

He parked at the hotel, then circled the car to her side and gave her a hand. The fact that she allowed him to help her spoke volumes about her emotional state. She was trembling as he guided her inside to their adjoining rooms. He rushed to the bathroom and turned on the shower.

"We need to warm you up," he said quietly.

She moved on autopilot and began to strip. Bastard that he was, his body hardened, instantly coming alive.

But a sliver of guilt wormed into his consciousness, and he hesitated, refusing to take advantage of her in this vulnerable state.

She looked up at him with helpless vacant eyes, dropped her hand as if she was too tired to even undress, and he removed her clothes, forcing himself not to stare or touch her sexually when his balls ached and throbbed and his cock pressed against the fly of his suit pants.

When he'd spotted her in this delicious dress earlier tonight and made love to her, he'd imagined removing it at the end of the evening, but not like this.

Moisture glistened in her eyes, and her chin quivered as she climbed beneath the spray of water. But she didn't move to bathe, she simply stood there shaking.

A snap decision made, he stripped off his clothes and climbed into the shower with her. She faced the wall, her head thrown back as warm water sluiced over her body.

He soaped the cloth and slowly ran it over her shoulders, her back, gently bathing her, then lower over her buttocks and legs. His cock twitched and pulsed, wanting between her legs, the urge to push her against the wall and drive himself inside her so strong that he sucked in a deep breath.

Then he turned her around slowly and bathed her shoulders, her arms, then trailed the bubbles over her breasts. His breath hissed between clenched teeth at the sight of her nipples budding and rosy under the warm water. But he didn't linger. He traced a path with the bubbles over her stomach, thighs, and legs, avoiding touching her heat. Although his gaze fastened on the tattoo and he traced a finger over the design, wanting more, wanting to kiss her bare flesh.

If he did, he wouldn't be able to resist prying her legs open and touching her intimately. He wanted to be inside her, to make her forget the pain for a moment as they'd done earlier. To take whatever little she could offer tonight before they faced another gruesome day tomorrow.

To give to her as he'd never given of himself to a woman before.

Suddenly her expression softened, and she seemed to realize they were naked and wet together, and she arched against him, hunger flaring in her eyes.

He kept his hands gentle as he tilted her chin up to search her face. Was she asking for his loving?

"Please touch me." She closed her eyes, and he sucked

in a sharp breath. He couldn't deny her any more than he could deny himself.

His need raged, dark and raw, driving his movements as he trailed his hands over her shoulders, down her arms and to her breasts, where he cupped the heavy mounds in his hands.

"Quinton..."

"I'm here, Annabelle. It's all right."

He touched her tattoo again, then soothed her with soft whispers, her quiver telling him that his hands were awakening erotic sensations along her spine.

She slowly opened her eyes and looked up at him, and he heard her thoughts as if she'd spoken them aloud.

She wanted him. A man who could kill coolly without blinking an eye, without an ounce of remorse, but a man who'd saved her life more than once now.

A man who elicited erotic sensations in her belly, and made her feel more alive, more aroused, than she'd ever thought possible.

A threat to her—yes.

Would she have him?

She had to.

———

Dr. Wynn picked through the dozens of bones, trying to decide which one to add to his collection. So many bodies to choose from. So many pretty bones to add to his wall. Some large, some small, children's, women's, men's...animals'.

Like fine art, he selected each one for its shape and texture. A finger that had been severed, the bone jutting in jagged lines. A kneecap, once round now distorted.

A splintered rib. A femur carved with the imprint of shattered glass. A tibia marred with the vulture's teeth prints.

A fractured skull, the eye sockets torn out by the birds of prey.

The vultures had done a number on them, but that was their primal nature, to clean up after death. Just as it was his.

Chapter Twenty-four

Annabelle's heart thundered in her chest. Quinton's gaze locked onto hers, his hunger evident in the deep blackness of his eyes, and sensations stirred low in her belly, rippling through her in erotic waves.

"You're shivering," he mumbled in a fierce tone.

She shook her head. "Because I want you."

His jaw tightened, the scar along his neck glistening with water. "You're in shock. Let's dry you off and put you to bed."

"I don't want to go to bed," she whispered roughly. "I want you inside me."

"Annabelle." His voice rumbled out, deep and throaty, and he stepped back, dropping the washcloth. Water cascaded over his rippled, muscled chest, down his washboard stomach, over his engorged penis, which twitched with arousal as she blatantly stared at it.

She started to reach for him, but he held up his hands in protest. "Look, I'm not a good guy, Annabelle. But I'm trying to do the right thing here."

She licked her lips, desperate for comfort. "Why in the hell would you start doing the right thing now?"

A hint of a smile lit his devilish eyes, but he still shook his head.

She didn't care. Her body craved his, and the dark hunger in his eyes promised her another mind-blowing orgasm.

She knew how to seduce him, how to make him break. Licking her lips, she slid her hands over her breasts, cupping them, twisting her nipples to stiff hard peaks that begged for his mouth. His eyes tracked her movements, his breath hissing between clenched teeth.

"You want your hands on me, don't you?" she whispered.

His throat muscles contracted visibly as he swallowed. "Yes."

Forgetting all thoughts of caution, she teased the nipples again, then slid one finger to her center and stroked her clit, moaning as sultry sensations flooded her.

"Don't make me do this alone," she whispered. "You know you want me."

He swallowed again, the raw need in his tautly controlled face exciting her and driving her to a frenzied heat. She lifted her fingers from her damp center and slid them over his length, tracing a finger over the tip of his penis and circling the enormous head.

Then she blatantly parted her legs, displaying herself and begging him with her eyes to take her.

A low groan tore from his throat, and he suddenly snapped. "Dammit, Annabelle. I can't just watch. Not with you."

His gruffly spoken admission sent a frisson of fear and pleasure along her spine. Then he jerked her into his arms, dragged her mouth to his, and thrust his tongue into her mouth. His movements were no longer gentle but laced with desperate, raw passion.

She met his tongue thrust for thrust, moaning as his hands splayed over her breasts, teasing her, twisting her nipples until she cried out and ran her foot up his calf. His hair-dusted thigh brushed hers, stirring her hunger.

Then he lowered his mouth and kissed the tips of her breasts, licking and suckling until pleasure overtook her, and she began to quake with the first hint of an orgasm.

Enflamed by her moans and her hands frantically reaching for his cock, he shoved her against the tile wall and wedged his thigh between her legs, parting them for his invasion.

"You really want this?" he mumbled huskily.

"Yes, please," she whispered, hating to beg but knowing she'd do anything now to have him.

Anything he wanted.

The thought sent terror through her, but also a tiny thrill that tripped her orgasm over the edge. She cried out, trembling as he slid his fingers inside her and stroked her deep and hard.

When he withdrew, her body protested with a moan. But a second later, she realized he'd reached into his pants on the bathroom floor for a condom, ripped open the package, and pulled it on. With a growl from deep in his throat, he ground his big body against hers, but still didn't penetrate her, simply teased her inner thighs with his sex, stoking the flames again, arousing her to the point of nearly pleading.

He bent and suckled her nipple into his mouth again, then trailed kisses down her stomach and she realized his intention. "No, I want you," she hissed.

Frantic for fulfillment, she grabbed his arms, pushed him against the wall, and lowered her hand around his thick hard length. His cock surged and pulsed beneath her fingers, his look feral as he lifted her and she impaled herself on him.

She wrapped her legs around him, clinging to him as he stretched and filled her, their bodies slapping the tiles as they ground together.

A million butterflies danced in her womb, as he bit her neck and pounded into her. It was fast, furious, passionate, mind-boggling in its rawness.

Everything she'd ever wanted.

He buried his head against her, nibbling at her ear, his hands cupping her ass and shoving himself so deep inside her that she cried out with the impact, felt as if he was tearing her apart, and knew that she'd be empty without him inside her if he left.

Tingling sensations spiraled through her, her body quivered, her womb clenching around him, her head spinning as another orgasm claimed her. She threw her head back in wild abandon, unashamed at the guttural shout that erupted from her.

He drove deeper, harder, faster, pushing her over the limit, then his body jerked and he growled her name as his own pleasure mingled with hers, his big body rocking with his climax.

Amazing sensations overloaded Quinton's body, triggering a flood of emotions, and he gripped Annabelle tighter. Dammit, he didn't want to let her go. And he sure as hell didn't want another man having her.

He tensed, troubled by his thoughts. She wasn't his to lose. Sex was the only thing they could have together.

Instinctively, he knew Annabelle would want more. A family.

Her thoughts fell open to him.

She cared about him, needed him, wanted him to love her. But she was scared as well. Afraid of getting hurt.

He couldn't let her need him too much because he would have to let her go.

A man with demon blood running through his veins didn't have the right to make promises of happily-ever-after. And what if he brought a demon child into the world?

Why the hell was he thinking such nonsense? He was a loner. When this ended, he'd return to his solitude.

But Annabelle's pain mingled with his own, and his knees nearly buckled.

The water was turning cold, and she sagged against him, stroking his wet hair, shivering. He flipped off the water, slowly let her slide to her feet, then reached for a bath towel and dried her off. Her nipples were stiff from the cold, goose bumps dotting her beautiful skin, his love bites marring the perfect flesh.

Guilt slammed into his gut. He had bitten her like a damn animal.

Her eyes were glazed with passion, her lids drooping, but her face also looked haunted, a reminder of her anguish.

He quickly dried off, swept her into his arms, and carried her to her bed. Needing to put some distance between them, to compartmentalize, he started to walk away, but she gripped his hand.

"Please, don't leave me."

His throat thickened. He needed to talk to Vincent, ask him about Gryphon. Do something to find this demon.

But she tugged his hand again, and he couldn't resist. He climbed into bed, wrapped his arms around her, and held her until she fell into a deep sleep. Even then, he lay watching her, wondering how he'd gone from a killer who'd contemplated taking her life to a man who would give his own life to save hers.

The ringing of his cell phone broke the silence. He cursed, wanting to ignore it, but he couldn't. What if it was the police about the bombings?

He slipped from bed and retrieved his phone from the pocket of his jacket, then checked the number. Vincent.

He connected the call. "Yeah, it's Quinton."

"What happened last night?" Vincent asked. "According to the news report, Annabelle's father almost set off a bomb."

Quinton scrubbed a hand over his neck then explained what had happened. "I think the demon used Armstrong to get to me."

Vincent sighed in agreement. "How's she taking it?"

"She's devastated," he said, his gut clenching. "But her father responded to her in the hospital, hopefully a sign that he'll recover. The staff has instructions to phone me the minute he regains consciousness so I can question him."

"This could be a break," Vincent said. "So how did you stop him?"

Quinton relayed the incident in detail. "I don't think anyone saw or understood what I did."

Vincent cursed. "Hell, Quinton, you can't expose yourself. That could be even more dangerous."

"Don't you think I know that?" Quinton said in a low

voice. "But what was I supposed to do? Let him blow up the room?"

A tense second passed, then Vincent spoke. "Any leads on the demon's identity? Do you think it was Reverend Narius?"

"No. Armstrong took him hostage and planned to blow him up with him."

"Shit. So that eliminates him as a suspect."

"Exactly." Quinton paced to the window, not surprised at seeing the vulture perched on the windowsill, its beady eyes staring into his own.

He snatched the sheers together, but even as he did, the monks' warnings rose to taunt him, and he went to his bag and pulled out *Deadly Demons*.

Quinton exhaled in frustration as he flipped through the pages, searching for more information on the vulture and the Death Angel. "Listen, Vincent, at the shelter, I met this woman who said she's a descendant of a voodoo priestess. She knew about us and our father, said that she was a witch and a demonslayer."

Another long silence, then Vincent's hiss. "What's her name?"

"Shayla Larue. She was the social worker at a homeless shelter."

"I'll check her out," Vincent said. "What else did she say about us?"

"Just that the demon would use Annabelle to get to me."

Vincent grunted in acknowledgment. "I'll pull a list of everyone who attended the fund-raiser and look for a person of interest."

"Have someone study all the posts on that online PTS

support group, too. Dr. Gryphon visited the group and is top on my list of possible suspects." Quinton explained about the information he'd tapped from Gryphon's mind involving his past and his research efforts.

"I'll put someone on it ASAP," Vincent said.

"What about a common denominator with the cities?" Quinton asked.

Vincent hesitated a minute. "All of them are historically haunted cities."

"And New Orleans is often called the city of the dead for its aboveground cemeteries."

"I'll get a warrant for Gryphon's office and home," Vincent said. "And I'll find out where he's conducting these experiments."

Quinton halted as he located the page in the book describing the Death Angel and an adjoining page about the vultures. "Vincent, get this. Old-world vultures were gryphon vultures."

"Gryphon?"

"Yeah. If Gryphon is the demon, he used Annabelle's father to hurt her. And Annabelle to get to me." A pain shot through Quinton's chest. "Which makes me responsible for her father's current state."

"Did she see what you did tonight? Does she know what you are?"

"You mean that I'm not human, but part demon?"

Vincent muttered an obscenity. "It's a curse we have to live with."

"She saw, but don't worry. I took care of Annabelle. She won't tell anyone."

"I hope you're right," Vincent said. "Can you imagine

if it leaked that we're demonic? The FBI, police, scientists, they'd all want to get a piece of us."

"Trust me. I just came from her bed. The situation is under control."

A strangled gasp made him jerk around, and he went stone-still.

Annabelle stood in the doorway, her hair tousled, her eyes blurry, her complexion ashen as she stared at him.

Apparently she'd overheard everything.

Part of him wanted to deny what he'd said.

But the smart, rational trained agent in him told him not to. To let her think the worst.

Because he had to let her go to protect her and her father, or the demon would come after them both again.

Annabelle flinched as Quinton's words echoed in her head.

She'd known he had powers but had never really believed he was demonic. Or had she just buried her head in the sand because he'd seduced her?

Hurt splintered through her. He had seduced her to keep her quiet.

How could she have been such a fool?

She'd chased him down for a story, but she'd gotten caught up in the danger, the messages from the bomber, and in . . . Quinton.

In his tough facade. His masculinity. His raw sexual power.

But he'd been playing her all along, just as he played his targets for a kill.

God . . . He was the reason her father was in the hospital, in all this trouble.

She wet her lips, determined not to reveal how much he'd hurt her. "Who was on the phone?"

A detached look settled on his face. "Vincent. He called about the bombings."

She paused at the edge of the bed, searching his face for answers. For hope that this nightmare would end. "Does he have new information?"

"He's searching for connections between the cities targeted so far," he said instead. "He'll call if he finds something new."

"Tell me the truth, Quinton. Do you know who's responsible?"

He shook his head. "No, but I'll find him."

"But it is a demon."

"I told you that, yes."

"And you're part demon?"

"You saw what I did with my mind and my hands."

"Yes, you climb into people's minds and bend them to your will. That's what you've been doing to me all along, isn't it?"

He hadn't meant for her to hear his phone call. Hadn't meant for her to know. Hadn't meant to get involved because he wouldn't stick around.

"I am what I am," he said instead of denying her accusation. "You came for a story. I told you from the beginning that I couldn't let you print it."

She wanted to scream and cry and force him to admit that he cared.

But he obviously didn't.

The way she'd tracked him down still disturbed him. "Just how did you find me, Annabelle?"

She squared her shoulders. "What? You think a demon led me to you?"

He shrugged. "If not, then who did?"

"One of the guys who served with you in the military. He apparently had a beef with you."

He cursed. Probably Olander North. They'd never gotten along.

"What did you do to him to make him hate you so much?" she asked.

"I used my power against him," he said bluntly. "But I let him live. That was my mistake." He shoved the *Deadly Demons* book in front of her. "Take a hard look at these demons, Annabelle. Getting in bed with me puts you right in the middle of my world."

Apprehension crawled up her spine as she opened the book and contemplated his words, that she'd be in his world. A world of demons and danger.

Detailed sketches of monsters filled the pages. Creatures that looked half human, animals that shape-shifted into people, a serpent who was the devil, werewolves and vampires, a sex siren, an incubus, the Death Angel, Soul Collectors, Shadowmen, guardians of the portal between the mortal world and the underground, vampires, witches and warlocks...

And vultures.

"I've seen this before," she said, refusing to be intimidated.

"But you haven't really considered the consequences. Play with sharks and get bitten."

And play with demons and get killed.

"I'm sorry for you," she said. "Sorry that you're incapable of loving anyone."

His eyes glittered darkly, dangerously, and he fisted his hands by his sides as if fighting for control.

"You want to know the reason, I'll tell you, Annabelle. My father was a spawn of Satan, my mother an Angel of Light. My father abused my brother and mother, and my mother sent me and my twin away to keep us safe. Then he killed her."

His heart hammered, but his voice remained calm, steady, devoid of any feeling. He'd never shared his past with anyone before, but she had a right to know.

"The monks isolated me, locked me away for days and nights in the darkness, taught me how to control my dark urges, how to put them to use. Their spiritual lessons trained me to school my emotions. But that dark side lives in me, never doubt it."

She was holding her breath. "What kind of training?"

"Spiritual enlightenment exercises," he said. "They trained me to rely on my inner being, my chi, to relate to nature and call upon its forces to strengthen my power."

"I thought monks were spiritual beings, not demons."

"They are, but they knew what I would one day face. They put me through rigorous physical training. Torture, at least for a small child. Locked me in the darkness for days, forced me to meditate. To remain silent. Then threw me out into the wild to survive off the land or die." He paused, hands knotted by his sides. "And the military taught me to kill. To be tough so I could one day fight the demons that would come for me."

"Did they ever come for you before?"

Memories suffused him, ones he'd tried to banish from his mind, yet they were stored there permanently. "Twice.

Once when I was four. You know the bogeyman that all kids are scared of?"

She nodded.

"Well, there really is such a thing. He takes children in their sleep."

Annabelle's chest squeezed <u>as</u> she imagined the child he might have once been, and how someone had stolen that innocence from him.

Yet he was what he was. And loving him hadn't made any difference.

Her lungs tightened. Did she love him? Had she allowed herself to fall for him?

His throat muscles worked as he swallowed. "Another time I was held for days by a demon, but I escaped. And in the military, I was subjected to brainwashing exercises. Beatings. Drug experiments. Sensory deprivation torture."

No wonder he'd been so cold at times, then hot at others.

But any tenderness had been an act. The art of seduction.

All to keep her quiet.

"So why are you telling me this now?"

He chuckled. "Because you deserve the truth. But...no one will believe you if you print it. And Homeland Security has no knowledge of the Ghost team that I work for. They would never allow that kind of clandestine operation."

"Then why sleep with me? Just to keep me quiet?"

That dark hungry look returned to his eyes, then a sinister smile followed. "Because I wanted you," he said simply. "It didn't mean anything, though, Annabelle. So don't make out like it was more than it was."

"You really are a bastard," she said.

He nodded. "I know."

There was nothing else to say. She wouldn't beg, argue, or confess that she loved him.

"I'm going to concentrate on getting my father well." She folded her arms across her chest, struggling to remain cool. "And I don't ever want to see you again."

"I told you I'd protect you until I caught this demon, and I intend to."

"I don't want or need your protection," she said. "So stay away from me, Quinton. Now, I'm going to get some rest so I can visit my father later."

She gave him a glacial look, then turned and went into the other bedroom. But this time she locked the door between the two rooms, and he didn't follow.

The monks gathered in the deep chambers of the stone monastery, cold air swirling around them as if death had just placed its icy finger on the room. Whispers of the evil roaming the world echoed from the hollow chambers, threatening taunts flowing through the walls, tapping incessantly as if they intended to rip away the stone and mortar and climb into the minds of the monks themselves.

"Duna Florence, Duno Dain," Father Robard said in greeting as his comrades and sisters and brothers began to file into the room, their robes flowing as they nodded. Their vows of silence had stretched on, the power of meditation and prayer their weapon against the demons knocking at their door.

"Our protégé Quinton served us well, and the Death Angel failed at his latest attempt."

Silent murmurs of hope and thanks rumbled through the cavernous walls.

"But Quinton didn't vanquish the Death Angel," Father Robard said. "Now he is enraged and wants Quinton. As does Zion. We must continue our prayer vigils day and night."

He stepped to the front of the common room, encased in darkness, and lit a candle then bowed his head. One by one his fellow monks strode forward and followed his actions.

Yet the stone structure trembled, the earth shifting as the enemy shouted its attack call from below.

Chapter Twenty-five

Quinton fought his gut instinct, which urged him to go after Annabelle. To apologize, ask for her forgiveness and admit that he did care.

That yes, at first, he'd intended to seduce her to keep her quiet. Only somewhere along the way, things had changed, and he'd wanted her for himself.

But caring was trouble.

He couldn't afford it.

Still, he would protect her from this demon if he had to die doing it.

So what was his next move?

He had to think of this case as a mission. Scope out the target and take him out.

Dammit, if he knew the target's identity, he could do exactly that.

He sat down at the computer and began to methodically outline what he knew so far. He drew a line to the suspects on his list. Reverend Narius—he'd pretty much ruled him out.

Dr. Gryphon. He certainly fit the profile.

He needed to find out exactly what he was up to. He found the business card he'd given Annabelle lying on the end table and dialed the man's number.

"Dr. Gryphon speaking."

"It's Agent Valtrez. I talked to Miss Armstrong and she's reconsidering your offer of help. Is there a clinic nearby where I could observe your work in progress?"

Dr. Gryphon hesitated. "I can't compromise my patients' confidentiality."

"I understand. But if you want to help Mr. Armstrong, and clear yourself of any suspicion, you'll give me a tour. Once you've been eliminated as a suspect, you might be able to assist us in finding the person behind these attacks."

A reluctant sigh. "All right. Meet me in an hour."

Quinton jotted down the address, then hung up and tried to call Shayla Larue to go with him. If she truly was a demon slayer, he could use her as backup.

But she didn't answer so he left a message.

He started to knock on Annabelle's door to tell her where he was going. But she'd said she was going to get some sleep, so he didn't disturb her. If her father regained consciousness, the doctor would call him.

Until then, he'd try to solve this case. Finding the Death Angel and destroying him was the only way to keep Annabelle safe.

The sound of a tree branch slapping the window woke Annabelle a few hours later, hazy evening shadows streaking the room, the sun having faded.

A vulture pecked at the window incessantly, the scratching giving her the creeps as memories of the night before assaulted her. The ballroom, her father's gaunt life-less eyes, the bomb.

The near explosion that Quinton had stopped by using

his power. Quinton holding her, comforting her, making love to her.

Then the conversation she'd overheard. She'd been ready to accept that he was part demon, but he'd used sex to keep her from revealing his secret.

He didn't care about her at all.

She rolled over, aching for him again, but the bed was empty. His masculine scent lingered on the pillows and the sheets.

Sighing in frustration, she sat up and dropped her head into her hands, willing herself to forget.

But reality crashed back with a vengeance. Her father was in the hospital, disoriented and confused.

The reporters would already have outlined the story for the world to know. And they'd hound her for the truth.

Her phone rang and she checked the number. Her boss, Roland. He was obviously wondering when he was going to get her story.

She had no idea what to tell him, so she ignored the call. She couldn't talk to him yet. Not until she decided how to handle the things she'd learned about Quinton.

Maybe Roland would be satisfied with human-interest pieces on the victims. And she could offer some follow-up pieces on post-traumatic stress syndrome.

Still, she had to find out who'd turned her father into a killer and clear his name.

But if Quinton was right, and it was a demon, what would she report?

Her phone trilled again, and she frowned, expecting it to be Roland, probably calling back to leave a caustic message. But the hospital's number flashed on the display.

Her palms began to sweat as she snatched up the phone and connected the call.

"Annabelle Armstrong."

"Miss Armstrong, this is Dr. Andradre at the hospital. I hate to tell you this, but your father didn't make it."

Annabelle's stomach knotted as grief filled her. "What?"

"I'm sorry. The medical examiner is going to do an autopsy, and we'll notify you of the results."

No...She doubled over in grief. He couldn't be dead. He'd squeezed her hand, sent her a message.

She had to see him for herself. "I'll be right there."

She disconnected the call and glanced at the closed doorway between her room and Quinton's. She wanted to go to him, ask him to come with her.

But he'd made a fool out of her, and she refused to beg for his help. She'd call a taxi and go on her own.

She wanted to say good-bye to her father in private.

Quinton studied Gryphon, his mind struggling to read the doctor's thoughts.

The research hospital where Dr. Gryphon was conducting his experiments wasn't what he'd expected. He'd imagined hearing tortured cries and screams from the end of a corridor of dark hallways and locked doors. Instead, the facility appeared normal, quiet, a working medical environment staffed with professionals who would draw no suspicion.

Or was it a cover?

Gryphon settled his wiry frame back in the chair. "How are Miss Armstrong and her father doing?"

"Naturally, she's upset about her father. I phoned the

hospital on the way over, and Mr. Armstrong's condition hasn't changed."

His brows furrowed together with his frown. "In cases like these, it's hard to predict how long it will take for the patient to recover, or if he ever fully will."

Quinton tensed slightly. Was that a warning? "I'm sure Annabelle will see that he receives the best medical care available."

Gryphon's eyes narrowed as he leaned forward in his seat. "And you obviously don't think that's me. So why are you really here, Agent Valtrez?"

"We know you conferred online with the first two bombers, who were homeless men. We have agents studying those posts to determine if they might have hinted at their plans."

"We've been over this, and I found no signs of suicidal thoughts or hidden agendas." Gryphon drummed his fingers on the mahogany desk and sighed. "It's a shame that some prey on the homeless and aging. That's one reason I decided to focus on geriatrics and am working on treating memory disorders."

"You're making progress?"

He gestured toward several files on his desk, then his computer. "Some, but not as fast as I'd like. Medicine has helped increase our life span, but that fact also has its downside. Many elderly are left alone with no one to care for them. And more diseases result from the aging process, especially dementia and Alzheimer's." A self-deprecating smile tilted his lips. "Then again, you didn't come for a sermon on my personal mission."

Quinton studied the nuances of his words, his

expressions, his silent thoughts, but everything seemed...
sincere.

"It's doubtful these homeless men created this plan on
their own," Quinton said. "Someone else masterminded
the attacks."

Gryphon steepled his fingers. "Do you think a terrorist
cell is behind the bombings?"

"The FBI is investigating that theory. But I have another
one."

"Care to share it?"

Quinton shrugged. "I think someone may be drugging
or hypnotizing these men, exerting mind control, if you
will. I mentioned this to you before."

Gryphon frowned. "Yes, you did. And I suppose that's
possible."

"With your expertise and research experiments, have
you conducted mind-control experiments?"

A second passed, then a wary look flashed across Gryphon's features. "Are you asking if I know of a drug that
could make that possible, or if I've been experimenting
with mind control?"

"That is what you're doing here, isn't it?"

Gryphon leaned back in his chair with a dismissive
shrug. "I can give you a list of drugs that physicians
use in therapy, ones that would assist in hypnosis, but I
won't acknowledge your implication with a response." He
quickly clicked a few keys on his computer, hit Print, then
handed Quinton the list.

"How about the names of other doctors you think
might be conducting experiments with mind control?"

"If I suspected any of my colleagues were doing anything inappropriate, Mr. Valtrez, I would report them to

the police." He gestured toward the door. "Now, please leave. I have patients to see."

"I came here to observe your work," Quinton said. "You agreed to give me a tour of your facility."

Gryphon hesitated as if weighing his decision. Then Quinton read his thoughts.

Why not? He had nothing to hide.

Quinton gestured for him to lead the way. Gryphon seemed resigned as he stood and started down the hall. He showed Quinton two of the treatment rooms that he used for relaxation therapy and hypnosis, introduced him to two of the nurses on staff, then they walked down the hall housing the patients.

No electric shock treatments or anything that looked illicit. No demonic stench from Dr. Gryphon or the patients.

"Most of my patients are admitted on an outpatient basis," he said. "But I have rooms available for the patients taking part in my current research project."

Gryphon escorted him into a solarium where he spotted two men playing chess, an amputee in a wheelchair reading the *Wall Street Journal*, an elderly gray-haired man nodding off in a lounge chair, and a fourth younger guy staring out the window.

Quinton greeted the men playing chess, but they barely acknowledged him. He touched their shoulders and sensed they were troubled, but detected nothing odd about their skin coloring or scent. He walked over to the guy in the wheelchair and noticed he was reading about the stock market.

"I may be in this chair," the man said, "but I still have to manage my investments."

"Right." Quinton forced a smile, then went to the young guy staring out the window. He seemed the most depressed, but when he looked up at Quinton, he realized the guy was blind.

"I like to feel the sun on my face," he said quietly.

"I understand," Quinton said and placed his hand on the guy's shoulder, reading his thoughts. He felt trapped, was suffering from flashbacks of the explosion that had caused his sight loss. But he was determined to get his life back.

No suicidal or homicidal thoughts.

Quinton's cell phone buzzed, and he quickly checked it, hoping for a lead.

He had a text.

His nerves instantly sprang to alert.

More fireworks on the way. A private show—just for you. Watch Annabelle die.

The scent of death and formaldehyde suffused Annabelle as she exited the elevator in the hospital basement and walked down the hall toward the morgue. She inhaled, trying to settle the nausea in her stomach as images of her father taunted her. What had gone wrong? Why hadn't he held on?

The cabdriver had wanted to talk about the near bombing the night before, and had tuned the radio to a discussion of its disastrous effects on a city that had already seen enough trauma for a lifetime, while she'd wanted to hear anything except the news.

Her hands were sweating as she pushed open the door to the front office. A drawing of the human body and skeletal system hung on a faded chipped wall. A sickly smell greeted her as a doctor appeared, ripping off a pair of plastic gloves and tossing them into a bin designated for biohazardous material. The room felt icy cold, the smell sickening.

The doctor smiled, an odd smile revealing jagged front teeth. "Hello, Annabelle. Welcome to the morgue."

"Dr. Andradre, phoned and said my father died," Annabelle said, her heart in her throat. "Is he here?"

In a flash, he closed razor-sharp nails around her wrists, then a sharp sting pierced her arm and the world spun in a drunken rush.

She clawed for control, for something to hold on to, but a world of black drew her into its terrifying abyss.

Quinton phoned Annabelle as soon as his feet hit the pavement outside Gryphon's office. Five rings later, and her voice mail picked up. He left a frantic message warning her that the killer might be after her and to call him back, then jumped in his car and drove to the hotel to see if she was there but just avoiding him.

After the way he'd left her, he wouldn't blame her if she didn't even want to speak to him.

He honked his horn and sped around slower traffic, careening into the hotel parking lot on two wheels, then jumped out and ran to the entrance.

His pulse pounding, he raced inside. But Annabelle wasn't in the room.

He punched in her cell number again, but was once more connected to voice mail. Sweat beaded on his brow and neck as he ran back to the car. She must have gone to the hospital to see her father.

She was safe. She had to be.

Vultures soared above the car as if they were dogging him as he raced toward the hospital. Partygoers already clogged the streets in the evening hour as dark descended, embracing the charm and culture New Orleans offered. He wove through the throng, wondering where the Death Angel would strike.

If he had Annabelle, where would he take her?

Gears ground and his tires screeched as he drove into the hospital parking lot and jumped out. Again, he hit the ground at a dead run, racing past nurses and orderlies, shoving past a medicine cart to reach the elevator. Perspiration trickled down his forehead as he took the elevator.

When the elevator door dinged open, he jogged to Armstrong's room. The older man lay in the bed, still unconscious, but Annabelle wasn't inside.

Grinding his teeth, he rushed outside to the nurses' station. "Have either of you seen or heard from Miss Armstrong this afternoon or evening?"

A blonde looked up and wrinkled her nose. "No, not today."

The brunette nodded agreement. "I figured she'd be back by now."

Panic tightened Quinton's chest. He didn't know where to turn. Where to look.

If only the message had told him something specific.

He had to call Vincent. Ask for his help. He was the only one who understood that they were looking for a demon. He clenched his cell phone and punched in Vincent's number. His brother answered on the first ring.

"Quinton, I was just getting ready to call you."

"Listen," Quinton said, cutting him off. "I just questioned Gryphon. He's not our perp. And I received a text message. I think the Death Angel has Annabelle, but I don't know where he took her."

"I have another person of interest," Vincent said.

"Then tell me, dammit."

"I cross-checked the list of guests attending the ceremony last night with a massive list of volunteers, doctors, social workers, all who'd aided the homeless in the last year, along with their schedules, looking for someone who travels around."

"And?"

"Guess whose name came up?"

"Fuck, Vincent. I'm not in a guessing mood. He might have Annabelle."

"The forensic specialist, Dr. Wynn. He's been in all the targeted cities the past few months, does consultant work on various cases. He tends to rent a place when he's in town, and I'm at his rental in Savannah right now."

"And?"

Vincent exhaled. "Sam Wynn died over twenty years ago. This demon, the Death Angel, may have possessed his body from the grave."

Quinton's head reeled.

"Sam Wynn was a piece of work," Vincent continued. "He had Asperger's syndrome."

"That's a form of autism, right?"

"Yes, he was highly intellectual but couldn't relate to others, to humans. Quinton, this guy was a serial killer who liked to chop his victims into pieces, then eat them."

A cannibal? Quinton's stomach turned. "Just like the vulture. He cleans their flesh. Then he collects the bones as his trophies to showcase his hunt."

"It fits," Vincent said. "He needs to be destroyed, Quinton. You won't believe what I'm looking at."

"What?"

"Bones," Vincent said. "The man collects bones from various crime scenes. My guess is from those he's killed."

His stomach knotted. "The bones are his souvenirs."

"Hell, yeah. This is one sick son of a bitch."

"He owns a place in New Orleans?" Quinton asked.

"Yes. But if you're at the hospital, I'd check the morgue first."

Holy hell. The morgue—a perfect place to hide a body. Was Wynn going to set off a bomb in the morgue and watch the bodies explode?

"If he's not there," Vincent said, "he might have taken Annabelle to his rental property."

Quinton memorized the address as he raced toward the elevator to the morgue. Impatience gnawed at him as he waited, so he took the steps, jogging down them two at a time.

At the landing, darkness engulfed him, the scent of death, vile body odors, and chemicals wafting toward him. He pushed into the hallway, checked the signs, turned left and jogged down the corridor, then through a set of double doors. Someone should have been at the office desk, but it was vacant. He pushed through another door to the back cold room, scanning it for Annabelle, for Wynn. But the room was empty.

Except for the body bags in the storage room.

His breath tight in his chest, one by one, he forced himself to check each body bag.

Thank God, Annabelle wasn't inside.

Heart racing, he headed outside to his car, punching in Detective DeLang's number as he went.

"Detective, it's Quinton Valtrez. We have reason to believe that Dr. Sam Wynn may be behind the bombings."

"Dr. Wynn from the FBI?"

"Yes. I think he has Annabelle Armstrong. Send a crime unit to the hospital morgue to check for forensics."

"Got it. I'll put out an APB on him as soon as I hang up."

"Thanks. Wynn has a rental house in the bayou. I'm going to check it out now."

"Call me if you need backup."

"I will." Quinton hung up, knowing he wouldn't call. If Wynn was there, if he'd hurt Annabelle, he'd forget the police. Demon or mortal—it didn't matter.

He'd kill him.

Chapter Twenty-six

Fear snaked through Quinton. Annabelle could not be dead. Not the beautiful gutsy woman who'd had the audacity to challenge him. Not the one who'd willingly given herself to a dark man like him.

He ran to his car, frantic. Traffic crawled through the city, bright headlights nearly blinding him as he drove toward the bayou. Dilapidated and storm-tattered housing bled into view, and the smell of the backwater rose like a murky stench from the ground as he neared the dirt road leading to Wynn's place.

Horrid images bombarded him. Did he have Annabelle? And if he did, what had he done with her?

He'd dealt the hand of death plenty of times without batting an eye, but a cannibalistic demon?

He slowed the car, flipped off the lights, and stopped. Once out of the vehicle he approached quietly, his gaze scanning the weed-infested yard, the strip of a muddy walkway leading to the river, and the gator-infested swamp. Eerie eyes peered up at him, and water splashed as a gator floated toward the bank, its sharp teeth gnashing as it whipped its tail and screeched an attack call.

Gators gathered at the bank, hissing and snapping at him as if he'd come to rob them of their meal.

Inhaling to control his temper, he knelt and focused on summoning strength from nature, on calling to the bayou and the gators and the spirits that drove them all. To the loup-garou who haunted this land with the swamp devil's cry.

I am not your enemy, he willed them silently. I am your friend.

One gator whipped its tail, slapping the muddy Mississippi viciously, and water splattered his face. He brushed it off, didn't have time for these games.

Utilizing every ounce of his physical, spiritual, and mental powers, he silenced their hisses and sent them floating back through the water on their backs, completely at his will.

Silently, he inched through the overgrown weeds and tupelo trees, letting the spidery moss of the giant oaks shield him as he approached the weathered shack. His training as a Ghost kicked in and he moved silently, his feet barely making a sound as he crossed the rocky path littered with dried leaves and twigs.

The biting wind brought the scent of a dead animal to him, reminding him of the dangers of the bayou and the cycle of life and death.

That death couldn't be stopped.

Maybe not forever. But dammit, he refused to let it have Annabelle tonight.

Gray shadows hovered like clawing hands surrounding the rotting shanty, spiderwebs covered the porch awning, and inside, the place looked black. The stairs leading to the front porch creaked beneath his weight. He gripped his gun at the ready as he climbed them and peered through the fog-coated window.

From where he stood, the shanty appeared to be empty, but he prepared for attack as he tried the doorknob. The frame was so rotten that the lock sprang free with little force, and he scanned the interior.

Nothing.

He inched into the space, listening for a breath, a sound, but a cold, empty mustiness greeted him along with the acrid scent of death.

Cursing, he found a frayed old lamp and turned it on, the dim light it cast radiating across dingy walls.

Walls covered in bloodstained bones.

Annabelle struggled to regain consciousness, to understand what had happened to her, but the dark cavern was so black she couldn't see two feet in front of her. And it was cold, so cold her body was numb, as if it had been frozen in ice.

Her limbs felt paralyzed as well, her lungs battling for a breath. Inhaling only drew rancid odors that sent bile rushing into her throat.

She opened her mouth to scream, but the sound died, echoing in the frigid empty darkness. Then reality returned. She had driven to the morgue to say good-bye to her father.

But she'd been attacked instead. The call had been a trap.

Tears blurred her eyes, freezing on her cheeks, and another blast of cool air assaulted her, sending a chill through her already numb body.

"Why are you doing this?" she cried. "Are you such a coward that you won't show yourself?"

Suddenly the brush of sharp points—fingers, no, *tal-*

ons—made her skin crawl. They jabbed her skull and fire singed her nerve endings, sending a jolt of unbearable pain through her temple. She screamed, her body trembling as the pain sizzled through her head.

She had to fight. She wasn't a quitter. Somehow she knew this madman or creature, whatever it was, had destroyed her father, and she wouldn't let him win now.

As if to defy her courage, a vulture's screech reverberated through the darkness, and she cringed, knowing he was stalking her, waiting for her to die.

Quinton's face flashed in her head and she whispered his name.

"Please, Quinton, save me ... I don't want to die."

Quinton stiffened, the faintest whisper of Annabelle's voice breaking into his conscience.

"Save me ..."

His gut tightened. "I won't let him kill you, honey," Quinton whispered. "Just tell me where you are. Give me a clue."

But only the sound of the wind rattling the trees met his request.

And the broken and mutilated bones on the wall mocked him, nearly choking him with fear.

His mind raced with panic; he couldn't think, didn't know where to turn.

He had to call his brother again. He was the only one who understood what they were dealing with. The only one he could trust.

"Did you find him?" Vincent asked.

"No, but I just reached his cabin. You were right—the walls are covered with human bones. But he's not here and neither is Annabelle." His voice cracked. "I don't know where to look now."

"Listen, Quinton, I checked into that woman you talked to, Shayla Larue."

"What does she have to do with this?"

A nervous pause. "Quinton, Shayla Larue has been dead for fifty years."

Quinton's shoulders tightened. "There has to be another Shayla Larue."

"Maybe," Vincent said. "Or maybe she rose from the grave on All Hallows' Eve just as Wynn did."

A bead of sweat slid down Quinton's brow. "You think he took Annabelle to the shelter?"

"No. Shayla is buried in a graveyard in New Orleans, the same one where the famous voodoo priestess Marie Laveau is buried. Larue was rumored to be one of her descendants, a very powerful voodoo priestess with supernatural powers."

Quinton rammed his hand through his hair. "What does this have to do with Annabelle?"

"Dr. Wynn...was buried in that same cemetery."

Quinton's blood ran cold. "You think Wynn might have carried Annabelle to the cemetery? That Shayla Larue knew his spirit had risen but didn't know what body he had possessed?"

"It's the best theory I've got," Vincent said.

Quinton took off running toward his car. "Which cemetery did you say it was?"

"St. Louis cemetery. It's one of the oldest in New Orleans." Vincent's voice dropped a decibel. "People say they see apparitions there at night in the passageways between the tombs."

Quinton started the engine, sped down the dirt road and onto the highway, then raced past a slow-moving car, blew his horn at another to move out of the way. Precious minutes crawled by as he maneuvered through traffic. Sweat beaded on his neck and trickled into his shirt, and for the first time since he was a child locked in that dark closet, his hands shook with fear.

Dammit. He was never rattled like this on a mission. But he'd never tried to save anyone before.

And if Annabelle died, it would be very personal.

He had to reach her in time.

A dozen scenarios flashed into his mind. Annabelle being tortured, her brain fried in her head. Annabelle with a bomb strapped to her chest.

Annabelle burned at the stake as Vincent said their mother had been, screaming his name.

Him being too late.

Chest heaving, he parked along the edge of the cemetery, searching the bushes and trees beyond. Instead of being laid out in a grid pattern like most cemeteries, this one consisted of a labyrinth of narrow walkways that wound through massive wall vaults, dilapidated tombs that were unmarked, and marble mausoleums.

Shadows slithered between the tombs, a chill rippling through the frigid night air, while above a vulture flapped its wings and coasted as if to watch over the dead.

He inched slowly through the narrow passageways, glancing quickly at names etched in marble. There were also unmarked tombs. He wondered who they held as he listened for Annabelle's voice.

For her cry for help.

Bones and chicken feathers were piled at the foot of

Marie Laveau's crypt. Some kind of voodoo offering, he assumed. Small x's had been scratched on the tomb. The monks had mentioned that believers knocked three times when leaving their offering in order to make a special request or invoke a voodoo spell.

The vulture probably lived on the offerings made in the dead of night. Quinton froze as a shadowy mass—an apparition—floated between the crypts.

Marie Laveau? Or was it Shayla Larue?

Loose stones scattered beneath his boots, cutting into the grisly silence as he turned through the labyrinth of graves, searching. The wind tossed the scent of decay, then smoke as if flesh was being charred.

His chest clenched. Annabelle?

Suddenly he heard her thoughts, her fear, the terror in her pleas for him to save her.

"Help me, Quinton..."

"I'm coming, baby. Where are you?"

The apparition shimmered ahead, long black dread-locks, silver eyes glowing in the night, the wisp of magic. Shayla Larue.

She was leading him toward Annabelle.

He quickened his pace, the scent of burned flesh growing stronger as he approached a tomb, then Annabelle's scream of pain wrenched the air, and he ran toward it and yanked at the closed entrance.

The stone door weighed a ton, but adrenaline churned inside him and rage fueled his power as he tugged the heavy door open and stepped inside.

Annabelle was lying limp on a stone slab, her body convulsing in pain as Wynn splayed his talons against her temple.

*   *   *

Annabelle had to fight; she couldn't die here in this crypt.

She felt Quinton's strength, his anger, the force of his powerful presence reach out to her and bolster her courage.

But where was Dr. Wynn?

Voices swirled around her. Some madman issuing an ultimatum to Quinton—follow his father or Annabelle would die.

Outside, the hideous screech of vultures rent the night, one pecking viciously at the crypt, trying to claw its way in. Anxious to taste her.

Another fiery blaze shot through her head, and she jerked in agony, screaming for the burning torture to stop.

"Release her now," Quinton shouted. "And I'm yours."

Zion watched through the Seer's visions as his son Quinton stood inside the crypt.

Quinton had come to save the woman.

The Death Angel turned and watched the Dark Lord enter, then he sent another jolt of fiery pain slicing through the woman's head.

"She will belong to the otherworld soon. Already she has lost consciousness. With it goes her will to live," the Death Angel murmured. "She has mere seconds left until she succumbs to death."

"No, she's stronger than that," his son bellowed. "And so am I."

Zion smiled, enjoying the battle.

The Death Angel began to morph into the vulture,

shedding his human skin. "You want to save her?" the Death Angel asked.

Quinton nodded. "Yes."

"Then you must walk with your father."

Zion waited, his breath erupting in fiery spurts in anticipation of the victory ahead.

Chapter Twenty-seven

Quinton couldn't let Annabelle die.

Not the woman he loved.

The amulet pulsed inside his pocket, and Quinton probed Wynn's mind. The bastard had been the one who sent her the text messages all along.

Had used her because he knew that Quinton was connected to her.

Then he'd trapped Annabelle into meeting him by telling her that her father was dead. The fun, after all, was in watching the target squirm in pain before the kill.

Quinton understood that greed and thirst.

"Yes, I had to get your attention," the demon said. "Torture is such sweet pleasure."

Quinton understood torture, could endure any pain. Except the pain of watching this demon hurt Annabelle.

A burning, mind-numbing sensation seared Quinton's skull. The demon's power—he was trying to destroy Quinton's free will.

Quinton fisted his hands. He had to fight back. Use his own power to stop the demon and rescue Annabelle from the demon's force.

Wynn's transformation into the vulture was almost complete. His bald head gleamed in the dark, feathers covered his hands, and his talons jutted out from his fingers, sharp spikes digging into Annabelle's skull.

Quinton slid his hand into his pocket, withdrew the amulet, and gripped it in his palm. The angel wings glowed, burning fiery hot, reminding him that he was part good inside, that good also held strength.

Use your power. The whispered words echoed from the cavernous tomb—his mother's voice emerging from the heavens.

A sob echoed in the air as the vulture lifted his talons from Annabelle's head. She suddenly opened her eyes, but they looked foggy, tormented with pain and terror.

Rage shot through Quinton, along with every dark craving he'd ever possessed. The need for revenge, for blood, for the vulture to experience the same kind of agony he'd inflicted upon Annabelle and his other victims.

Driven by the need to kill, he focused his energy on the vulture, tapping into Wynn's mind and twisting it to his own vengeful hungers. Using his hands, he threw him away from Annabelle. The vulture-man's body slammed into the concrete wall with such force that the ground trembled.

Burn. The man needed to burn; his demonic brain should fry, as had the brains of the innocent homeless people he'd inflicted so much pain upon.

Suddenly the vulture's head reddened as fire seeped into his brain matter. The scent of seared flesh, skin, and feathers, of rotting insides and death, engulfed the room, and the Death Angel—Wynn's body with the bald head of the vulture—shook. Then a shrill inhuman scream pierced the air.

Quinton continued channeling his powerful energy

into vanquishing the demon until the vulture's feathers singed and flew off him, swirling around the darkness and falling to the cement like black ashes.

Wynn cradled his head and fell to his knees, his body quaking as his mind gave way to emptiness and the fire that scorched his brain consumed him from the inside out. His eyes bulged, blood vessels rupturing, the whites exploding, brain matter flowing out. Then he collapsed into the dirt and concrete and his body jerked once and then exploded.

Outside, the vultures screeched as if protesting their leader's demise, a reminder that death and evil lived on.

But Quinton had extinguished this Death Angel.

At least until another one was named.

His head started to throb, his energy draining as he rushed to Annabelle. She trembled with horror as he lifted her in his arms and carried her outside. One vulture, then another, swooped into the crypt to feast on Wynn. Blood dripped from the vultures' mouths and talons as they sank their teeth into the demon's flesh.

Quinton wrapped Annabelle tighter in his arms, shielding her from the attacking vultures that swarmed and pecked at them as he raced toward the car. Using what he had left of his mental force, he sent the ugly black birds flying against the ground and into the sides of the tombs, fending them off until he reached his SUV and tucked Annabelle safely inside. She lay limp, fading into unconsciousness, her pallor chalky as if close to death.

He had to get her to the hospital. Had to make sure she lived.

If she died, he'd travel to hell and back to get his revenge.

*　　*　　*

Annabelle roused from a restless sleep, her head aching, her vision blurring. The first strains of daylight slashed through the blinds, and the scent of antiseptic and the drone of hospital machinery surrounded her.

Nightmares of the night before crashed back, robbing her breath, and she clenched the sheets, searching for the monster who'd attacked her. He had looked half human, half like a...vulture.

Had she been hallucinating, or was what she had seen real? A demon as Quinton had said?

And how long had she been here?

She searched the room and found Quinton sitting in the chair in the corner, a hulking mass of strength, his black eyes boring into hers, his jaw set in a hard line. "What...happened?" she whispered.

"You don't remember?"

"I'm not sure if what I remember was real." She massaged her temple. "Dr. Wynn...he was evil. He looked like a vulture."

His breath hissed out. "That was real."

Her head spun with questions. How was it possible?

Quinton had told her that supernatural forces were threatening the city. That he had powers and could read minds. And he'd shown her the book of demons.

He'd tried to warn her, but she hadn't believed him.

"You killed him," she said.

"He deserved to die. He was behind all the deaths these past few days."

Annabelle's chest ached. "And my father's."

He rose and moved to her, then stroked her hair. "Your father isn't dead, Annabelle. He's alive."

"What?" A tear slid down her cheek. "Dr. Andradre called and said he passed."

He wiped away the tear with the pad of his thumb. Wynn was the one who called, pretending to be Andradre. "It was a trap to lure you to the morgue."

She nodded, the pieces falling into place.

"In fact, your father is doing better," Quinton said. "I also saw Dr. Gryphon's work, and he's on the level. You may want to ask him to help your father."

His expression turned closed as if he was withdrawing from her again, yet the savage need in his eyes drew her as it had in the beginning.

"Thank you for saving me again," she whispered hoarsely.

"Don't thank me," he said in a harsh voice. "You wouldn't have been in danger if not for me. It was my father who sent the demon after you. And he'll come after me again."

She licked her parched lips. She didn't know how to respond to his comment because she sensed it was true.

Memories of the last few hours haunted her. She was terrified of what she'd witnessed. Of what he was, and the threat in his eyes. But the fact that she'd seen this demon, that he'd used mind control and turned her father into a killer, proved demons were real.

And being with Quinton meant becoming entrenched in this terrifying world forever.

Besides, he didn't love her. He'd claimed the sex meant nothing to him.

More tears threatened, but she blinked them back. She wouldn't beg. And she wouldn't admit that the sex had meant everything to her.

She'd let him go, and she'd move on with her life without him.

He never should have stayed at the hospital. But Quinton hadn't been able to drag himself away from Annabelle's side. Not when he'd feared that the demon might have caused her irreparable harm or brain damage.

Not when Annabelle's death would have been his fault.

Dammit. He preferred the old Quinton, the one unencumbered by guilt and self-recrimination, by worry and fear.

He almost reached for her, but he knew she would be safer if he left, that another demon would come one day. Maybe his father next time, as his premonition had shown.

Resigned to his fate, he walked out the door and forced himself not to look back.

For the first time in his life, he understood what his mother had gone through. How much she had loved him, and how much it must have hurt her to give up her children to keep them safe.

As he drove back to the hotel to pick up his things and book a flight home to Savannah, he phoned Vincent and explained the confrontation, and that he'd destroyed the demon. Unfortunately Vincent had no more leads on the stolen blood.

The air seemed fresher this morning, the sun bleeding through the gray skies, yet an ache enveloped him. As he let himself into his cabin, the silence felt suffocating.

He was alone again. Just as he'd always liked it.

Exhausted, he fell into bed and slept like the dead for

most of the day, then decided the only way to get Annabelle out of his system was to move on.

Fuck another woman.

But when he punched in Fancy's number, his hand shook. All he could think about was Annabelle. Hell, he felt...guilty—as if he was cheating on her.

He didn't want that kind of guilt.

When he needed a lay, any ripe, warm, willing woman could accommodate him. Her name or face didn't matter.

At least it never had before.

He cursed, dropped the phone, threw on jogging clothes, and ran for miles. Remembering the punishing physical routines the monks and the military had put him through, he hoped the physical torture would purge the images of him and Annabelle together from his mind. Of Annabelle's erotic body and tongue against his flesh.

Loving him...

Yes, he'd told Annabelle the sex hadn't changed anything between them.

But dammit, he'd lied. Sleeping with her *had* changed everything. It had changed *him*.

Done something to the dark need inside him. Softened him. Resurrected his humanity.

Annabelle made him want things he'd never had—like love and family. A woman who'd stand by him no matter what. One who wouldn't throw him away as his mother had.

He tried to deny that *pain* from long ago, just as he had denied the *pain* of being tortured and left alone as a child.

Caring only brought suffering, and he didn't want that

anguish. The very reason he couldn't have a relationship with Annabelle.

He had to stay away from her to protect himself.

But most of all, to protect her.

⌒

Zion roared his displeasure, the underworld shaking with the force of his wrath.

The Death Angel had failed to win Quinton.

Did he have to do everything himself?

The Seer waved a black clawlike hand, and Zion strode toward her, his scales itching and flaming hot with his ire. "What?"

"Your son Dante. I have found him."

The anger rolling through Zion couldn't be tempered, but excitement stirred in his demonic mind. "And?"

"He is well versed in his powers as a firestarter."

She flashed a vision of a post with a woman's body dangling from it, her hair singed, flames dancing around her in the ghostly night as a man watched the flames grow closer to her bare feet.

So sweet. Just as his own wife's death had been.

Screams tore from the woman and the flames shot higher. Then he saw his son. Dante looked more like him than the other two sons.

Pride swelled in Zion's chest.

Dante would come to his side, and together they would rule the world.

Chapter Twenty-eight

Quinton had waited for two long weeks, wondering what Annabelle would report on CNN. Wondering if she'd expose him.

He had meditated and prayed that the demons and his father had accepted that he didn't care for her and they'd leave her alone.

He poured himself a scotch and stared at the television screen, soaking up every detail of her beautiful face. Her physical bruises had faded, but had the mental scars from being tortured healed?

"I'm Annabelle Armstrong, reporting from CNN," Annabelle said into the camera. "The FBI has now concluded its investigation of the recent Savannah and Charleston bombings and determined that a forensic specialist, Dr. Sam Wynn, was responsible for orchestrating the mass suicide bombings. Apparently Dr. Wynn suffered from Asperger's syndrome, a highly functioning form of autism, often characterized by superior intelligence with an inability to connect to other humans." She paused. "Unfortunately, Dr. Wynn preyed on the homeless, especially those suffering from PTS, by using drugs to hypnotize them into committing violent acts.

"Agents found collections of bones Dr. Sam Wynn had kept as souvenirs from his victims on walls in several of his temporary residences."

Her tone grew low, controlled, although a slight tremor twinged her voice when she continued.

"It is a matter of record that my father was one of Dr. Wynn's victims and almost carried out a suicide bombing in New Orleans. He is now recovering and undergoing treatment for trauma.

"A team of private investigators working in conjunction with FBI special agent Vincent Valtrez and Homeland Security agent Quinton Valtrez traced Dr. Wynn to a shanty in the bayou in New Orleans, but in Wynn's attempt to escape, the gators killed him.

"While the events of the past few days were certainly tragic, heroes have emerged from all walks of life. Rescue workers, paramedics, police officers, and others in law enforcement rushed to save individuals. Also, countless citizens selflessly stopped in to help. I'll be bringing you stories of some of these silent unsung heroes in human-interest pieces over the next few weeks.

"Some may question how these innocent people so easily became Dr. Wynn's victims. We'll discuss this more in a special report to come, but for now I think it's safe to say that the events of the last couple of weeks have sent a clear message that we need to take better care of our elderly and our veterans, for they are true heroes themselves, if not of wars, then of life."

She thanked everyone, then the screen switched to the local weather forecast.

Quinton exhaled in relief as she finished. So she hadn't reported the entire story, how the Death Angel, working in the human form of Dr. Sam Wynn, had met his end.

To protect him or because she thought no one would believe her?

He stood and paced his den, feeling caged and antsy, then opened the sliding glass doors. Outside the wind roared, the waves crashed, the tides changing as they would forever do.

He heard the soft whine of the sea serpent demon carried on the salty air, and he cursed.

The demons were all around him.

And that was the reason he could never see Annabelle again.

Fatigue weighed on Annabelle as she finished the report. She'd gone seeking one story but found so much more.

The ordeal had made her realize that the hard-hitting stories were at heart about the people involved, that she *wanted* to showcase those individuals who had helped others for no reason other than that they still had their souls.

"Good job," Roland said. "You've definitely earned a solid reputation now."

A bittersweet feeling filled Annabelle. She'd thought a career was what she wanted, would fulfill her. But she'd never felt more alone in her life.

Images of Quinton still haunted her.

She'd never imagined that when she got the scoop on the real story behind the man, that story would open her eyes to an ugly world of demons she'd never known existed.

Or that she'd fall in love with him. The man...and the demon.

Weary and glad the story had aired, she caught the Marta train to her midtown Atlanta loft, let herself in, then kicked off her shoes and checked the message machine.

One call. Not Quinton.

The nurse at the hospital. "Miss Armstrong. I'm calling about your father. He's becoming more responsive and asking for you now. I hope you'll come to visit."

She smiled and hugged her arms around herself, grateful to know that even though they had a long road to travel, he was on his way back.

A headache pulsed behind her eyes so she stretched out on the bed to take a nap before she went to the rehab center.

She closed her eyes, wondering if Quinton had seen her story. Unwillingly, other memories flooded her mind. Memories of him watching her undress. Touching her. Kissing her.

Making love to her.

She suddenly sat up, her pulse pounding. She'd wanted to uncover the story behind the killer and she had. Only Quinton wasn't coldhearted. He cared about innocents. That concern drove him to be an assassin, to kill bad guys, terrorists, and...demons.

And he had protected her at every turn. Had fought a demon to save her.

He'd even offered to trade himself, to walk with his father, to keep her alive.

Wasn't that love?

She paced for an hour, wondering what to do. She loved Quinton, but was she afraid of what he was?

Part of her wanted to go to him and declare her love, demand that he admit he loved her, too.

But what if she was wrong?

He hadn't asked her to stay. Hadn't admitted feeling anything for her other than lust.

No, she had to stay away from him to protect herself and her father. She'd just gotten him back. She couldn't lose him again.

Exhausted, she lay back down, closed her eyes, and fell asleep. Still her dreams were filled with fantasies of the man she couldn't have.

But an hour later, she jerked awake. A noise had startled her. Something at the window, a scraping sound. The wind—or was someone trying to break in?

She jerked up, searching the shadows, then inhaled the scent of a man. Sweat. Skin. Raw animal.

Smoke.

The intruder's breath rattled in the quiet.

She started to scream, but a large hand clamped down over her mouth, and a hulking figure loomed over her.

"Be quiet." The man's brusque tone sent a chill down her spine.

Terror sucked at her nerve endings, and she struggled against his hold, but he pressed his knee into her chest and slid his free hand around her throat.

"Fighting me is useless, Miss Armstrong."

She searched his eyes in the dim shadows of the room, thought they looked familiar, and for a moment thought she was looking at Quinton. Had he succumbed to the darkness he'd claimed lived inside him? Had a demon possessed him?

But a sliver of light sliced across the man's face and she realized it wasn't Quinton. This man's hair was wiry, short and spiked, and he was older, at least by twenty years.

A deadly evil radiated from his eyes.

"I'm going to move my hand," he said in a gritty voice, "but if you scream, I'll break your fucking neck. Understand?"

She nodded, and he slowly moved his hand an inch, testing her. "Who are you?" she rasped. "What do you want?"

He gripped her jaw so hard she expected to hear bones crunching. "Zion. We're going to see my son."

She nodded, desperately choking back her fear as he clamped steely fingers around her wrist and dragged her off the bed.

Quinton ran for miles and miles, the wind beating his chest and sand swirling around his feet, the waves crashing and rolling out to sea. Night had set in again, the sky a deep purple streaked with shadows of seagulls circling the sky.

No matter how far he ran, nothing could alleviate the anxiety in his body or the loneliness in his soul.

Yeah, he had one. He didn't like it, but Annabelle had awakened the conscious he thought he'd buried long ago. Still, each time he remembered the demon's talons against Annabelle's temple, the darkness sucked at him.

But he refused to give in to it. If he did, his father would win.

Then he would become a monster just like the ones he

hunted, and the demons would rule the world, the innocents unprotected. Annabelle especially...

A vulture screeched and soared above the edge of the waterfront, sending the beautiful seagulls scattering.

He'd thought killing Wynn would send them away, but they lingered as if waiting for another feast.

He let himself into his cabin, but an odd smoky odor pervaded the room, and his instincts kicked in. Something was wrong.

Someone was in his house.

He reached for his weapon from the drawer by the door; it was gone. Shit.

His pulse raced, but he forced himself to remain perfectly still, to scan the dark interior. A breath echoed in the quiet, so low it was barely discernible, and Quinton braced himself for battle.

"Show yourself," he snarled.

The lamplight flipped on, and his stomach knotted, panic churning in his gut. Annabelle was sitting in a chair, tied down, a dark-haired man with fiery orange eyes holding a knife to her throat.

"Do you know who I am?" the man asked.

The blood roared in Quinton's ears, and he took a guess. "My father?"

A nasty leer made the man's entire body shoot off fiery sparks of rage. "Yes, Damn you for defying me. You are my son and were meant to walk by my side and lead the underground."

Quinton glanced at Annabelle and gripped his hands, willing himself to think. He had finally beaten the Death Angel.

But how was he going to defeat Zion on his own?

Zion was supposed to be the most powerful demon of all time.

"She is beautiful, son," Zion said in a voice that made Quinton's skin crawl.

A wicked look flashed in his eyes, and he leaned over, flicked out his tongue, and licked his way along Annabelle's cheek. "So sweet. I've hungered for flesh all these years."

Annabelle shuddered, and Quinton's body burned with fury and rage... and protective instincts stronger than anything he'd ever known.

Quinton focused on the knife and sent it flying from his father's hands onto the floor. "Leave her out of this. She has nothing to do with us."

Zion's nasty laugh echoed through the room, vile and wicked. "Yes, she does. I saw you with her." He held up his hand, fire spewing from his fingertips in a wide arc that sizzled in the darkness. "Don't even think of fighting me. I'll kill you and do as I want with her." He gestured toward the film rolling on the computer screen, the scene of Annabelle undressing.

"I liked what I saw." A smirk twisted his mouth. "And once I have her, she'll give me her soul and become my mistress of the underworld."

"You don't want her," Quinton snarled. "You only want to hurt me."

Pure hatred bubbled in Quinton's chest, and he focused all his energy to fling his father across the room. Zion bounced backward, hit the wall, then laughed and threw a fireball at Quinton. He dodged the fire and ran toward Zion, slamming his body into his father's. They rolled to the ground fighting.

Every touch from Zion's hand sent pain screaming through Quinton. But he summoned his strength and tried to throw his father off him. A loud roar rent the air as Zion grabbed him by the throat, the heat from his demonic hands sending a streak of pain through him that cut off his breath.

Zion's human body shimmered into demonic form, his eyes a fiery red, the devil's face ugly and scaled.

His grip on Quinton tightened, and Annabelle screamed his name. Zion tossed a fireball at her feet, and rage sparked Quinton's adrenaline. He cursed, pried his father's hands off his neck, and threw him aside.

He heaved for a breath, but before he could attack Zion again, Zion tossed fireballs around Annabelle in a circle that lit up the room.

Damn the bastard.

With a roar and a flick of his hands, Zion threw another ball of fire at him, the flames rising at lightning speed. Quinton used his power to hurl it back, but Zion caught it, then laughed again, a hideous sound that echoed shrilly into the sizzling flames as he flung it onto Quinton.

"Quinton, help!" Annabelle was struggling to untie herself, but the flames were growing closer, licking at her feet.

Quinton turned to go to her, but Zion grabbed him by the throat again, the flames eating at his arms and legs. Their gazes locked, and fear clutched Quinton. His father was stronger than him, could beat him.

He needed Vincent.

Zion knew it as well. "We could play this game all day," Zion roared. "But it will be more fun once I have your brother Dante by my side. He and I will make you and Vincent pay for defying me."

Quinton focused on the firepoker in the corner of the room and flung it at his father's back, but Zion was too fast and sent it flying into the window with a crash.

"I should finish you now," he snarled, but he suddenly released his hold. "But I want you to squirm. To have to face your brother and me together."

Flames burst higher between them as Zion headed to the door, and Quinton knew he had to make a choice.

Save Annabelle. Or go after Zion.

He rushed to Annabelle and swept her from the flames just as they caught her clothing. He snuffed out the sparks as Zion disappeared out the door and into the night.

Quinton cursed, then extinguished the flames on the floor with his mind as quickly as his father had created them. But he was shaking with fear and anger as he dragged Annabelle into his arms. His father's words reverberated in his head. Zion would be back.

He gripped Annabelle tighter and hugged her in his arms. "Dammit. He could have killed you."

A sob tore from her. "Quinton, are you okay?"

"Yes. No..." He kissed her, a kiss so full of hunger that it left him weak and wanting more. Made his cock twitch for the warmth between her thighs and the light in her eyes.

But her gaze flickered to the monitor and hurt crossed her face. "Why did you keep that?"

He buried his head against her neck, his throat thick as he inhaled her erotic scent. "Because it was all I had left of you." He stroked her hair, treasuring the silky softness, wanting her so bad he thought he might beg. "I thought by letting you go, you'd be safe."

She pressed her palm against his cheek. "You left me to protect me? That means you do care. That…"

"That it was more than sex," he ground out, his voice choking. "I love you, Annabelle." He dropped his forehead against hers. "But I'm not a good man. I don't deserve you."

"You've done some bad things," she whispered against his neck. "But you are a good man, Quinton. An honorable man. Everything you did, you did to save others." She clung to his arms. "Sometimes there are grays. I understand that now."

His gaze met hers, searching, wanting so much that he felt weak inside. He didn't deserve her love or anyone else's. But damn if he had the strength to refuse it now.

He crushed her in his embrace, his head throbbing, his body drained from the fight. He needed rest. Needed replenishing.

Needed sex, to be with Annabelle. But God, he didn't want to hurt her. "You've seen the world I live in, Annabelle. You should walk away from me. You deserve better."

She brushed her lips against his neck. "I deserve to be with the man I love."

He swallowed hard. His father knew who she was, understood their connection. Whether she was with him or not, Zion could find her. "I swear, Annabelle, I'll protect you until the day I die."

"I know, and I love you for it, Quinton." She cupped his face between her hands, then kissed him tenderly, and he fused his mouth with hers.

In the back of his mind, reality registered. He needed to call Vincent, tell him about his encounter with Zion. Warn him that Zion was going to try to win over Dante, then the two of them would come after him and Vincent. That Vincent was right—they needed their combined strength to beat Zion.

But Annabelle was here, in his arms, and he couldn't release her yet. His body hummed with arousal, needing her closer, needing to be inside her to make her his.

The phone call would have to wait. He'd missed Annabelle so damn much. "Are you sure?" he said gruffly. "You know what I am, that I have demon blood in my veins. That demons may come after me again."

Tears filled her eyes, but she stroked his jaw with the pad of her thumb. "I know, but I'm not afraid of you. And I can't think of any safer place to be than in your arms."

Quinton's throat closed, emotions pummeling him. He wanted to do the right thing for once in his life.

But his need, his dark hunger, for Annabelle overcame his reservations, and he stripped off her clothes, cupping her breasts in his hungry hands as he bent his head and drank from her. She moaned and clutched his shoulders, tearing at his clothes. Within seconds, they were both naked, flesh to flesh, light to dark.

She groaned as he sucked a nipple into his mouth. His lust for her would never be sated, just as his dark hungers would thrive as well. With a low moan, he kneed her legs apart and slid his cock inside her.

He finally had a home.

Her orgasmic cry as he pounded inside her resounded off the walls, and her body spasmed around him, the two of them joined as one.

It was the closest a Dark Lord like him would ever get to heaven.

He buried his head against her and feasted on her goodness, hoping it would be enough when the demons and his father came for him again.

It was only a matter of time before they would.

Until then, he'd take refuge in Annabelle's body and arms.

And in her love.

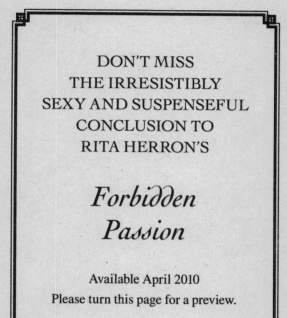

DON'T MISS
THE IRRESISTIBLY
SEXY AND SUSPENSEFUL
CONCLUSION TO
RITA HERRON'S

*Forbidden
Passion*

Available April 2010
Please turn this page for a preview.

Dante sniffed the scent of another demon as he entered Marlena's house. An odd odor permeated the air, but he couldn't quite put his finger on it.

A demon? No . . . a spirit?

Papers had been tossed onto the floor in front of the oak desk, the drawers open as if someone had been searching for something.

Bracing his gun at the ready, he sized up the space. A mystical sense hovered in the corners of the old house, and the floor creaked as he walked through the rooms downstairs. With a trained eye, he quickly noted the homey furnishings: the antique armoire holding the TV, the pine kitchen table with fresh flowers in a blue vase, and the crisp white cabinets. Then he silently inched upstairs.

To the right, he spotted what must be the master bedroom. A four poster bed draped with a white lace canopy dominated the center, the white curtains flapping from the heat vent working to warm the old house. The adjacent bathroom held blue and white towels and a shower and antique clawfoot tub.

But both rooms were empty and seemed undisturbed.

He paused to listen for sounds from the other room, but only the whistling wind and creak of the furnace filled the air. He stepped back into the hallway, then inched to the room on the opposite side, a guest room with girl wallpaper that must have been Marlena's room when she was young. Stuffed animals lined a white wicker bookcase and a teddy bear with gauze wrapped around its leg sat on the bed.

Marlena must have played doctor as a child.

The memory of her grief-stricken face on the news after her mother and sister's deaths flashed back, resurrecting the old guilt.

Guilt he'd never expected to feel in his first years with Father Gio.

The kind of guilt that made a man human, not a monster.

But he was a demon. He lived with the monster inside him daily. The ugly voices never let him forget his evil side.

Remembering that Marlena was waiting in her car and that she had called because she might have information on Jodie McEnroe's murder, he hurried down the steps. Marlena opened the car door as he approached and climbed out, a relieved look crossing her beautiful face.

If she knew what he was, that he'd been there when her family was killed, that he was one of them, she wouldn't feel that way. She'd hate him.

Straight jet black hair illuminated by the slightest hint of sunlight shimmered down her back, and her frightened eyes were still the palest, oddest shade of green he'd ever seen.

He'd never forget those eyes. They haunted him day and night.

She'd been a homeless child because of him and the demons.

"You didn't find an intruder?" she asked.

"It's clear." He swallowed again, disturbed by his reaction to her. The slow burn of arousal heated his blood. He'd never expected the adult woman to make him feel like this, to have this immediate attraction to her. This dark . . . lust.

From her heavy breasts to her narrow waist to hips that flared enticingly, she was a package of seduction. And the last woman on earth he could even think about taking.

The wind whistled shrilly, catching her hair and swirling it around her face. Reining in the fire in his fingertips and inwardly adjusting his body temperature, he cleared his throat. "Did you see anyone when you arrived?"

She shook her head.

Another gust of wind sent snow swirling around her, and she shivered.

"Let's go inside," he said. "Then you can check and see if anything is missing and tell me what you know about the McEnroe murder."

She clutched her coat around her and rushed up the drive and porch steps, and he followed, stowing his gun in his holster. Not that a gun would have been effective against a demon.

His hands would though—they were lethal weapons, always ready.

She immediately went to the hall table in the foyer and retrieved a box sitting by the lamp, then led him to her den. A troubled expression tightened her face as she glanced at the papers scattered on the floor.

"Nothing looks disturbed in any of the rooms except this one," he said. "But you can check."

She gave a nod, but glanced down at the box in her hands, her frown deepening. "I don't know why anyone would go through my desk."

"Do you have work documents here?"

She shook her head. "In my laptop but nothing in that desk. My confidential files are at my office. And I don't have any valuables."

"Maybe you forgot to lock the door," he suggested.

"No," Marlena said. "Someone was here. I saw a shadow in the woods outside. And the wind didn't open those drawers."

He conceded that point with another nod, but kept his suspicions to himself. A spirit of some kind was here, watching her. Watching him.

A spirit with sinister motives.

"So why did you call?" he asked, turning his focus back to the case.

Her breath rattled out as she pushed the box toward him. "This morning I found this gift box on my doorstep."

He narrowed his eyes, noticed her hands were shaking.

"What does this have to do with the McEnroe murder?"

"I heard the news report about her murder. The reporter said that her mother claimed that she always wore an antique pearl ring, and that it was missing." Marlena pushed it into his hands with another raspy sigh. "I think this is her ring. That for some reason, the killer left it for me."

THE DISH

Where authors give you the inside scoop!

♥ ♥ ♥ ♥ ♥ ♥ ♥ ♥ ♥ ♥ ♥ ♥ ♥ ♥ ♥

From the desk of Rita Herron

Dear Reader,

I have to admit that I'm a TV junkie. I love comedies, dramas, crime shows, and paranormal series, especially those with a romance in them. Of course, I always find myself drawn to the strong heroes.

Two of my favorites are Jack Bauer from *24* and Cole Turner from *Charmed*. Both are charismatic, tough, sexy, dark tortured guys with tons of emotional baggage. In fact, my husband, who is also a huge *24* fan, named our cat Jack Bauer.

When I first decided to write about demons, I wanted my heroes to have the same qualities as Jack and Cole, to be larger-than-life men who risked their lives to save the world—and of course, the women they love.

In DARK HUNGER, the second book in my paranormal romantic suspense trilogy *The Demonborn*, (out now!), I combined Jack and Cole and created Quinton Valtrez, Vincent's lost long brother.

Quinton is a loner, a government assassin, and a man determined to keep his job and supernatural powers secret. Like Jack, he fights terrorists. Like Cole, he battles demons—as well as the pull of evil inside him.

Pit him against a sassy, tenacious, struggling reporter named Annabelle Armstrong who is determined to unravel his secrets, and the sparks immediately fly. Quinton doesn't know whether to kill her or love her.

Quinton also faces a new kind of terrorist—a demon who has the ability to exert mind control over innocents and turn them into killers. Soon he and Annabelle realize they must work together in a race against time to stop this demon. But Annabelle isn't quite prepared to be thrust into this terrifying demonic world, or to face Quinton's father Zion, the leader of the underworld, who will use her to get to Quinton.

For any paranormal story, setting and world-building is important. Blending the real world with paranormal elements makes the stories more frightening. In DARK HUNGER, I also take you to three of my favorite southern cities: Savannah, Charleston, and New Orleans. All three are steeped with folklore, ghost legends, history, and a spooky ambience that adds flavor to the world of *The Demonborn*. If you haven't visited those cities, put them on your TO DO list. And don't forget to take one of the ghost tours and be on the lookout for demons!

Enjoy!

Rita Herron

♥ ♥ ♥ ♥ ♥ ♥ ♥ ♥ ♥ ♥ ♥ ♥ ♥ ♥ ♥

From the desk of Robyn DeHart

Dear Reader,

I've always been a huge movie buff and my very favorite genre is romantic action adventure; think Indiana Jones and *The Mummy*. Toss together some archeology, a dash of history, and a nasty curse, add in two protagonists with lots of sizzle and I'm one happy woman. I suppose it's this love that brought me to my Legend Hunters and the first book in that series, SEDUCE ME (on sale now).

I admit I'm a geek at heart, but there's something so compelling about old things: ancient texts, antiques, dusty old tombs. I mean, who hasn't dreamt of going on a dig and unearthing something so amazing it changes your life? Well, this is precisely what happens to our heroine Esme Worthington. She ends up getting herself kidnapped, but in doing so she comes face-to-face with the object of her lifelong obsession, Pandora's box.

Enter our hero, Fielding Grey, a treasure finder-for-hire who is none too happy that his latest assignment comes with a damsel in distress. But he can't walk away from her while she's literally chained to a wall. So he snags Esme and the fabled box and thus begins an adventure neither could have imagined.

Not only does the box come with a unique curse that has Esme acting the wanton, but a nefarious villain is hot on their trail and will stop at nothing until he possesses Pandora's treasure.

This new series is about Solomon's, a luxurious gentleman's club equipped with all the accoutrements one would expect from such a fine establishment. Membership is by invitation only, because in this club there's a hidden room where secret meetings occur. In these secret meetings some of London's finest gentlemen gather to discuss their passions; their obsessions. Some are scholars, some collectors, some treasure-hunters, but each of them is after the find of the century. I can't wait for you to meet the Legend Hunters . . .

Visit my Web site, www.RobynDeHart.com for contests, excerpts, and more.

Robyn DeHart

♥ ♥ ♥ ♥ ♥ ♥ ♥ ♥ ♥ ♥ ♥ ♥ ♥ ♥ ♥

From the desk of Diana Holquist

Dear Readers,

When my family moved from the big city to a tiny rural town for my husband's work, there were no jobs for me. I wept for about a week. Okay, maybe two weeks. Then I realized that this was the perfect time to start something new. Because I was incredibly naive, I opened a file on my computer and typed, "Chapter One."

Uh-oh. Now what? I needed a story. But what? What did I care about enough to pour my heart and soul into? Later, I learned that what a book is about—what it's *really* about—is called a premise, and every good book has one. What was my premise?

I started lurking on the Web site of a woman who was looking for her soul mate. She wanted him to be a certain height and make a specified income and on and on. But no matter how hard she looked, she couldn't find her "one true love."

What if there was a soul mate put here on this earth just for this woman, but he wasn't tall and rich? This woman needed a guide to the world of love.

Thus, Amy Burns was born, the psychic gypsy who can tell you the name of your One True Love. She starred in my first three books, creating chaos, love, and a premise I could believe in: only when we face our true desires can we find happiness.

In my first book, MAKE ME A MATCH, Cecelia Burns is a doctor about to marry the "perfect" man: a rich, successful, handsome, charming lawyer. Along comes her psychic sister Amy, to announce that Cecelia's one true love as destined by fate is not only an underemployed single father, but that he might be dying. If she wants her one shot at experiencing true love, she's got to act fast.

In SEXIEST MAN ALIVE, Jasmine Burns, the shyest woman alive, learns that her one true love as destined by fate is Josh Toby, *People* magazine's Sexiest Man Alive. Uh-oh. She can't talk to a regular man; how will she ever get near this one?

HUNGRY FOR MORE is Amy's book. She has to choose between learning the name of her own one true love or keeping her psychic powers. When she meets a sexy French chef, she realizes that accepting true love is harder than she thought it would be.

The One True Love series got great reviews, a RITA nomination, and won awards like the New York Book Festival romance award. But more important, this series introduced me to so many wonderful readers, some of whom I now count among my friends. When I look back on those first days of moving away from the city, I laugh when I think about how what I thought was the end was actually a new beginning. I didn't realize then that I was living my own premise: be careful what you wish for. Because when you try something new, open your mind to the possibilities that life offers, and focus on your true desires, good things happen.

Happy reading!

Diana Holquist